PRAISE FOR BECCA SEYMOUR

Refreshing, completely entertaining, and just a wonderful gay romance.

SIMPLY LOVE BOOK REVIEWS

This is my second foray into Becca Seymour's books and so far, they only get better and better. Give me Australian men ANY DAY!!!

OH YOU READ REVIEWS

I have waited YEARS for more basketball romance to come to MM. And Becca Seymour totally delivers in this hot new release! NO TAKE BACKS is fun, chatty, sweet, and has a great Australian flavor with hot basketball player and the boy back home!

ANNABETH ALBERT, AUTHOR

NO TAKE BACKS

BECCA SEYMOUR

RAINBOW TREE PUBLISHING

NO TAKE BACKS

ZONE DEFENSE BOOK 1

BECCA SEYMOUR

RAINBOW TREE PUBLISHING

ALSO BY BECCA SEYMOUR

Zone Defense

No Take Backs | No More Secrets | No Wrong Moves

Fast Break

Rules, Schmules!

True-Blue

Let Me Show You | I've Got You | Becoming Us |
Thinking It Over | Always For You | It's Not You |
Our First & Last

Outback Boys

Stumble | Bounce | Wobble

Stand-Alone Contemporary

Not Used To Cute | High Alert | Realigned |
Amalgamated

Urban Fantasy Romance

Thicker Than Water

Cover Design: BookSmith Design

Editors: Hot Tree™ Editing

E-book ISBN: 978-1-922679-04-8

Paperback ISBN: 978-1-922679-05-5

Disclaimer: *No Take Backs* introduces a fictional American pro basketball league, referred to as the League. Likewise, team names and universities mentioned are fictitious, allowing much more freedom in the rules and creation of the Zone Defense world.

For my son, Joseph. I love you despite no longer being able to jump on a trampoline without peeing.

PROLOGUE

NATE GRIFFIN

AGE 17

Me: What did McCormack want?

FOR THIRTY LONG MINUTES, THE BUTTWIPE DIDN'T respond. I watched my mobile, willing him to answer. I would have hung around after school to find out for myself, but Dad would have gone off at me if I'd shown up late for my shift at our family farm store.

Ryan: Be there in 10!!!!

I sighed, frustrated I hadn't a clue what was going on. When the head of PE had called Ryan out of our final lesson of the day, something was clearly up. The man hadn't looked annoyed, which was something, but it was now after four in the afternoon, and Dad kept throwing me frustrated glances, since I'd screwed up pricing up some new stock twice.

But hell if I could concentrate.

Since the first day of high school, Ryan and I had been all but attached at the hip. He'd been new to town, a place my family had lived for three generations. As soon as I'd seen the gangly eleven-year-old, dressed in the usual daggy Queensland state school uniform, but noticeably not new with the loose stitching on his shirt and the scuffs on his pleather shoes, he'd captured my interest. And when some ninth graders tried to give him shit, his mouth shut them down pretty damn quick. I'd decided there and then, I wanted Ryan to be my friend.

But me waiting to find out what was going on pushed my neediness to a new level. We didn't do anything separately, or near enough nothing. Seriously, we hollered conversations through the locked bathroom door to each other if one of us was taking a dump. Christ, I'd even joined the local under fourteens basketball team, which soon moved to the under eighteens, despite being so not interested in the sport, just because Ryan loved it and was crazy good at it.

Admittedly, Ryan had conned me when I was

twelve, and I'd half-heartedly said I'd join. As soon as my words were out there, he'd grinned before shouting, "No take backs."

And to this day, our "no take backs" rule stood firm. Neither of us was sure of the punishment involved should we defy our now five-year-old rule, but I had no desire to find out, not if it meant making Ryan unhappy.

So me not knowing what was going on with my best mate, and waiting for over an hour to find out, was a new level of torture.

When the bell on the door chimed, bringing with it a shimmer of winter warmth, I almost fell into a box of mousetraps in my rush to peer around the aisle.

"A minute longer and I thought Nate was going to have a meltdown or sprain his neck." My dad's tone held an edge of humor, and I caught his eye roll.

"Was not," I grumbled.

Dad scoffed. "Whatever you say, kiddo. Go take ten, as I'm convinced you're going to have an aneurism if you don't speak to Ryan."

Ryan's grin stretched wide. "Cheers, Mr. G. After, I'll make sure I help."

Dad threw him a friendly wink before turning his attention to Mrs. Henderson, who was dithering over some plants in our gardening area.

I indicated toward the back room, and Ryan followed, grin still firmly fixed. I examined him closely as soon as we were in the large storage area. "What gives?" He was all but vibrating. The grin didn't slip, and his eyes legit sparkled. Only twice had I seen him so excited.

One time was when he'd seen Lynn's boobs, though admittedly, there'd been a wide-eyed hint of wonder there too. I'd given him a high five when he'd told me while I'd swallowed my nausea. The other was four years ago when his mum up and left and his gran moved in to look after him and his little sister, Amber. That time my celebration had been real. His mum was a waster, and while his gran was strict, she loved her grandkids.

"McCormack pulled me into a conference call with a bloke from the college basketball league in Ohio and Coach Milton from Luton Vale University."

My heart slammed in my chest at the news. I knew what this meant, and while it was incredible, I struggled to catch my breath.

"I've been offered a full ride." Excitement lifted every single word, his whole body shaking.

"Shit, man." I shook my head, willed my smile to the surface, and swallowed the emotion clawing its way up my throat. I grasped him in a hug, squeezing hard and patting him on the back. "I'm so freakin' proud of you."

It was hard to get a basketball scholarship, and an Australian being able to score one, and in a division one school at that, was pretty much unheard of. Well, in our neck of the woods anyway.

I pulled out of Ryan's grasp, carefully arranging my expression and willing it to be real. "Have you told your gran yet?"

"Nah, you're the first." His words had me puffing out my chest, filling me with pride and a buttload of feelings I had no right to be experiencing. "I couldn't wait to tell you. Shit." He laughed and held out his shaky hand. "I can't stop shaking."

I reached out and squeezed his arm. "You're going to be amazing." He would kick butt in the college league. Hell, he had the skills to go all the way and make a career out of it. This time, a real grin appeared. "This is what you've always dreamed of. The pros, man. Like… college basketball… this is huge."

A flutter of happiness cut through my sullenness. It beat the misery back, reminding me my best friend was freakin' awesome. "And it's okay to leave at the end of the year, right? It doesn't matter about their term times or anything?"

"It's all worked out. I need to make sure I keep

my grades up, but that's what I've got you for." He swung a muscular arm around me and hauled me into a headlock, going to town rubbing his knuckles against my head.

I laughed, trying to shove away from him. The guy was too bloody strong for his own good, gangly limbs and all. Managing to break away with a curse and a "Piss off, Broadwater, before I take you down," I caught his gaze, and I begged my thoughts to not dip into territories of just how I'd like to take him down. It wasn't too difficult, not when he shot me a huge grin, his cheeks red, and a legit sparkle in his eyes.

This guy here was my friend, and I was okay with that. I always would be. I loved the guy, and I knew he loved my skinny arse right back. Platonic or not, that was everything.

"You wanna come with me to tell Gran and Amber?"

My heart leapt, wanting to be with him every step of the way and share in his excitement. "Hell yes. Let me beg off from work."

Once more, Ryan slung his arm over my shoulders, this time squeezing and not thinking he was a comedian. "How about I do the talking? Your dad won't be able to refuse."

I snorted, knowing he was absolutely right. When

his muscles shifted a little, becoming taut, I angled to look at him.

Ryan's smile slipped. "You'll find a way to come and visit, though, right?"

The slamming of my heart against my rib cage was almost painful. I wanted to celebrate with him, see him rise and take the pro ball world by storm. "Hell yes. Me and you, Broadwater, always. There's not a chance you're getting rid of me that easily."

"No take backs." His grin was wide and so disarming, I returned it immediately.

"In that case"—I nudged him—"best make it a first-class ticket as soon as you're rich and famous."

"Is that right?"

"You better believe it, hotshot. Nothing but the best from you to me. Think of it as payback for putting up with your weirdness all these years. And hell, you know how many ankle sprains I've put up with, just because you wanted to play basketball?" I rolled my eyes, earning me a nudge.

We stepped out into the storefront, laughing and shoving at each other. "Don't get me started on weirdness, Nate the Niplett."

"I do not have a third nipple!" I cringed, not realizing just how loud I'd defended my birthmark.

Ryan snorted just as Dad called out, "Yes, just get out of here."

"Ha!" Ryan glanced at me like he'd made that happen. "I don't even need words. Just my godly presence is enough."

"Godly, huh?" I rolled my eyes and puffed out my cheeks to stop the loud laughter threatening to spill. "And so it begins. I'm telling you now, Ryan, if you even think about getting a god complex and your ego grows to the size of Uluru, don't think I won't be the one to remind you exactly who you are. Remember, I know all of your weirdness."

His grin was broad. "Sounds like a plan. You'll be my very own Obsidian Blade. I'm feeling all kinds of special already."

I smirked at him. "I'll go all Skulduggery on your arse."

"Valkyrie. She's the only one who can wield the blade."

"You're such a dork."

"Me?" His wide-eyed horror didn't stick, not when his lips twitched. "I'm going to be the one playing pro ball one day. There's nothing dorky about that."

I tugged at his arm, as Dad was giving me "the look," the one indicating we were loud and ridiculous, and we needed to make ourselves scarce. "Come on, Faceless One, you keep telling yourself that while we make a run for it before Dad changes his mind."

Ryan's hand shot up in the air, and he waved it high and long and ridiculously over the top, shouting, "Bye, Mr. G. Nate can't come home tonight as I need help with my homework, so we'll see you tomorrow." He then snagged my arm, and we high-tailed it out of the store, ignoring Dad's grumbles and laughing like little kids.

PROLOGUE
RYAN BROADWATER

AGE 18

IN THE BLINDING LIGHT OF THE SUMMER SUN, I BLINKED rapidly, trying to keep my traitorous tears at bay. After already saying goodbye to Amber and Gran, I'd somehow managed to keep it together, until now.

Nate didn't even bother keeping the tears from his eyes, and when that first one slipped free, determination to keep my shit together nipped at me. I couldn't lose it. Not now, not with Nate's wet, sad eyes and his watery smile directed my way.

For the past five months, we'd made the most of every single moment together. We'd got through our dreaded exams, kicked butt in our basketball season, and had probably too many nights drinking stubbies out near the lake. It didn't make saying goodbye any easier, though. Looking at Nate's trembling lip and his damp cheeks cut me to the core.

Leaving him behind was the hardest thing I'd ever done. Throw abandoning my little sister and my gran in the mix too, and every swallow I made was like sandpaper.

With emotion bubbling in my throat, I attempted a smile that I expected looked like I was holding one in. For the life of me, I considered asking Nate's dad to take my bag out of the boot. So what that I was going to be playing the sport I loved like crazy? So what I was getting a full-ride scholarship to a kick-arse school, and in the States of all places? Did any of it really matter if I wouldn't see my best friend every day?

"Right." Nate huffed out a breath and rubbed his hand over his face. "Ignore me. You're going to be late."

I nodded silently, not sure I could speak, fearing an attempt at even a single word would break my composure.

"Dad's waiting."

Numbly, I nodded again. Mr. G was driving me to Brisbane airport. It was a couple of hours drive, and already I was relieved knowing Nate wouldn't be joining us. Last week I'd asked him not to see me off at the airport for precisely this reason.

Nate stepped forward, his arms wrapping around me, his face fitting perfectly in the crook of my neck. I inhaled deeply, not even giving a shit if he figured out what I was doing. His stupid scent—the weird organic shower gel his mum bought him combined with his natural scent—always could calm me. It always had, and for the past year or so especially, it did the job even better.

"I'm going to miss you so much." Nate's whispered words tickled my skin, and I hugged him harder. "Be a legend out there, got it?" I nodded against him, not able to let go. "Make sure you let me know when you're off the plane, yeah?" Another nod followed, but this time I managed an inhale and a grunt.

When I felt his arms shift, I considered hanging on and may have even tensed a little. His soft chuckle brushed across my neck as he pulled away, angling up to look at me. One of his hands freed itself from my shoulder blade and found purchase on the back of my head. He squeezed lightly, maintaining eye contact.

"Dead set legend, yeah?"

"Yeah," I whispered.

He shifted up to his tiptoes and pressed a kiss on my forehead. Just as I sighed into it, he was gone, out of my space, and a few steps back.

"Get your backside into gear, Broadwater." His gaze roamed mine, some of his tears clearing as he offered me a soft smile. "You're doing the right thing."

I formed a half smile. "I am?"

Somehow he managed a chuckle and a shove. "Yes, you are. Stop being lame. This, everything, is incredible."

My smile felt less like a grimace when I let his words flow over me, ease into my system with his warmth and familiar support. My heart spiked. "I'm going to play college basketball."

Nate's laugh was loud. "No shit. You're just figuring that out now?"

"You know what I mean." My throat constricted. "I just can't believe it's actually happening." His nod, his smile, the absolute faith he directed my way as he stared at me eased the noose around my heart. A thrill bubbled in my abdomen, growing big, separating and having a merry old time as they started popping, having a little party, reminding me *this*, this huge move and chance I'd earned, was fucking epic. Excitement built, a flood of happiness crashing through me. "I'm really doing this."

"Yeah, you are." Exhilaration lit up his eyes as he peered back at me, a lopsided smirk quirking his lips. "Was Gran okay when you said goodbye?"

This time I laughed. Sure, we'd all shared a few tears, but my gran was almost as excited as I was, and when she'd followed up with how proud of me she was and gave me this whole speech of following my dreams and my heart, I'd almost burst right then and there. "I expected her to pull out notes for the speech she gave me."

Nate snorted. "I bet. You keep that speech in your head, hell, maybe get that shit written down to whip out to remind you of how—"

"—*godly* I am?"

With a roll of his eyes, Nate punched my arm gently. "Hardly. But you're doing this for you—"

"And for them. If I can go all the way, just think of everything I can give them."

Nate's smile was soft. "I know, and they'll be proud as hell, but you loving it is important."

I scrunched my face and tutted at him. I'd swear Nate was ten years older than me. "Put your wise away. Yes, I love it. And I'm good at it." His mouth twitched at that, but I ignored him and kept going. "And if I can earn a heap of money doing it after college, then double the win, right?"

"Right. And just so you can sort my private jet."

"Private jet? You changing the goalposts there, 'cause dude, how much money do you think I'm going to be making?"

"Enough for a private plane if I want one," he joked.

My smile wilted when I heard Mr. G close the car door. "So, this is it."

With a tilt of his head, Nate nodded. "Make the most of a beer at the airport in Brissie before you're underage." He then stepped even farther back, out of reach. And thank Christ he did. It would have been so easy to latch back on to him and squeeze my friend to death. I knew I'd have to cope and get on without him, but it didn't mean it would be easy.

I shoved aside the ache in my chest, knowing I wouldn't see his stupid face every day or hear his voice while he got up me to finish my homework or whatever I was being lazy about. "I'll make the toast to you," I managed to say. Without another word, I got into Mr. G's car and strapped myself in, offering him a tight smile and a dip of my head.

And I didn't look back.

Couldn't.

If I did, I'd struggle to breathe, knowing I was leaving behind the one person who'd been my rock for the past seven years, the one person who simply got me.

As I focused ahead, I realized I hadn't said good-bye. I huffed out a laugh. Maybe that was a good thing. I didn't think I'd ever truly be able to say goodbye to Nate Griffin.

CHAPTER 1

NATE

EIGHT YEARS LATER — NOVEMBER

EXHAUSTION BEAT AT MY HEELS. REGARDLESS, I OPENED up the main entrance and stared bleary-eyed around the store. Immediately, rightness settled in my chest. While work was busy, this place was pretty much my second home. Whenever I was here, whatever stress I was feeling melted away. Maybe not all of it, but certainly enough to help me breathe.

If only it could help with my sleep-deprived state too.

It had been another night of Amber being uncomfortable and calling me at almost midnight, worried she'd gone into labor.

After checking on her, and me and her gran reassuring Amber that perhaps the curry she'd eaten may have been responsible for the grumbling stomach pains and not the baby ready to say hello, I'd finally dropped face-first on the bed in their spare room and crashed. Six hours later, I was going through the orders, preparing for a big delivery from our produce guy while yawning like it was an Olympic sport.

"Coffee?"

I glanced up at Patrick. He carried my saving grace. "Please tell me you got me a double shot and vanilla?" My voice was scratchy, lack of sleep doing a number on more than my attention.

"The gross sugary syrup is most definitely in there." He wrinkled his nose, and I didn't have a single thing to say in my defense, not when staring at the order sheet was already addling my brain.

Instead, I grunted, "You are a rock star," and took the coffee from him.

"That I am. Don't you forget it when it comes to Christmas bonuses."

I snorted before inhaling the scent of coffee deeply once I clung to the cardboard cup. I took a tentative sip, unable to wait until it cooled. The splash of frothy coffee, with the bitter tang of caffeine barely disguised under the vanilla, hit my tongue. I sighed happily.

"Amber again?"

I nodded, gaze resting on Patrick, a small smile

forming. He was one of two full-time staff who worked for my dad and me. He was young, early twenties, and from a local family. I knew his big sister from high school, which had helped me decide to give him a chance, and I was so pleased I had.

Most of the day-to-day management rested on me these days, which I was more than okay with. While Dad was still young in his midfifties, he'd had a few health issues over the past couple of years, so he had stepped back a fair bit.

But this store was all I'd known, so running the place was as easy as breathing. It meant even when struggling to function, I could just about manage. It also helped that I took comfort in being here. I loved the familiar space, loved hearing the gossip from the locals, loved interacting with so many people.

"Is she okay? The baby?"

"Both fine. She just had a scare. It's getting close, though."

"What is it now, a month?"

I bobbed my head, my heart leaping a little when I thought about Amber. In just over a month, she'd be a mum. I still struggled to wrap my head around that. Hell, she was still a kid herself. Admittedly, she was a lot more grown up than most eighteen-year-olds I knew, but she was like my kid sister and absolutely my family, which meant she was still practically a child. Her being a parent would change it all, though. And hell if we weren't all excited for the new addition.

"Are things still difficult at home?"

A chuckle spilled out of me. It was no secret Gran Broadwater was a force of nature. When Amber had asked me to be with her when she told her gran she was pregnant, I was sure I'd been more nervous than she was. But Gran had surprised us both that day. She'd listened to her seventeen-year-old granddaughter tell her she was pregnant without batting an eyelash. And when Amber had admitted it had happened when she'd gone to a festival, where she'd done the deed with two different guys, neither of whom she was in contact with, I'd been the one who'd winced and could have broken out into a full-on lecture. But Gran had listened to every single word before asking what she wanted to do about the pregnancy and saying she'd support Amber whatever decision she made.

Knowing that Amber had been as safe as possible by using condoms perhaps helped. But that tiny percent chance of protection failing was a shit of a thing.

Eight months from that festival that changed her world, Amber had finished up her final school exams last month and was waiting for her results. Always focused, she'd already put in her applications for studying next year to start her veterinary nursing course, and had even maintained a part-time job until last month.

I was so bloody proud of her.

"I don't even know why I'm laughing." I shook my head, becoming somber. "Gran's health isn't great, and you know how stubborn she is. I honestly don't know how Amber is going to manage being a new mum and studying while trying to make sure Gran is taking her meds and following the doc's orders." Yeah, there was nothing funny about any of it really. And while I did know Amber would cope, my concern was she'd struggle and not ask for help. Asking me for a Big Mac from Maccas at ten at night was a bit different from admitting she struggled with new-mum duties.

Since Amber's brother left—the only way I thought about him these days—I'd stepped up. Admittedly, it was my decision to do so, but with Amber being so young when he'd gone to America and her gran getting on in years, I'd felt responsible, and there had been a kinship in our sorrow those first years after he'd moved to the US.

There was nothing I regretted about forcing myself more firmly into the Broadwater home either. I spent more time—more recently especially—with them than my blood family. And I loved every moment of it. Well, the late-night calls from Amber I could do without.

Amber's gran had become my gran somewhere along the road, and while I had my parents who had also helped them out over the years, the past couple with my dad's heart issues meant my folks had his well-being to worry about.

"I imagine it's the only way you won't lose your mind," Patrick said, referring to my previous comment.

"Yeah. I just know something is going to give, and I'd prefer for that to be handled before it all turns to shit, you know?" My concern just wouldn't budge and was making me increasingly uneasy.

"Has Amber spoken to Ryan?" My stomach dipped at the mention of his name. Oblivious to my internal battle, Patrick continued, "Maybe if he knew how worried you were, he'd, I don't know, help them out or something."

My snort was bitter. "All Ryan thinks about these days is himself. He's not interested in being there. Throwing cash at a problem is more his style." While I was sure he worked his arse off for it, he'd hurt his family by breaking promises of seeing them often. Having already been abandoned by her mum, Amber felt that more acutely than anyone.

While he'd done an amazing thing a few years back and bought a new home for his family, which I knew Gran was beyond grateful for, Gran had still worked her full-time job to pay the bills and had only recently taken late-retirement. I'd asked more than once if she was okay financially, but she'd reassured me she had a decent superannuation fund, enough to keep her and her granddaughter going.

Patrick's brows shot high. The venom in my words left little to the imagination where my feelings were concerned. Patrick had no idea of my history with the prodigal town hero who'd up and left eight years ago, never to return. All the town knew was that Ryan was the basketball star who'd made it big in America.

A simple Google search on the sports pages could give them an insight into who Ryan Broadwater was. All of which I actively avoided, but temptation was a bastard of a thing sometimes.

The clean-cut, true-blue Aussie was an elite pro basketballer. He kept his nose clean and was only in the celebrity magazines for charity work and being arm in arm with the occasional supermodel at a party.

But I knew a different version of the guy.

When he'd first been drafted out of college in the early days, he'd flown Amber out when she was only fourteen or so to visit him. She'd returned early, upset she'd spent only a handful of hours with him in the five days she'd been out there—having been left alone for the majority of that time. Me? The first year he was away, we'd spoken at least once a week while he was at college. The second year had dwindled to once a month—him regularly not returning my calls.

At first I'd understood. I could only imagine the pressure he was under to perform, to play his hardest and make the cut. By the third year, though, I was surprised he'd remembered my birthday. After that, my back was up, and my heart was broken when he finally told me he didn't have time to talk to me anymore, so it was best if I stopped calling altogether.

It hurt a lot, and I still spent too many hours reminiscing about our time together, but grieving over a lost friendship and an unrequited love only led to bitterness. And based on Patrick's surprise, the bitterness held strong. But I never regretted his family or being so close to them.

"Oh wow, okay."

"Do you want to go and prepare the delivery area? The truck should be here in about an hour," I said, changing the subject altogether. Thoughts of Ryan would lead to nothing good. And I was already worried enough about Amber and Gran that my blood pressure remained high.

"Yeah, sure." Patrick dipped his head in agreement and left me to it. A quick glance at the time told me I needed to unlock the front doors. With my coffee in hand, I opened up and tried to concentrate on surviving the day without finding a spot to hide and curl up to sleep.

THE BIG, BREEZY VERANDA WAS ONE OF MY FAVORITE spots to kick back and sip beer. It just so happened to be at Gran's house. I tried not to overthink who had bought it for her and Amber three years ago.

The large Queenslander was a new build, with all the traditional charm but less maintenance than an original. It was stunning. Not only that, but it felt like home, and pretty much was these days with how much time I spent here.

Amber was another week closer to her due date. Honestly, I was surprised she hadn't gone into early labor after the stress of the past twenty-four hours.

"Gran's taken her meds and is having a lie down."

Amber waddled onto the whitewashed area and

to the overstuffed chair. She wedged herself in before lifting her feet onto the footstool with a sigh.

"And how are you?"

Another heavy breath escaped her. "Okay, now, but finding Gran like that last night…." Tears filled her eyes, and she shook her head. Amber released a humorless laugh. "I just don't know what to do anymore."

When Amber had called me panicked and crying last night, my heart had frozen for too many beats, thinking something was wrong with the baby. And while it had started again once she'd reassured me she and the baby were fine, my gut had clenched when she'd told me Gran had taken a fall.

We'd only just brought her home after a night's stay in the hospital. Miraculously, she hadn't broken a bone, especially considering her osteoporosis. But she was bruised and sore and still stubborn as hell. I owed the nurse big, though, for finally getting the truth out of Gran. She'd had a dizzy spell, and apparently, this hadn't been the first time.

"I'm moving in." Since waiting in the ER for news, I'd racked my brain, trying to figure out what to do for the best. For Amber, for Gran, and in some ways, for me too. Moving in would mean I wouldn't get late-night calls, for a start, and these guys were my family. I wanted to be here for both of them.

"You are?" Wide-eyed, Amber focused on me, a hitch in her question.

"Yeah. I'll collect a bunch of things tomorrow. It won't take long to settle in." There was no way I could let her do it herself. Me offering to do this wasn't even about me doing a good deed or the right thing. I loved Amber fiercely, loved her unborn baby too. Being a dad had never been at all in my plans—even if I fell head over dick for a guy. But an uncle... now *that* I could get on board with.

A loud sob escaped Amber. She clamped a hand over her mouth, her tears gushing freely over her tired face. "Really?" Her shoulders shook, her eyes wide and red.

I stood quickly and made my way over to her, kneeling at her side. I grinned at how she blubbered, but only because this girl rarely cried, so it was only right I teased her hormonal state. "Hey... really. It's all going to be okay. Promise." I scrunched my nose. "The tears are freakin' me out, though." My words earned me a laugh. "Don't laugh while you're doing that. Think of the snot, and I know you peed yourself last week. To be clear, I won't be cleaning up piss puddles."

"You're a dick." She rubbed at her eyes and smiled. "You know I've heard that peeing only gets worse after I've had the baby."

"Really? You know how gross that is." My brows shot up, deliberately comically high to get a rise out of her. "Please let me know if you need me to get those TENA things from the store. I have no shame in telling everyone they're for you."

She reached out and pinched my nipple.

"Ouch."

Her smile softened. "I don't know what I'd do without you." She reached out and took my hand. "My brother's the biggest dick in the world."

I snorted a laugh and squeezed her hand. "Do you need to call Ryan and tell him what's happening?"

She shook her head. "There's no point. It's not like he'll jump on a plane." The words were so matter-of-fact that I couldn't help but grimace. It didn't help that I expected she was right. "But seriously, Nate, thank you. You're the best big brother ever." Sorrow shadowed her words. I hated them as much as I cherished them. That she felt abandoned soured my memories of Ryan. I hated how those seven years of friendship—some of the happiest of my life—were tainted.

"We'll all get through this. More than that, we'll rock it. You need to just focus on that growing alien of yours and let me figure out things with Gran, okay?"

"She is not an alien."

"The last scan didn't prove anything," I jested, standing and pressing a kiss to her forehead before retreating to my seat.

"P-*lease*, you've just been watching dodgy sci-fi shows again."

I gasped, flipping her off. "Screw you, ET's mum. There's nothing dodgy about anything I watch."

She narrowed her gaze at me, her lips twitching, and I dreaded to think what she was going to say next. "You know it's important to clear your search history before loaning out your laptop, right?"

An honest-to-God dip in my stomach followed as I racked my brain. Amber had borrowed my laptop about four months ago after hers had shit itself.

"Who knew monster and alien gay porn was a thing."

I burst out laughing, despite my heating cheeks. "I have no idea what you're talking about."

"Uh-huh. Sure thing."

CHAPTER 2
RYAN

DECEMBER

Adrenaline raced through my veins as I pulled up into the underground parking lot of my condo. "Fuck." The one word punctured the air in my Audi R8. I inhaled deeply before exhaling and shaking out the tension, cracking my knuckles and stopping my hands from shaking.

I'd been ten seconds away from exiting my car to head into the discreet gay bar when I'd spotted the guy with the camera across the street. He appeared a little too casual to be anything but suspicious. Spotting him stopped me from destroying everything I'd worked hard to avoid.

Somehow, I'd pulled away slowly, as though the snarling, mocking shadows hadn't been chasing me every yard I'd moved away. Once in the clear and on the highway, I'd taken the risk and pushed hard to get back home.

With unsteady hands, I exited my car and locked it before stepping toward my front door. I pulled out my keys, pissed off I'd let the rush and exhaustion of the individual workouts and media week push me to chase head.

"Dickhead," I mumbled and entered my security code, opening the doors to my large home. I threw my car keys to the side, barely even checking they'd hit their mark on the console table, which was apparently some limited-edition, bespoke thing that I simply "had to have" according to the designer I'd hired when I'd bought the place. What once I'd thought was the height of luxury and maybe even class, now made me feel uncomfortable.

It was all bullshit.

The lies, the gossip rags, the empty existence I was living when not on the court. Everything about the game I loved. Hell, I could cream when I thought too long and hard about just how damn lucky I was to be living the dream.

I snorted as I tugged off my shirt, dumping it on the end of my bed. Basketball, playing professionally, playing in the big leagues, for shit's sake, was "it." It was certainly more than I'd ever dreamed of. But with the first week of workouts and media time done and next week another hit of hard yakka with group workouts before preseason games, a ball of unease formed in my gut.

Feeling heavy and sour, I wasn't sure how much longer I could keep smiling for the cameras—ones I avoided like the plague—or how much longer the dream job would be enough. Loneliness was a brute of a thing, and away from the court, it gnawed away at me like an incessant bug.

If I could spend fourteen hours a day on the court, I would do so in a heartbeat. I sighed at the thought, a genuine smile forming. Sure, I would be so tired and practically on my knees, but I'd be able to snatch on to the happiness, the adrenaline that sparked through me when we were playing a game.

Stripped and needing to find my breath, I slammed my eyes shut as I switched on the sprays to my walk-in shower. I knew it was just the media part of the week that always got my back up and that I was simply feeling sorry for myself. I reminded myself of that as the hot water, hotter than was comfortable, sprayed down on me.

Pro basketball had to be enough. It was everything.

I exhaled, turned the temperature down, and angled my face. Once the season kicked off properly and I was with the team, traveling from town to town, not knowing what day of the week it was, I'd feel better. I'd be content once again and in my happy place.

The problem lay in my downtime, which made it more frustrating that I'd let my need to have my dick sucked bring me down.

I angled my head from side to side and turned under the stream. I changed the setting of the fancy shower, and the water stung my muscles and the sensitive ink of my latest tattoo marking my left shoulder blade. I winced a little and shook my head at myself.

It was foolish to get inked up just before the start of the season, but last week it had been eight years since I'd left Australia, and the date had hit me hard. It usually did. A bender with some of the guys usually prevented me from thinking too hard about who I'd left behind.

This year, though, I'd felt the punch when I'd looked at the date. Guilt and self-loathing battled brutally for center stage. The numerous shots of JD and cola hadn't helped break my funk. It had meant I'd rocked up to Wizard's tattoo parlor, begging him to fit me in. I'd knocked back a coffee and a couple of bottles of water, pressing the fact I was sober enough to make the call. While Wizard had looked unsure, my desperation and pain had been plain as day if anyone looked hard enough.

A few hours later, I really had been sober. But more than that, I'd felt content, loving the escapism, the steady sting of the needle as it pierced my skin. While I didn't have that many tattoos, I had enough that I recognized the escapism it offered and would perhaps one day get ink on more visible areas of my body.

As it was, the ink I had was all for me.

That night I'd walked away with a tattoo of a griffin with such beautiful artwork that every time I looked at the damn thing, I was terrified I'd fucking cry. And how ridiculous was that!

And now, with the bittersweet sting of the steaming water pounding into the fresh ink, I didn't even overthink what I'd done wrong. There was no need for that. Every call I missed, every time I let down my best friend—the man who'd started to make my heart beat in the scariest of ways—and the too-many-times-to-count moments my callousness had left my sister in tears were ingrained in my skin. In my soul. They sometimes kept me awake at night and snatched at my dreams, leading them into shadowed despair that had me gasping for breath and hurting when I woke.

I attempted to shutter my thoughts, which led too

often to Australia, especially in recent months, and focused on washing away the sweat from my too-close call. Once done, I dried off and headed to the kitchen to grab a light beer—the single one I could allow myself when training—before swiping up my phone and throwing myself on one of the chairs on the back porch.

Looking at the wash of moonlight across the large lake where the city curved in the distance, I opened the app store and hesitated before downloading Instagram. I'd deleted the thing about a year back, not wanting to risk the temptation of checking in with Amber where I knew she tended to hang out, but more specifically, I didn't want to catch a glimpse of Nate. Doing so would have brought my homesickness once again to the surface.

It didn't matter that more years than I was comfortable in admitting had gone by. Whenever I thought of Nate and now looked at the stunning griffin on my shoulder, longing and guilt slammed into me. The last thing I ever wanted to become was a martyr, but I was on the cusp of being one. I wasn't sure I liked that look on me at all.

I barely dropped Amber a quick text, which I tended to do every Christmas, but she gave me noth-ing, no details beyond her doing well at school, which she'd just graduated from, and an update on

Gran. Anything more I couldn't handle, needing to protect my heart and my hide by effectively disappearing.

The knowledge sent a fresh punch to my gut. She'd graduated high school, and I hadn't even congratulated her properly. It didn't matter that my need to support Gran and Amber had almost equal weight to why I was here, so far away from home.

I wanted to give them the world. Wanted to pay back Gran for all that she'd done when she'd taken in my sister and me. That I had no regrets about. I knew that looking after them financially was one thing, but abandoning them by not being present was something I'd tried to make peace with. I wasn't doing so great a job at that.

After three failed password attempts, I was finally granted access to the app. I scrunched my nose at the notifications, ignoring them all, and instead searched for Amber. Her name popped up immediately, and I hit her profile pic.

Images bombarded me, my gaze traveling from one to another with increased shock. That shock fluctuated, a flash of heat hitting my chest, morphing into white-hot anger alongside my curdling stomach.

My sister was fucking pregnant.

My mind spun, struggling to comprehend what I was seeing. I zeroed in on the image that had the red blurring my vision. Nate with his arm around Amber, his hand resting protectively on her stomach.

With a shaking hand, I clicked on the image, waiting to read the text.

@amberkicksarse: Final stretch and this hottie @nategriffin_oz is the best. #bestbabydaddyever LOL

I shifted to the comments. My eyes widened when I landed on an exchange between my sister and Nate.

@nategriffin_oz: I'll remind you of this next time I refuse to buy you Maccas at 2 in the morning.

@amberkicksarse: Gasp. You wouldn't.

@nategriffin_oz: Snort. Try me.

@amberkicksarse: Don't tempt me. I have my ways of dragging your butt out of bed. Plus this baby needs Maccas. You'll break both our hearts.

@nategriffin_oz: *rolling eyes* I wouldn't want that.

Squeezing my eyes tightly, I exhaled deeply.

Nate and my sister?

Fucking pregnant?

I just couldn't.

Nothing about any of this made sense. For a start, my kid sister was knocked up. That was enough of a mindfuck to last me a lifetime. But Nate? I shook my head and all but charged to the kitchen, where I pulled out a bottle of vodka.

This called for a complete bending of the rules.

I swigged directly from the bottle, wincing and welcoming the burn. Reopening my phone, I stared once more at the image of the two of them that I was sure I wouldn't ever be able to erase from my memory. Another swig, and I went into my contacts, finding Nate's name. With no idea if the number was still active, I touched his name.

After a couple of rings, a hesitant "Hello" carried down the line. The sound of his voice, one I'd foolishly believed I'd forgotten, wrapped around me in an instant, the single word a balm to my hurting heart. "Ryan?"

The sound of my name dragged me back to reality. "What the fuck have you been doing with my kid sister, you fucking prick? I swear to God, I'm going to kick your ass so damn hard you won't know which way is up."

Silence filled the line.

"Seriously, she's eighteen. *Eighteen.* What the hell were you thinking! I just... can't—" I broke off, running out of steam while my gut twisted and turned with betrayal.

Betrayal that my friend would take advantage of my kid sister.

Betrayal that the one person who'd first made me question everything about my own sexuality was going to be a dad.

Emotion clung to my words as my voice dipped and wobbled. "How could you? I trusted you."

The silence remained, the sound of whatever was going on in the background drifting away. It was already Saturday in Australia, but I had no clue what time.

A heavy sigh finally split the empty air between us. "You finished?"

The tone was one I remembered well, even after all these years. Nate was pissed, exasperated, but I wasn't quite sure if he was rolling his eyes, clenching his teeth, or vibrating with some emotion. Maybe it was a combination of all three.

When I didn't respond, the previous white heat charging through me fizzling out with renewed exhaustion, Nate snorted.

"Figured." This time I was convinced he shook his head. "It's been, what, six, seven years since you picked up a phone, you dickhead, and it's to what? Slam me for shit you know nothing about? Unbelievable." Another heavy sigh followed, but his next words didn't carry the same frustration. "Amber didn't tell you she was pregnant?"

"No."

His humorless laugh flowed down the line. "Figures. Honestly, I'm not even surprised at this point."

"Why didn't she?" As soon as the words escaped, I clamped my mouth shut, already knowing the answer.

"You wanna retract that?"

Shit, how he still knew me so well was beyond me and more than I deserved. "I suppose, yeah. I'm not exactly up for the brother of the year award." My treatment of Amber a few years back was something she'd never moved on from.

"And some."

"You're the dad?" The words tasted sour, wrong. And selfish or not, I wished with everything I had that he wasn't. His reaction had given me hope, but his following words would either destroy me all over again or, hell… I didn't even know anymore.

"You really need to ask me that question?" Disgust registered in his voice, the timbre causing the hairs on my arms to stand on end. "If that's the case, you really have changed and never knew me at all."

"No," I rushed to say, all but hearing him making a move to end the call. "I don't, not really. I just…

reacted." I rested my forehead against the kitchen counter and closed my eyes, the phone still to my ear. "I just saw a picture on Instagram, saw an exchange, and freaked out."

Nate made a sound in the back of his throat.

"I'm sorry. I know you'd never do that. I know you look out for her."

"She's practically my kid sister."

His words stung, the truth of them clogging my throat with emotion. For years I'd been avoiding him and putting distance between my family and me. It had reached the point where I didn't know how to make everything right, unravel this lonely existence I'd made for myself, correct the harm I'd done, the hurt I'd caused.

"Perhaps you should finish this conversation with Amber."

"Yeah, maybe." I angled up and took a seat on the stool. "I'll give her a call."

"Give her twenty. She's having a bath."

"You're there?" I frowned before shaking myself from the direction my emotions attempted to tug out of me.

"For the foreseeable future."

My back went ramrod straight. "What's wrong?"

Nate sighed once more, and while it was beginning to rankle, I got it. "I'm so pissed that you have to even ask that." Sorrow blanketed his tone, carrying his words to me and threatening to suffocate me. I'd hurt Nate so badly.

"I know. I wish I didn't have to ask," I said honestly, trying and struggling to remember when I last bothered to pick up the phone to call Amber or Gran.

"Gran's not great. She took a fall a couple of days back, but she wasn't doing brilliantly before that either. And Amber's due soon. She's big and cranky, and she's got no one but Gran and me."

"I'd be there if I could—"

His laughter cut me off. "That right?"

I clenched my jaw, hating he was right. The last three times I'd promised to visit, I'd canceled my plans, and when Gran offered to come out, I'd put her off. "Listen, I know I fucked up."

"And some."

"I get it, but I'm trying here."

"Right, one call with you accusing me of knocking up your sister and asking a few questions means you're trying. I suppose it's good to have expectations."

God, I hated he was right, but that didn't stop my hackles rising, trying to defend myself, even knowing my own arguments were hollow. "They don't want for anything," I gritted out.

Hell, I'd bought Gran a house a few years back. I'd offered a couple of times to give them money too, but every time Gran refused. My gut tightened. Gran had retired last year, and I didn't even consider if she was still okay financially.

"That's right. I don't suppose the love and support of a brother or a grandson rank so highly these days. Whatever makes you sleep at night. Just call your sister. I'm done."

He ended the call. I pulled my phone away and stared at the screen, not quite sure which emotion to settle on. The worse thing was knowing anything Nate threw at me, I deserved.

CHAPTER 3
NATE

"I THOUGHT I WAS GOING TO LOSE YOU THERE FOR A minute."

I looked up from staring at the floor where I'd been cradling my head, taking deep breaths. Amber was pale, her voice sleepy, yet the biggest grin I'd ever seen her wear stretched wide on her young face.

"I love you, Amber, but never again." I chuckled lightly, struggling to get to grips with the mixture of horror I'd witnessed, along with the absolute awe and beauty of the moment.

"Thank you."

I frowned at the catch in her voice.

"For being here, for everything."

"Hey." I stood quickly and returned to her side,

stroking the hair off her sweaty forehead before smiling softly at the incredible baby in her arms. "You can count on me, always. You're amazing." She seriously was. How she'd got through this—pushed Ivy out of her like that—was as mind-blowing as it was harrowing.

Amber sniffed and wiped a tear from her cheek. "I promise you'll never have to get close to my vagina again, okay?"

I laughed loudly before cringing when Ivy made a squeaky sound in her mum's arms. "That would be great. She's worth it all, though, right?"

Amber looked down at her sleeping daughter, affection in her eyes that squeezed at my heart. "She really is."

"I just can't believe how perfect she is." I really couldn't. She was pink and squishy and had a mass of brown hair. I was sure that meant she should have looked weird and more like the alien I'd declared her to be, but bloody hell, she was beautiful.

"I keep just staring at her."

I chuckled softly. "Right." On cue, my gaze drifted back to Ivy. Jesus, this kid wasn't even mine, but already I loved her. "I'm worried we're not going to be able to stop. You know, when she's fifteen, and we're still finding it difficult to not look away, she's going to want to leave home, right?"

Amber gave a tired snort. "I think maybe our fascination will wear off."

I scrunched my nose, not convinced. "Maybe it's her smell. Don't people go on about baby smells or something?" I went to lean in, but Amber's words stopped me.

"You know she smells beautifully of my vagina and amniotic fluid, right? And I think I may have shit myself too."

I stared in wide-eyed horror at Amber. The nightmare woman that she was, she quickly clamped a hand over her mouth. I expected so her loud-arse laugh wouldn't wake her baby.

"The hell you say that for?" I complained.

She shrugged and finally seemed to calm herself enough to speak. "Will you collect Gran and call Ryan and let him know?" Her gaze locked on mine, and I was sure she was waiting for a grimace or something. While my stomach flipped at reaching out to her brother, I'd do so for Amber.

"Sure thing. You need anything from home?"

"Nah. I think I have everything I need in my bag."

"Text me if you change your mind."

"Thanks," she said as I dotted a kiss on her forehead and brushed a finger tenderly over Ivy's super-soft hair.

It didn't take long before I was in the car and heading to pick up Gran. Amber had already laid down the law about her gran not being with her during the delivery, worried about Gran's health and the dizzy spells that hadn't improved. Gran had been miffed for sure, but she'd taken her granddaughter's request in her stride and had sat this one out.

I'd already called Patrick, asking him to open up the store, and Dad said he'd head on in during the busier hours to cover me. With those bases covered, there was just Ryan to deal with.

While I'd yet to speak to him again after his first call, he'd made an effort with Amber and his gran, calling them regularly, even though the game season had officially started. While I hated taking sneaky looks to check how his team was doing and if his name was mentioned in gameplay write-ups, I actively avoided any game footage. Seeing him would be too hard. Moving on was difficult enough, and I couldn't lie to myself; I'd spent too much time over the years fantasizing about what could have been with Ryan Broadwater.

I hit Bluetooth, asking Siri to call Ryan B. A quick glance at the time, and I figured it was late afternoon in the US, and he didn't have a game today—or yesterday, since he lived in the past. I snorted at the irony, sure I was still stuck firmly there with him.

"Nate, everything okay?"

That he'd answered immediately was a start. Ignoring the way my heart picked up speed, I replied, "Yeah, all good. Amber's good; so is Ivy."

"Holy shit, she's a mum? I'm an uncle?"

"Yeah." I huffed out a laugh as I hit the indicator and turned right. "They're both great. Took a few hours, and Ivy was born about an hour ago. I've just left to pick up Gran. The midwife said she can go home tomorrow if she wants."

"Already?"

"Yeah, apparently she can. Though she can stay longer if she wants. She seems keen to get home, though."

"Can you send me a pic?"

My smile was automatic at the softness evident in his request. "Will do as soon as I pull over, sure."

Ryan cleared his throat. "Were you there?"

"Sure was."

"Oh, wow, and uh, how was it?"

"Gross and strangely amazing. Made me kinda relieved there's no chance of me ever getting a woman pregnant." I snorted, only becoming aware of the strange quietness that met my words.

"You won't?" Curiosity colored his response, and I held my breath, realizing what I'd said. Ryan had no idea I was gay. I supposed it made sense Amber wouldn't have told him. Why would she, considering their distance?

"I'm just pulling up now," I answered, avoiding his question. "I'll text you a photo. I expect Amber will give you a call when she has the energy. Bye, Ryan."

There was a moment of hesitation before a quiet "Yeah, okay, thanks, Nate. Bye," followed.

With a heavy breath, I exited my vehicle and rubbed a hand over my face. I was bone-weary, so I couldn't even begin to imagine how Amber must have been feeling. I pushed my tiredness aside, which honestly seemed to be my new state of being of late, and headed up to the doorway. As soon as I entered, Gran called out to me, "About time!"

I grinned, hearing her shuffle around. I picked up my pace to get to her, not trusting she wouldn't hurt herself in her rush.

"I got here as soon as I could." I held back my smirk at the stink eye she shot my way. "I don't suppose you're going to give me ten minutes to grab a shower?" Her snort was my answer. "I guess not. Come on, then. It's time you met your great-grand-daughter."

A flash of warmth appeared in her eyes, gone but a moment later as she bobbed her head. "Let's get a move on."

I helped Gran into the car, then shot off a cute photo I'd taken of a smiling Amber and Ivy, who'd been midyawn, to Ryan. We headed to the hospital, picking up some chocolates and a balloon en route.

Amber smiled when she spotted us both, and I hesitated when I realized she was breastfeeding. "Don't even think about running, Nate. It's okay you're here. I'm sure you'll get used to seeing my boob out."

I grinned and stepped fully into the room, looking on as Amber inhaled two chocolates and chatted quietly to Gran. After a couple of winces from Amber, Gran called me over to help her stand so she could help her granddaughter latch Ivy on. I did so immediately, not overthinking the weirdness of this situation, but through it all, I smiled, amazed at this whole feeding thing, this baby actually being born, and I'd been lucky enough to have witnessed the entire thing.

"I just can't get over how she just knows how to do that." I shook my head once I retook my seat, Ivy seeming to be feeding a little easier.

"Amazing, right?" Amber glanced at me, the darkness under her eyes not dampening her happiness.

"Sure is."

"Did you talk to Ryan?"

"Yeah. He asked for a photo." Amber's teary smile told me it was the right thing to share with her. I tugged my phone out and opened up my messages, having heard the notification alert on the drive back. I read the message over once before smiling, saying, "Ryan thinks Ivy is beautiful, and he can't wait to meet her. He also said how proud he is of you."

I glanced over at Amber, who was gazing down at her suckling child. She was a picture of contentment, and I was relieved Ryan had changed his tune from the call we'd had a few weeks back. While I knew he'd made an effort, considering the mass of baby gifts he sent over for Christmas, letting his sister know she mattered and he cared for her was important.

This was good for them, reconnecting. Envy fluttered to life, and my heart panged. What I wouldn't give for things to be different. I just didn't know if that would ever be possible for the two of us. Twice Ryan had broken my heart—the first time when he'd left, the second two years later when he'd distanced himself.

I'd be a fool to allow it to happen a third time.

FEBRUARY

Broken sleep. Inhaling coffee. Stained shirts. My life in a nutshell, but the smiles made it all worthwhile. While Ivy was still far too young to be smiling, her farts made it look that way, which was super cute, and every time I heard her gurgle, my grin came fast.

Amber was incredible. She was knackered and grumbled like the rest of us but quickly reined herself in and got on the best she could. She also stopped being a dick after the first three days of being home and accepted our help more readily when we reminded her she didn't have to go this alone. As far as I was concerned, I was this kid's uncle, and I'd do my best to make sure she and her mum were happy and well cared for.

But those smiles weren't all about Ivy.

Ryan Broadwater was doing a hell of a job at worming his way back into my life. This morning was no exception. I glanced down at the text.

Ryan: Did you catch the result?

I smirked. I expected Ryan would be back on a bus or in a hotel or something, since his game had finished about an hour ago. Our time difference worked out well, considering when he played, it was usually late morning here.

Me: Did I miss something?

I was an arsehole. I'd been following the updates as they came in on ESPN, the notifications popping up on my desktop while I worked in the office. When his team had won, a fist pump may have happened, and that he'd finished with a triple double had got my heart racing.

Ryan: Nah. Not much, just me being a dead set legend.

My heart squeezed tight and had done so constantly over the past few weeks since Ivy had been born.

Me: Legend, huh? How'd those misses work out for you?
Ryan: Flipping you off right now, wiseass.
Me: Wise*arse*... It's pretty fine and definitely wise.

As soon as I hit Send, I froze. What the hell was I doing? Was I flirting, or was this simple bantering, the usual sort of shit we got up to and said to each other as kids? I frowned hard, not quite sure anymore.

Ryan: Not sure about the latter.

I shoved away from my desk, my office chair rolling backward, more than aware I was over-thinking and quite possibly freaking out about this unnecessarily. This was just us having a laugh, right?

"Everything all right in here?" Patrick stuck his head around the door, his brows dipped low.

I nodded quickly, realizing my movement had been somewhat dramatic, and had pushed a box of papers onto the floor. "Yeah. Just knocked this over."

"Need a hand?"

"Nope. All good, thanks."

He remained in the doorway a beat, looking me over. I bent and focused on placing the papers in the box while willing the heat in my cheeks to bugger off.

"Okay," Patrick finally said. "Give me a yell if you need anything. You also wanted me to remind you about the mower rep coming in. They should be here in an hour."

"Great, thanks." I risked a look in his direction, relieved I was alone. Once I sorted the box, I resettled behind my desk, finding new messages waiting for me.

Ryan: Have I lost you?

Ryan: Where'd you go?

Ryan: Gotta go. Coach wants a word. Chat later.

I exhaled and stretched out my neck before flicking off a message.

Me: Good game, Broadwater.

I distracted myself from Ryan's text as best as I could, trying not to wonder if he was saying my butt was fine. That line of thinking would only drive me to despair. I was sure of it. When Patrick appeared in the doorway again, saying Tallis had arrived, I stood up quickly, relieved for the break.

Once in the storefront, I caught sight of the guy I assumed to be Tallis, the rep from John Deere. "Tallis?"

"Yeah, mate. You Nate?"

"Sure am." I gripped his hand and gave a friendly shake, my gaze glued to his piercing green eyes. They contrasted to his dark skin so dramatically it was hard to not stare at just how mesmerizing they were.

"Thanks for agreeing to meet," he said, his broad grin friendly and seeming genuine.

"No worries. You wanna grab a coffee first?"

"That would be great. It's been a long morning."

"Let's get you caffeinated then," I said with a chuckle, heading to the kitchenette out back. "Grab a bottle of water from the fridge too." I indicated in the direction of the small fridge. "One of these pod things okay?"

"Sure. A little more upscale than a heaped scoop of the generic stuff I'm used to."

Tallis's laughter was light, nice; he was also easy on the eyes. Just the thought of that was a reminder of how long it had been since I got myself out there. It had been a while since I'd been to Brissie. The Zone was my not-so-usual haunt, since it had been over a year. Considering my appreciation of the handsome man casting what I thought was an interested glance my way, it was in my best interest to take a visit to the city sooner rather than later.

After our coffees were poured, we took a seat, generally shooting the shit before we got down to business. After thirty minutes of chatting and another two hours of talking mower models and stock, Tallis said, "Perhaps one night you want to head a little further south and join my boyfriend and me for a beer." While his friendly smile was still fixed in place, I didn't miss how he eyed me, perhaps waiting for a reaction at the mention of his boyfriend and making sure he'd read me right.

I grinned immediately, right along with my brows shooting high. "Yeah, that sounds great," I replied, surprised by his offer.

His shoulders relaxed. "Sounds good. There's a decent LGBTQ bar we tend to go to. I'll invite a couple of friends too. Are you dating anyone?"

I shook my head. "Nope."

A mischievous smile appeared when he spoke. "In that case, I'll make sure at least a couple are single."

I snorted. "Uhm, okay. It'll just be good to hang out and great to check out a new bar." Was it crazy that the thought of hooking up made my stomach swirl with unease? I couldn't even fool myself about the reason why that was, either. Ryan bloody Broadwater filled my thoughts far too often.

"Sounds good. I've got your number, so we'll make plans soon." He left with a friendly handshake.

I grinned after him, stoked that less than an hour away, I had a new connection and the possibility of a fun night out. As much as I loved my town, there wasn't much happening in terms of a queer community. While I was out and didn't keep my sexuality a secret, I expected many steadfast locals would be happy not to be reminded of the fact either.

A night out, maybe even a night away from being a dependable uncle, would do me a world of good. It may even help get my mind off the man I'd never really let go.

CHAPTER 4
RYAN

END OF FEBRUARY

IT WAS EASY TO LOSE TRACK OF THE DAY OF THE WEEK, but having no idea which city we were staying in was a given. It was so good to be back on the court and well into the season. The days, the games, the training all blurred into one. My focus was fixed on the team, the players; there was barely time to shit, let alone think about anything else.

Like every year at this time, I felt more relaxed and together, completely in my element.

Almost halfway through the season, and our team had suffered too many injuries to be comfortable. It was to the point where everyone was stressed to hell and Coach was pushing us hard. There was a challenging battle to come for a playoff spot, and honestly, with Higgins and McGuire out, the whole team was feeling despondent.

That hadn't impacted on the satisfaction I experienced every time I stepped onto the court, though.

"Just get your ass to Lucas's, no excuses," Jayden called out before he left the change room. He'd been giving me shit for ages about not joining him and a bunch of the other players for downtime drinks. My excuses were wearing thin, and it was clear he wasn't going to let me keep giving him and everyone else the brush-off. It wasn't like I didn't love hanging out with the guys. I seriously did. But it was the whole drama of fending off women or dealing with digs from my team about me needing to get laid.

It was hard to believe that as a teenager, I'd lapped up attention. These days, I was all about keeping my personal life—and absolute lack of it—completely private.

"I'll be right behind you," I hollered in defeat. It wasn't the worse thing to be doing after a game, especially as practice tomorrow wasn't till the afternoon, and our next game wasn't for another three days.

The players on my team were good guys. When I was traded to the Minnesota Eagles, it had been the right call, even though the team was in the infancy of a big overhaul three years back. Back then, we were far from a championship team, but we were definitely heading in the right direction three years in, despite the smattering of injuries. And I liked to think I played some part in the turn.

But injuries, bad games, as well as shit-hot ones, were just part of the journey. I'd discovered that early in college and had it reaffirmed when I was lucky enough to be drafted. My focus had been absolute and unwavering. Time and time again, that had been my excuse for the distance I'd put between me and home, and there was some truth to it. Had I stayed in touch, been more invested in my family and Nate, there wasn't a chance I could have lasted so long in the States, even in pursuit of my dream job.

That first year in college, I'd made myself sick with homesickness and loneliness. While I'd covered up, played the role of happy, carefree, put-together jock, nothing could have been farther from the truth. By my second year, I'd known in my gut the only way to make a go of it was to all but cut ties. It was shit and wrong and made me feel sick to my stomach even today thinking about it. But I'd done it, believing it was the only way to survive, and for the most part, it had worked.

I cut off my engine in the parking lot of Lucas's, a small bar not too far from the court. It was a local hangout for the team; it meant everyone was usually left alone. The security helped with that, for sure.

I headed inside, greeting one of the security guys at the door. I wasn't here regularly enough to know if he was new or not, but he was built like a brick shithouse and had a handsome smile, as well as ink running from beneath the collar of his black shirt along his neck.

"Broadwater," he greeted, surprising me.

"Uh, hey." Even after years of being in the spotlight, it still boggled my mind that people out in the street knew who I was. While in and around the court I expected it, I'd deliberately lain low, keeping out of the press as much as possible, only ever really being photographed when out on official team dinners, usually with a girl my agent had organized to be my plus one.

Mickey and I weren't close. We didn't have that friendly relationship some of the other guys had with their agents. Probably because I wasn't interested in media attention or making more cash in sponsorships. Not being his money cow meant I was pretty low on his priority list.

The only thing I'd asked him for—apart from

good transfer deals—was my name out of the press and for a trustworthy plus one for dates. He did so, all without question.

"Your team is out back."

I dragged my gaze away from the bouncer's tattooed flesh and smiled. "Yeah, thanks."

A small head bob was my acknowledgment. I headed inside, the sound of my team enough to draw my attention and make me head in their direction.

"Dude, you showed. Pay up, Sutton," Jayden said, throwing me a shit-eating grin and holding his hand out to Gale Sutton.

"Seriously, Broadwater, today, the first time I've bet in ages, you decide to show up." He scowled at me, but the humor was there all the same.

I snorted as I stepped closer to the guys. "Looks like Jayden's buying, and I like to keep you all on your toes. Keep you guessing."

Sutton rolled his eyes before placing a beefy arm around my shoulder. "You can keep us guessing all you want. Just show your ugly face here more often."

"Aw, you missed my pretty face? If I'd have known, I'd have organized a poster or something, or maybe one of those life-sized pillows of me for you to take home with you," I razzed.

"The Aussie has jokes, everyone. Mind yourselves, he's going to go into Aussie mode anytime soon, and we're not gonna understand a lick of what he's saying." Sutton squeezed my shoulder lightly, leading me to the bar. "What's Jayden buying us? Shots?"

I chuckled. "Hell no. Training might not be till four, but I'm still knackered and need sleep without waking with a hangover. Just a beer, whatever's on tap."

"Make that two," Sutton said to the bartender. "And put it on Jayden's tab. His treat."

"The fuck, how much was your contract worth again, yet you're not buying your own beer?" Jayden grumbled at Sutton's side.

"You just won my last hundred-dollar bill." He shrugged, as though that explained it all.

"And your credit card?" Jayden's brow lifted.

Sutton shrugged again, not bothering to answer. Instead, he picked up the beer the bartender placed in front of him and took a huge swig.

"Tight-ass."

"Thanks for noticing, Jayden, my man. Buns of fucking steel right here," Sutton shot back. I snorted loudly—probably a mistake, since both guys zeroed in on me.

"What did I do?"

"Other than losing me a hundred bucks?" Sutton

quipped. "Not a lot, apparently. Where have you been hiding? Beyond practice and games, you're a damn ghost."

Jayden grabbed his beer and indicated toward an empty booth. Sutton and I followed, beer in hand, and took a seat.

"So what gives?"

My attention shifted to Jayden, who'd asked the question. I angled back in my seat, glancing between the two of them, and frowned. "You know, this feels like an intervention or some shit." While there was a lightness in my tone, it really felt that way. These two players had joined the Eagles when I had, and before that, we'd run into one another a time or two. After playing alongside each other for the past three years, we knew each other well. Or at least as well as I'd been willing to share, since there wasn't a chance I'd be outing myself.

There wasn't a single professional basketballer in our pro league currently out. Sure, there were a handful of gay or bi players out, a couple in football and hockey, even a baseballer. From what I understood, they dealt with homophobia regularly—usually after having a poor game—but the teams were supportive and cracked down on any homophobia from fans and the press pretty damn quick.

The media frenzies had calmed, usually after an interview or something.

More power to them.

I loved that a few pro players were living how they wished, openly and without apology, and rightly so. But I had no interest in being the only out basketball player. More than that, I had zero interest in being talked or gossiped about. And honestly, I just didn't want the attention. Not now. Not ever.

One day I'd live an authentic life, but while playing professionally…. I shuddered at the thought. That would not be happening. Ever.

"You need an intervention?" Sutton eased back and stretched his arm out across the booth.

"No." I rolled my eyes and took a swig of beer.

"Seriously, man, I know you've never been one to party, but… I don't know, since the beginning of the season, something's changed."

Knowing he was right, I held my breath, my gut somersaulting. And looking at these blokes who I considered friends, maybe I could share a bit of honesty. "I became an uncle just after the New Year."

"No shit!" Jayden's brows rose high, while Sutton's plummeted so low I could barely see the whites of his eyes.

"Why the secret?"

I lifted one shoulder in a barely there shrug. "Not

a secret so much as a surprise and me getting my head around it."

"Explain."

I smirked at Sutton's one-word order before telling them about my little sister and her not telling me she was pregnant. I explained how she was already doing an online course studying to be a veterinary nurse. As I spoke, I saw questions forming in their eyes. The big one was why the fuck I hadn't known.

"Photos." Sutton held his hand out, indicating my phone.

So relieved the questions I was sure were coming hadn't started yet, I tugged my phone out of my jeans and opened it up to my text messages. I hesitated before clicking on Nate's name. He was the one who regularly sent me photographs and short videos, and when I thought about it, it was usually a few times a week.

I touched the photo of Ivy I'd woken to this morning. She had the basketball player plushie I'd sent in her hand, the foot of it in her mouth. "Here." I handed it over. "Work backward."

The pair of them did so, heads together and mouths tilted in goofy smiles. I couldn't help but grin that these two guys, both over six foot five and solid and focused men at that, were all but clucking over the photo.

I got it, though. My niece was the prettiest baby ever, not too dissimilar from her mum. My and Amber's age gap had meant I'd looked after her, cared for her a lot from the moment she was born. It wasn't till we'd moved in with Gran and Mum had finally up and left—perhaps the nicest thing she'd ever done for us—that I'd come to appreciate my little sister was kinda sweet rather than being a burden.

"She's a cute kid," Sutton said, looking at me. "Fortunately, there's no resemblance to her uncle."

I flipped him off.

"Hell, your sister's hot, man. No wonder you've been hiding her away." Jayden bounced his brows up and down.

"Stop doing that. You look ridiculous and gross, man. She's eighteen, my kid sister."

"Looks like a MIL—"

Sutton smacked Jayden around the head before I could, cutting him off.

"Hey, I was only saying she's hot."

I rolled my eyes at him.

"So, who's the guy?"

I frowned at Sutton's question. "I already told you she doesn't know who the dad is." While that wasn't the greatest thing ever to admit about my sister, I wasn't ashamed of her. Despite her falling pregnant, she'd promised she'd been as careful as she could be with condoms, but clearly one just didn't work out. The last thing I wanted to think about was her sexing it up either, especially with a couple of guys, but hell, I'd got my cock sucked by absolute strangers in incognito gay bars over the years. I was the last person to judge.

"No." He shook his head and thrust my phone out so I could see. "This guy here."

I zeroed in on a photo of Nate cradling Ivy against his bare chest. When I'd opened the text, I'd almost swallowed my tongue at the sight of so much flesh. My gaze had then drifted to my niece, and my heart had flipped that he was stepping up for my sister so massively.

I'd never be able to repay him for all he'd done, *was* doing.

I cleared my throat and dragged my gaze away, looking up to see both men's focus was intent on me. "That's Nate." Both sets of brows lifted, making it clear they expected more from me. "We were best friends growing up. Since I left, he's been looking out for my sister and Gran. He, uhm, actually moved in with them just before Ivy was born." And wasn't that something.

Nate was still the best man I knew, and that he was still there, looking after everyone, something I should have been doing, made my insides twist in knots.

"Right," Sutton said, "and he's not the kid's dad?"

The word "No" shot out a little vehemently.

Sutton didn't respond immediately, staring a little too fixedly at my face for comfort. Unable to stop myself, I shifted, disconcerted under his scrutiny. "What's his story?" he finally asked.

I shrugged and took a gulp of beer, not quite sure how I felt about telling the guys about Nate. Since Nate and I had reconnected, with admittedly me being the one chasing the contact and throwing him a text whenever I got the chance, it hadn't taken long before longing stirred in my chest for the man I expected I could never have.

"We went all through high school together. Had each other's backs. When I left, we sort of lost contact, and he's been helping out with everything." There was so much left unsaid, so much I didn't share, couldn't share.

"Sounds like a good guy. He ever been out to visit?" Sutton asked.

Before I could respond, Jayden spoke. "Hang on,

when was the last time you visited Down Under?" he said with a god-awful Aussie accent.

I smirked at him and shook my head. "I'm not from South Africa," I jested.

"Whatever." He flipped me off. "But when was it?"

My mouth went a little dry before I answered. "Never."

Sutton's brows sprang high while Jayden said, "For real?"

"Nah, I just… I brought my sister out once, years ago. I had to organize the whole chaperone thing on the plane for her." I winced when I admitted, "She ended up leaving early." It was hard acknowledging just how much I'd fucked up to my friends who only knew me as a kick-ass player.

Unsurprisingly, it was Sutton who indicated with a flick of his hand for me to continue, with a one-word instruction of "Speak." The guy could be intimidating as hell at times, and while I could have walked away, verbalizing my downfalls and just how much I'd messed up was weirdly cathartic.

I spent the next fifteen minutes or so telling them half-truths. My homesickness, my distance, my effectively cutting off the three people I cared for. The only thing I kept close was how I'd admitted, realized, or whatever epiphany I had during that first year in college, that I was gay. It was that year, when I thought long and hard about my feelings for Nate, that the jigsaw piece I'd struggled to find clicked into place. Not only was I gay, but my feelings for Nate went so beyond those of friendship that even speaking to the guy pulled at me, made my new life in the US all but unbearable.

"And so you're back in touch," Sutton said, indicating toward my phone as he passed it to me.

Even though it wasn't a question, I confirmed with a nod. "Yeah."

"That's a good thing, right?"

A whisper of unease unfurled in my stomach. Talking about Nate, especially now we'd reconnected and he hadn't seemed to have changed a bit, was tricky, since it would be too easy to gush about the guy. Somehow I contained the soft smile that had been forming more and more lately, usually when I read one of his texts. "It is. He's one of the best guys I know," I admitted.

"You know, I've always wanted to visit Australia," Jayden said, cutting through the tension that had built by talking about home. "The place where everything tries to kill you. Sounds pretty fucking wild."

I snorted a laugh. "Not quite sure it's that bad, but it's an awesome country."

"You going to head back in the off-season?" Sutton's gaze remained unwavering. I had no clue what he was seeing or thinking, but goose bumps broke out nonetheless. The guy was freakily intuitive and good at reading people. I had no desire to be the next person whose barriers he broke down.

"Yeah. While Gran's on the mend now that they've figured out the stuff about her blood sugar, I still need to spend time with her. Plus there's my niece."

"And Nate."

Sutton snagged my gaze, and I swallowed hard. Shit, I really needed to get out of this place and away from the intensity of his gaze. "Yeah." I offered a too-casual shrug and looked down at my phone. "I think I'm gonna head back. Call it a night."

Jayden's groan was over the top and enough to make me smile. Some of the tension in my shoulders drifted away. "You've had one beer, dude!"

"I know, *dude*," I said with emphasis. He narrowed his eyes at me. "But I'm knackered. I need to get in a good sleep, ready for tomorrow."

While they were in the same boat as me, and it wasn't even nine thirty, they said goodbye without too much fuss, and I hightailed it out of there, my mind turning the night over. I hadn't told anyone I'd be heading back to Queensland to see them yet, still in two minds, but as soon as I'd answered yes earlier, I knew I couldn't not visit.

The only difficulty was, after seeing my family again, spending time with Nate, would it be too difficult to once again say goodbye?

CHAPTER 5
NATE

EARLY MARCH

T̲here'd been no more texts that made me second-guess if Ryan was flirting or not, and I wasn't sure if I was relieved or disappointed by that. It also made me wonder if I'd read far too much into that one text, which was likely, since Ryan Broadwater was very much straight. There'd never been a moment to make me consider otherwise.

While there'd been no specific texts that made me overthink, there'd been plenty that gave me a buzz of hope that our reconnection was real. Last night he'd messaged to let me know he had plans to come home at the end of the season. That was another couple of months away, and I could still hardly believe it.

I headed out of the store, calling out to Patrick

that I'd grab him a muffin and coffee, and stepped out onto the main street. It was only just gone nine, yet there were plenty of people around. Since a new housing estate opened up just a couple of kilometers out of town, it meant there were a heap more people around, which was good for business, especially when it came to gardening, as the new residents were landscaping.

Cooroy was a great place to live. With only a couple of thousand residents, it was easy to know lots of the locals, and considering how long the store had been open, which was since before I was born, it was a staple. There were usually lots of tourists around too, though.

Maple Street had an old-school charm to it. As I passed the estate agents and the small clothing store, I appreciated the collections of "Hellos" a few faces I recognized sent my way. With the sun already pressing its heat onto the sidewalk, I kept to the shade the store canopies provided. While we were officially in autumn, that didn't make much difference to our Queensland heat.

I headed into the bakery, my stomach grumbling and letting me know it was morning tea time. Ivy had been up every couple of hours. I'd taken over at five this morning so Amber, who was dead on her feet, could attempt to get a couple of hours of sleep before I left for work.

"G'day, Hattie."

The rosy-cheeked woman glanced up from what she was doing, offering me a friendly smile.

"Morning. The usual?"

"Yes, please, plus Patrick's."

Hattie immediately organized our coffees and our snacks, calling over her shoulder, "How's your morning going?"

"Not too bad. A steady stream. You know how it goes on a Friday."

Friday mornings tended to be super quiet until around eleven, when customers visited thick and fast, usually preparing for their weekend activities.

"That I do." She finished making our coffees while I angled to look out toward the street. A few people were milling around, parents with pushchairs, several elderly folks getting on with their day to buy their morning newspaper and fresh produce from the local grocer.

The normality of it all had me thinking of Ryan and the message I had yet to answer for no other reason than it had been a busy start to my day. I rolled my eyes at myself, calling BS. I had plans this weekend to head out again with Tallis, his partner, and a group of their friends. It was ridiculous, but I felt kinda weird saying as much to Ryan, sure he'd be asking questions.

Coming out, yet again, was endless as well as exhausting. Doing so to Ryan seemed a lot more significant than it had to anyone else, ever, including my parents. The possibility of him freaking out, especially knowing all the times we'd shared a swag and undressed in front of each other growing up, wasn't something I wanted to deal with. But I would. I had to. Knowing he now planned to visit in a couple of months cemented the idea.

"Here you go, Nate." Hattie placed the take-out cups in a cardboard carrier and the muffins in a bag for me. "Have a good one."

"Cheers, Hattie, you too."

I headed out, still thinking about Ryan, the unanswered text burning a hole in my pocket. A huff of breath later as I entered the store, I figured it was time to respond and get to the details. The cards would fall regardless, and I'd have to be okay with that. If Ryan was weird, he could go screw himself. Though even thinking that made my insides cramp uncomfortably.

"Don't say I don't do anything nice for you." I smirked at Patrick as I handed him his coffee and muffin.

He snorted. "Cheers, mate."

"I'm heading into the office to catch up with the quarterly statement. Give me a holler if you need anything." I glanced at the wall clock. "Dad's coming in early afternoon," I reminded him.

"I best go dust off the paint cans then, huh?"

I laughed, thinking about Dad and how he had this weird obsession with dust. "Best had." I continued into my office, closing the door before placing down my morning tea and tugging out my phone. Once seated, I reread the text, smiling as I caught a glimpse of an earlier message where he was bitching about dodgy bacon or something.

Me: Not a lot on tonight. Heading out to the Sunny Coast tomorrow night.

I smiled when dancing dots appeared. Ryan didn't have a game Thursday night, so I imagined he was already home, ensuring he got a good night's sleep for a fresh start tomorrow. The guy was nothing if not committed.

Ryan: Leave a guy hanging. *winky face* Anywhere decent to hang out on the Coast these days?

Before Ryan left, we'd just been on the cusp of

adulthood, so we had never ventured out to bars or clubs. Instead, we'd tended to grab the occasional sneaky beer to have at a friend's house or something. Ryan had been completely committed to making it in the pros, so he'd rarely drank anyway. Me? I'd been too shit scared to get pissed, afraid I'd end up a drunken mess and out myself.

Me: A few. Brissie's better. Just heading out with one of the John Deere blokes who's local, his partner—I hesitated over the use of partner, but swallowing back my nerves, I continued—**and some of their friends.**

Ryan's message took a minute or so to arrive while I sipped on my coffee and started overthinking everything again.

Ryan: Sounds good. A particular bar?

And this was it. While Ryan wouldn't know the place I mentioned, a quick Google search would tell him enough. And if Broadwater was the same guy as the version I knew all those years ago, he would absolutely research the hell out of the name I gave him.

Me: Bar QK. Should be a good night out.

I was really looking forward to it. When I received a text from Tallis a few days ago letting me know he was heading out Friday and asking if I wanted to come with him, he also mentioned the drag show. I'd been up for it immediately, having only watched a couple before, and both in Brissie. Plus, the last night out with him and his friends had been easy and comfortable, so I was happy to get to know them all better.

He'd offered me his spare room again, but I'd felt kinda odd accepting, since I'd only met the guy a couple of times, so instead booked a cheap Airbnb a short walk from the bar.

Ryan: I'll check it out online.

I held my breath, not sure if he intended to do so now or another time.

Me: Okay. If I don't chat with you before, be a legend tomorrow.

I grinned as I hit Send, ignoring the increased pounding of my heart.

Ryan: On it.

Setting my phone to the side of my PC, I ate my muffin while I waited for the Excel doc to open. It didn't take long to get my head around the details I needed to upload and work out. Once in the zone, I found my rhythm easily, punching in the numbers and double-checking I wasn't messing up. About half an hour in, my message alert went off.

I hit Save before picking my phone back up. A rush of air escaped me when I opened the message.

Ryan: Heading to bed. Just thought I should say I'm totally up for a visit to Bar QK when I see you. Night, Nate.

Heavy pounding erupted in my ears, blocking out all other noise.

What. The. Fuck?

Was this Ryan telling me he was gay? Or was he just reassuring me he wasn't an arsehole?

I stared at the message, unable to compute, unable to grasp which he meant, and too nervous to believe the former in case I was wrong.

With buzzing in my ears, I tore my gaze away, staring unfocused around my messy office. My fingers tingled, my heart fit to explode, all while my stomach somersaulted so fucking dramatically it thought it was in training for gold.

There was a moment's hesitation before my fingers flew across the keyboard on my phone.

Me: Ryan Duncan Broadwater, are you wanting to join me when I visit a gay bar?

I hit Send and waited, my body vibrating.

Ryan: With you?

The bastard. I shook my head and forced myself not to kick off a response. I didn't have to wait long.

Ryan: Abso-fucking-lutely.

Fuck me sideways with a double dildo. Dead. This arsehole, with all his perfection and wanker ways, was going to kill me. And right now, with my face flushed and a grin stretched so wide, I was at risk of causing permanent damage, I didn't want it any other way.

CHAPTER 6
RYAN

I'd told him. Sort of. Maybe. Okay, I actually hadn't at all, but I had absolutely no regrets about the tentative first step I'd made.

Forcing myself to ignore my pounding heart and the weird hum in my ears, I took a steadying breath. This was Nate. One, he wouldn't be telling anyone about what I texted. The certainty of that was as clear to me as the full moon that currently hung overhead, casting a bright glow onto my deck.

Two, I hadn't actually come out, per se. So, if by some freakish chance he lost his phone and someone read our exchange while figuring out who the hell I was, nothing would get out.

And three… for the first time in eight years, I felt like I could truly breathe. It was a taste of what it could be like living authentically, being my true self, out in the world without giving a shit what the gossip rags, fans, or the management would say. It was as liberating as it was terrifying.

For now, as I clung to my bottle of water, looking out across the lit city and the moon's dancing rays on the lake, I chose to latch on to the former.

What I wouldn't give to be liberated.

What I wouldn't do to have the guts to say screw it all and shout to the world I loved me some D.

I snorted as the thought filtered through me, amused at the possibility of "D." An errant thought traveled to Nate, sure he would piss himself laughing and rib me something rotten for spouting on about liking the D. With that thought came the slap of reality. Nate Griffin was gay. Right?

There were times I could get so caught up in my own world and own head that I could miss the blatantly obvious stuff. I wasn't arrogant enough to think otherwise. But Nate choosing to share with me the bar's name had to be his invitation for me to check the shit out of it. I always had… done research, that was. While I sometimes missed the obvious, share something with me that I didn't know, hadn't heard of, and I'd google the crap out of it.

Nate had ribbed me often enough when we were kids about that. There was no way he'd forget.

So of course I'd researched Bar QK. When I had,

and the gallery had popped up, color me fucking surprised. I'd spent about half an hour poring over images, practically inhaling the write-up and the various pages, and had come away shell-shocked. Right alongside that open-mouthed amazement that such a place existed not too far from where I was brought up, an honest-to-God sucker punch had hit me in the solar plexus.

Nate was gay, or maybe bi, or at least not straight.

I thought.

Hoped.

I had dreamed about the truth of those words since I was eighteen, and while those dreams hadn't ridden me hard the last few years due to my blocking the man from my life as well as my mind, the truth was, he was still there, buried under my skin, alongside what I'd thought was a futile hope.

I huffed out a heavy breath that carried a touch of laughter.

That text I'd sent him had been frantic, automatic after my research. There wasn't a chance I couldn't send it. By doing so, it felt like I'd changed everything…, but, I thought with a sobering swallow, I hadn't really changed anything at all.

I was still here, doing what I loved, playing the game, chasing the dream, or one version of it. The thing was, the other version was the one I'd tried my hardest to bury. Yet here it was, breaking free like some sort of zombie or vampire or some shit, crawling from solid earth after it had punched its way out of the coffin.

God, I needed something stronger to drink. When I started comparing my dreams to an episode of *Buffy the Vampire Slayer*, shit had seriously gotten off track.

As I made my way back inside, a quick glance at the time told me what I should be doing was heading to bed. It was only just gone nine, but my alarm was set for five thirty so I could fit a run in before training. We had a big game tomorrow, and like every other game, I needed to be focused.

Heading to bed rather than grabbing a glass of whisky, I glanced at my phone and read my last text. I expected Nate would be freaking out, which led me to wonder a whole lot more about Nate and his life.

Me: Nate's gay?

I paced the room, waiting for my sister to pull her finger out and text me back already. The couple of minutes felt like a million with how long she took. I'd hesitated a beat before sending the message, that slight concern about outing someone. A moment later, I'd dismissed the idea. My sister was nothing if not tenacious. If Nate was not straight, she would absolutely know about it.

Amber: And?

And? Was she serious? I flopped back heavily on my bed, pissed at my sister being facetious while my fast heartbeat started up again. She hadn't challenged, hadn't said no.

It was true.

Right?

Me: Why wouldn't you tell me?

Amber: Why would I? I don't go around telling you about people's sexuality. That's just weird. Hey, Ryan, my friend Pippa is straight. I repeat... and? What of it? And more to the point, why would I out someone?

I hesitated and hung my head, feeling like a prick for sending her the message in the first place.

Me: Just came as a surprise, is all. Heading to bed.

I had no idea if the brush-off would work, but a man could hope.

Amber: Snort. You're such a loser.

Me: Whatever. Give my niece a kiss.

After that, I turned my phone to silent and got into bed after washing up and brushing my teeth. As I expected, my brain worked overtime. Falling asleep thinking of a shirtless Nate and the new possibility that provided made my dreams ridiculously sweet and a lot dirty.

Me: So how was it?

I'd woken up Saturday morning more than aware that it was Saturday evening in Australia and Nate was out. And not just out, but out at a *gay* bar. Nate should have been the last thing on my mind as I'd pulled on my running shoes and completed a five-mile run. He definitely shouldn't have been on my mind as I drove to meet up with the team for briefing and basic warmups before our game this afternoon, but by midday, I'd sent the text anyway.

I figured it was early hours in the morning over there and hoped a little too hard that he was tucked up wherever he was staying—which I didn't want to think too hard and long about—all by himself.

There was a strong possibility Nate wouldn't be by himself. The guy was hot, and it was safe to say the few years that had passed looked good on the man. It gave me a new level of understanding of the saying about aging like a fine red, or however it was, because, yeah, an eighteen-year-old Nate had been sweetly sexy, but the twenty-six-year-old version was mighty fucking fine.

"Broadwater, get your head out of your ass and pick it up," Coach hollered at me. We were in the middle of drills, and what I should have been doing were sprints and free throws.

I hadn't been.

Instead, my mind was occupied with my unanswered message. That was a whole shitload of dangerous.

I was the king of focused, of switched on. Nothing messed with my games, ever. Shout shit at me? I could barely hear the words. A crappy personal foul, and I was motivated as hell. Nate possibly having a hot and heavy night, staying who knew where, *doing* who knew what, and I was in danger of making Coach's head explode and getting some bench time.

Forcing myself to get my head in the game, I pulled it out of my ass and worked through the drills. After that, Coach left me alone, and I continued my same routine, preparing to go back with the team in a short while before they opened the doors for the spectators.

With drills over, I headed to the locker room, Jayden at my heels.

"You doing okay there, Broadwater? What was Coach chewing your ass about?"

I shrugged. "Nothing, all good."

"You're the golden boy. That's the first time ever Coach has given you shit, so that's not nothing."

A barely there sigh escaped, embarrassment more than anything pushing the air past my lips. "I wasn't focused."

I cast a quick glance at Jayden, seeing his brows springing high in surprise. I would have laughed if I didn't feel so ridiculous.

"You focused now?" While worry wasn't in Jayden's voice, something close to concern was. I got it. My screwups were rare, and that wasn't arrogance talking. It was hard work and dedication. We were drawing in closer to the end of the season. These games mattered. The points *mattered*. While we weren't running for the championship, our performances would impact contracts next season. There were a few guys about to become free agents. I wasn't one of them, with a year left, but me messing shit up for them, potentially screwing up a pass, their chance to play their best, would not be okay. It never would be.

It was that I reminded myself of every single game, every single practice. So yeah, I understood Jayden's furrowed brow, the slight apprehension when he looked me over.

"I'm focused. You know we've got this shit. Dead set legend, remember?"

He snorted at that—one of the phrases I'd introduced to my American friends—Sutton joining us and releasing a low chuckle too, no doubt hearing the tail end of our conversation.

"There he is… the boy wonder from down under."

I shoved Jayden gently to the side—always fucking gentle, as I'd heard too many times about injuries been caused by the stupidest shit. "You're a dick."

"Yet again, you're confusing that with me having a *big* dick."

Jayden was incorrigible. "And I'm interested in knowing your dick size because?" Every single time I played this sparring game, I cringed on the inside. Such expected humor flew close to the radar.

"Any living soul would be goddamn lucky to get up close and personal with my giant dick. It's a curse, really, a cross I have to bear." Jayden tugged off his shirt once in front of his locker, a couple away from mine, Sutton between us.

Sutton piped up, his voice deadpan, "You put a whole new meaning to dribbling with all that leakage going on. I don't know if it's coming from your ass, your mouth, or your *giant* dick."

I laughed loudly. "Leakage? Gross, are you dribbling from an orifice, Jayden? Man, there's medication for that. Geez."

Jayden shot both of us the stink eye. "Fuck you, assholes. I fill fucking orifices, not the other way round."

My eyes shot up, and I gaped before I laughed so hard I was sure I was going to curl over.

"The fuck, that's not what I meant," Jayden shouted, backtracking unsuccessfully.

"So women don't have orifices?" Sutton looked at me with a smirk and threw me a wink before settling his gaze back on Jayden. "You don't need to explain yourself to me why you'd jump to that conclusion. You know the association has strict guidelines about supporting everyone and being inclusive," he said, and my laughter died away as he spoke, knowing while that may be the party line, a "don't ask, don't tell" culture was very much true.

I glanced away and grabbed my toiletries, listening in as Sutton continued. "We all know that's a crock, but anyone with big enough balls to come out in *our* team, they'd get our support 110 percent."

At some point, all amusement had gone. Jayden listened intently, no longer protesting, and a few other guys were clearly listening in too. Me? My whole body froze in a rush of fear. Why the fuck was he saying this? Was it me? Was he saying it for my benefit? Regardless of the reason, what he said was amazing, but still… had I said or done something that made him suspect?

Nausea grew thick and fast in my gut, a balloon of lead expanding, becoming heavier and heavier, and the sweat already covering my skin doubled its efforts.

"Too fucking right they would. One of ours will always be one of ours." The fire in Jayden's voice took me by surprise, but there wasn't a chance I'd look his way. I couldn't.

"Shower," I said, a little too loudly, drawing more than Jayden and Sutton's attention to me. I needed to chill out. "Get your asses into gear before Coach comes looking."

And thankfully, I wasn't wrong.

Coach had his own pregame routines he expected us to follow, and showering after our early drills was just one of them.

By some miracle, we won. While I wouldn't usually assume divine intervention, after the weird pronouncement from Sutton, my head wasn't where it should have been. I'd had two hours pregame to sort myself out, and while I'd shaken off most of Sutton's words, his voice echoed on repeat in my head.

While I didn't know if he was on to me or not, my nerves threatened to spill over and screw up my performance. One stumble, I'd thought that was it, but it had also been enough to shake me and remind me this was my job, my life…, my career.

I couldn't screw this up.

The game against the Knights had been tight. They'd had one too many breaks, making us pretty even at the half. With some smooth… hell, even enviable moves from Blake in the third quarter, the game finally tilted in our favor; by the fourth, we were on a roll, despite the last five minutes of always being in a clutch. Those five points rode us all heavily until a three-pointer from Jayden set us up for the win.

Tension—a combination of relief, anxiety, and a blast of fucking joy—buzzed in my veins as I left the stadium. There wasn't a chance I'd head out with the guys tonight. Jayden hadn't even pushed for it when I'd refused either.

A new message alert grabbed my attention, and I asked Siri to read it.

"Nate. Good game. Nothing like leaving it till the last second, though. Deakin is a turd. What the hell with that foul?"

I grinned as Siri read Nate's text to me. Not allowing myself to overthink, I directed Siri to call Nate. He picked up immediately.

"Shit, man, how's your ankle?"

I chuckled lightly. "All good. Nothing to sweat about. Deakin *is* a turd," I agreed. The asshole in the Knights had shoved me hard. My ankle had twinged in the fall, and for one heart-stopping moment, I'd hesitated over moving it, too terrified I'd sprained it or done a whole heap worse.

Thankfully, it was little more than a pinch. A quick strap during a time-out had meant I was good to go.

"Thank Christ for that. You heading out?"

"Tonight? No. On my way home. Tomorrow we're heading to Memphis for the game the day after. I need some downtime."

"I can't even imagine."

"What's that?" I ask.

"The traveling, the chaos during the season."

"It's something."

"You doing okay? Really?" The last word was offered tentatively.

I huffed out a breath, wondering that despite the years of disconnect, he could still read me so well. "Yeah." I wasn't ready to bare my soul to the guy. Maybe when I visited, I'd make a move and finally say the words aloud for the first time, and that included to myself. "Enough about me. How was your night?"

He hesitated a moment, probably debating whether to push. I was relieved when he gave me a break and answered with "Pretty fucking awesome, if I'm being honest."

My grin was immediate after hearing the smile in his voice. "Yeah?"

"Yeah. The acts were amazing, and the atmosphere… shit, it was good fun, mate."

"So definitely a place for you to take me when I visit?" My earlier warnings to myself flashed on red alert, but this wasn't the first I'd hinted. Perhaps I was a coward, but I kinda wanted Nate to just come out and ask. The thought of him doing so exhilarated me as much as made me want to shit my jocks.

"Yeah," he said, his tone changing, dipping quieter, lower. "There's nothing quite like a place where you feel safe, feel like you can be yourself."

I swallowed hard and forced myself to pay attention to the road before me. What it would be like to simply live authentically… one day. "Yeah, one day," I murmured, fully aware I was sharing my thoughts and giving him so much.

"What time are you heading out tomorrow?" he asked, changing the subject, allowing me the reprieve I needed to shake off the emotion and longing riding me.

"Training in the morning, then we're heading out for the next game, I think early afternoon."

"That's with the Tigers, right?"

Warmth unfurled in my chest that he knew the roster. "Yeah. It'll be a tough game, but we'll do all right."

"I've no doubt. Just keep that ankle strapped, and don't let a fucking loser push you around again."

I laughed. "I'll try my best. You know," I continued before I could stop myself or think clearly, "my last game is in LA, the closest state to Australia. If you want, you could, you know, come on out and visit." The words and the idea were out there and took shape immediately. Longing slammed into me. It had been so long since Nate had been courtside, the thought of him being so again sent a rightness through me, a desperate need to make it happen.

Two quiet beats passed before he cleared his throat. "You want me to watch you?"

"More than anything," I admitted. "My flight to Brissie is the week after, so, you know, we could make it a thing, a break for the two of us; let me show the sights, obviously back here where my team is. But we can then head home together for my trip." My words were a rush, and any chance of holding back my eagerness to make it happen was dissolved with the added, "Please."

"Let me think about it."

"Obviously I'll pay for your flight and—"

"Ryan," he cut in, "it's not about the flight or the money. Just let me have a think, okay?"

I nodded, despite being by myself, my eyes wide, wishing upon everything that he'd say yes. "Okay, I can let you think about it." I hesitated a moment, the next words dancing in my mind, ones that were at the core of our friendship. *No take backs, remember?* Before I'd left Australia, I'd thrown out our "unbreakable" promise to each other with the naiveite of a teenager. Back then, it had been about him heading to the States to watch me play.

The thing was, he would have done it in a heartbeat had I given him the chance. We talked about it that first year of college, but I'd thrown a spanner in the works by distancing myself and destroying our friendship.

I swallowed down the words instead, not wanting to push this with him right now.

"Listen, I've gotta go. My folks are expecting me for lunch."

"Sure. Say hi for me, yeah?"

"Absolutely." And imagining Nate's grin with that one word, I smiled again, some of the adrenaline pumping through me evening out. "Get home safe and look after that ankle."

I chuckled. "Will do. Talk soon."

"Talk soon."

When the phone cut off, I stretched out my neck, relieved my turn was coming up. Asking Nate to come out and visit may have been an impromptu request, but fuck if I didn't want it to happen.

CHAPTER 7

NATE

ANY EXPECTATIONS I HAD ABOUT THE DRAG NIGHT WERE blown out the water, and some. It had been forever since I'd laughed so much or had been hit on that much either. The night was a heck of an ego boost, something I hadn't realized I'd been missing.

I'd rolled into the cute Airbnb in the early hours of the morning after enjoying the show, dancing till my feet legit hurt, and having had so much to drink, my head had spun.

Tallis and John had taken me under their wings for a second time, simply by being so welcoming. Not only that, they'd introduced me to more of their friends, a couple of whom I'd grabbed numbers from.

I'd been missing out, having forgotten how

empowering and important a tight group of friends in the community was.

After my night out, I was on my way to getting that back.

A week had passed since then, and I'd texted a couple of guys I'd met and even arranged for a quiet drink at Bar QK one night. My week had also sped by with daily texts from Ryan, and his invite still unanswered.

Every time I thought I'd decided, I wigged out, doubting myself.

My phone pinged, and I opened the text, immediately laughing.

Ryan: Remind me never to eat grits again. I swear, they're the devil's cum.

Me: Shit, warn a guy with a text like that, mate. Nothing like opening a conversation with devil's cum. And grits?!? Is that the weird breakfast thing?

Ryan: Yep, also known as the devil's cum. That shit is gross. Went out for breakfast this morning, and I'm still gagging on the memory of the stuff.

I paused, my brain immediately drifting to Ryan tasting cum and gagging. I gripped my dick through the denim of my jeans, grateful I was in my office behind my desk. Dick twinges at work weren't the best at any time of the day, but when I was due to head out and cover Patrick for his morning break in fifteen, yeah, I needed to get on top of that.

Me: Best I don't touch on any of that. Shouldn't you be sleeping or something?

It would have been so easy to jump all over his words, and maybe ten years ago, I would have, but with the uncertainty between us, I didn't want to push it too much. My heart had been broken once already. Me flirting so obviously…. I shook my head, aware it hadn't been the first time we'd flirted by text, but fuck if I wasn't terrified I was heading for a fall.

Ryan: Too wired to sleep.
   Me: ???
   Ryan: Just thinking about my visit… and yours???

I winced. Ryan hadn't broached the subject since he'd asked. I wasn't surprised he'd let it slide for so long. While we'd both changed, grown over the years, some traits were most definitely the same.

Ryan's lack of tenacity being just one of many.

Me: I'm thinking about it.

Ryan: What can I do to make it happen?

I snorted a humorless laugh, aware I no longer needed to worry about my stiffening junk. The potential answers to Ryan's question were numerous. *Don't hurt me. Don't let me fall for you again.* Though for the latter, I wasn't sure I'd ever stopped. *Don't abandon me. Promise to always be there.*

I released a heavy sigh, hating I felt like a needy dickhead for my heart's inner ramblings. 'Cause that was definitely what they were. My heart was the driving force to all things Ryan-related.

Me: Give me time.

Dancing dots appeared immediately, and I swallowed hard, waiting for his response.

Ryan: I'll give you everything and anything I can. Including another sorry and a promise not to be a fuckhead again.

A loud snort tore out of me. I seriously wanted to visit and spend some time with the man. Get to know him all over again. He'd been my best friend once. After these weeks of exchanges, he was already vying for the top spot again. Not that there were any other contenders.

Me: Not being a fuckhead is a good quality. As is not complaining about the taste of devil's cum.

And I totally went there, already rolling my eyes at myself for my inability to stick to my word. That's what Ryan did to me, though. He drew out the playful side of me, the ridiculous flirting, and a little of my bravery too.

Ryan: Ha! If you do visit, we'll see how you handle it.
Me: The taste of cum has never been an issue, loser. Bring it.

There it was. Again. And when he responded with laughing emojis, I simply shrugged and laughed right with him.

LATE MARCH

Ryan: Why do kings always scream when they cum?

Ryan: Because it's customary to announce when royalty arrives.

Ryan: Why do cum shots drip into belly buttons?

Ryan: It's seamen trying to get to the navel base.

THE GRIN ON MY FACE WAS GOOFY, BUT HOW COULD IT not be when I woke up to these god-awful texts from Ryan. It was after six in the morning, so I had a little time to kill before I needed to get my butt into gear.

Me: Really?

I waited a few moments to see if he had his phone on him, but when he didn't respond after a couple of minutes, I suspected he was training or something. His next game wasn't until tomorrow, so I supposed he could already be traveling.

Still wearing a grin, I got myself sorted for the day and headed downstairs, greeting Ivy with a kiss on her head and the same to Amber, who was feeding her.

"Morning. Ivy didn't wake you in the night, did she?"

"Nope." I put the kettle on to boil and looked at Amber properly. "Rough night?"

"You saying I look like shit?"

I snorted a laugh. "I wouldn't dare."

Amber smirked. "Honestly, she wasn't too bad. Just once, but it took a while to get her to sleep."

"You have a busy day?" I asked.

"Not really. There's a module online I need to finish up, but I should manage okay between naps."

I nodded. "Well, if you can't, let me know by three, and I should be able to finish up early. Dad's in town today and can close up for me, so I can head home early and look after her for you."

Her smile softened. "Thank you. Seriously, I'm sure you'd prefer to be back at your own place by now. I already feel guilty that we're cramping your lifestyle."

I snorted. "What lifestyle?"

Amber raised her brows as she lifted Ivy to her shoulder to burp. "Exactly. You've been out twice… *twice*… recently. You're young and hot. Shouldn't you be going out and getting some? Hell, I really wish you would, as who the hell knows when the next time I'll be able to."

I scrunched my nose. "I really have no desire to hear about anything at all, as in *ever*, about you getting any. And there's not a chance I'll be sharing stories with you either." I shuddered. Amber was virtually my kid sister. While she was a mum, she was still a kid and probably still would be when she was forty.

"So, there are stories to tell?" Her brows waggled up and down. "Seriously, let me live vicariou—"

"Not a chance."

She huffed out a forlorn sigh. I laughed and went back to making my coffee now the water had boiled. *Stories?* I thought. Chance would be a fine thing.

Next weekend, I was meeting up with a couple of my new friends at the same bar, and Lenny, one of the guys who worked there, had been a little flirty. *But* there was a "but," one which pissed me off.

Ryan "pain in the butt" Broadwater was firmly back under my skin. And sending me jokes about cum. I shook my head at myself. Maybe I just needed to get him out of my system. Even with that thought in mind, I opened up Google and started a search on cum jokes.

EARLY APRIL

The bar was packed, but knowing the owner's husband apparently meant that Tallis had snagged a big booth. There were no complaints from me. I'd had a busy week at work and had got into the habit of staying awake late into the night texting or talking to Ryan, which meant while I was knackered and needed sleep, I was looking forward to a fun night while sitting on my backside.

"So, have you decided yet?" The question came from Tallis and pulled my attention away from Lenny serving at the bar. He'd caught my eye a time or two, had even thrown me a wink, but I was still unsure if he was flirty or friendly.

"About?" I asked.

Tallis rolled his large green eyes at me. "That friend of yours in the States and making a trip."

I grunted in response, choosing to take a pull from my bottle of beer instead. Tallis was a good guy; his partner was great too, but Tallis and I had become firm friends, resulting in me oversharing last week about all things Ryan.

"If you're still friends with the guy…."

I glanced back at him, understanding the direction of his trailed-off words. "It feels so much more complicated than that."

He nodded and leaned forward. "Complicated could be worth it, though, right? You get a trip to the States, spend time with one of your best mates…."

When he spelled it out like that, it seemed pretty straightforward, until I considered the ache in my heart the last time he'd left, and then the added pain when I had to accept I'd lost him for good. And that was just with friendship. Now, with the casual sharing of info, I was more and more certain that Ryan was not straight. But everyone knew how assumptions could make an ass out of… well, me.

"I'm leaning toward heading out to see him. It'll be good to spend some time with him before he heads home and is focused on his family," I admitted.

Initially, Amber had been a little leery once she'd learned of her brother's upcoming visit, but that hadn't lasted long. While the girl was as tough as nails, she loved her brother fiercely. Sure, she was pissed at him, but the look was there, clear as day, knowing she'd be seeing him again and that he'd meet her daughter. And Gran was crazy excited.

The old coot was as fearless and stubborn as ever, and while her meds had really improved her health over the past couple of months, we were all aware she'd never be a hundred percent again. Old age didn't stop for anyone.

"I say go for it. I think you're making a good decision," Tallis said. I smiled in response, hoping he was right.

"When he's over, we'll definitely make a night of it," I said.

"Damn straight we will," he declared, rolling his

eyes at me. "I need to check the guy out who's had you by the short and curlies since you hit puberty."

I snorted. "In that case, maybe not." My brain then stumbled. If Ryan wasn't straight, he wasn't out, so what I'd already sort of hinted at—my interest in Ryan—was already too much. It was something I'd need to be discussing with Tallis—the need for discretion—and of course Ryan, if it was evident I needed to.

Tallis grinned wide and leaned back, smiling at John when he returned with a round of drinks. "You're family now. There's no chance of us not seeing him."

A flutter of warmth unfurled in my chest at his words. I simply nodded, heat filling my cheeks, not quite sure how to respond without sounding like a tool.

As I thanked John for the fresh bottle of beer, my phone vibrated. I tugged it out, seeing an incoming call from the man who was always on my mind.

"That him?" Tallis leaned in and peeked at my phone, grinning widely when he spotted Ryan's name.

"I'll just step out—"

Before I could move or complete my sentence, Tallis swiped at the answer button. "We all want to say hi."

Amusement danced through me. I figured Ryan wouldn't mind at all, especially since he knew I was out, yet he'd video called me anyway.

As soon as his face came into view, my heart flipped over itself. His dark hair was damp, as if he'd not long showered. A tight, pale blue tee stretched over his tanned chest and biceps, providing a sexy image of the guy. His focus was connected firmly to me, his smile bright, wide, and real.

"Hey, you."

"Hey, Broadwater. Crashing my night out?"

He gave a light shrug, a smirk on his face. "Maybe. Thought I needed to check out who keeps stealing you away."

This time tiny wings took flight in my chest. I swallowed, my grin true and fixed. "Missing your early wake-up chat, huh?" Humor laced my voice, but I was sure my words carried truth.

"That's pretty much the gist of it. You having a good time?"

"Yeah. There's an act on in about an hour, so we're just shooting the shit."

Ryan's gaze shifted to my left, to where Tallis's face dipped into the screen, wearing a huge grin.

"G'day, Ryan. Tallis." Tallis followed up with a chin lift and a smile.

"Hey, Tallis, good to meet ya. Nate here's told me

a lot about you," Ryan answered. He flicked his gaze to me briefly before refocusing on Tallis.

"Back at ya, mate. I'm sure there's a shitload more stories I need to hear, but Nate's told us a few." Tallis chuckled and nudged me.

I snorted. "I've barely touched the surface."

"Just only believe the good stuff, yeah?" Ryan said, his smile still in place, but I saw the small shift in his gaze, already figuring what the "not so good" stuff referred to.

"Sure thing. Heard you've got another big game coming up on Monday."

"They're all big games," I answered for Ryan. At my words, Ryan tilted his head slightly, his gaze roaming my face before settling on my eyes. "What? They are. They all count, right?" Since reconnecting with Ryan, I made no bones about watching every replay and some games on livestream.

"Shit, I forgot Nate here was your biggest fan," Tallis jested.

My eye roll was teamed with a smirk, not even caring that he was right. The four beers I'd had probably helped with my not caring. That combined with the sweet smile Ryan cast my way, and I absolutely didn't care that he knew just how important he still was to me.

"You're still my biggest fan, Nate?"

For all that was holy and hot, Ryan's voice dropped a good octave when he spoke. And hello gruffness! I swiped my tongue across my bottom lip, finally thinking perhaps that fourth beer wasn't the best idea. I was far too needy and horny when I got to that fuzzy, happy place, the one I reached before I got hammered.

It was impossible not to notice the way Ryan's gaze zeroed in on the action. I swallowed hard before remembering to answer. "You're no longer so high on my shit list, so I thought I should make the effort."

Tallis snorted beside me, while Ryan's eyes narrowed a fraction just before he smiled once more. "Can't ask for more than that, and you know, that visit guarantees a good seat courtside."

"We were just talking about Nate's visit," Tallis butted in, and I cast a furtive look my new friend's way. His words sounded like it was a done deal. I sighed before returning to focus on the screen and the new light in Ryan's eyes.

Fuck.

Who was I kidding? There wasn't a chance I could not go and see him.

"Your visit as in when you arrive here?" Ryan directed his question just to me, an eagerness in his expression that once again sent those wings in motion.

Just as I started to nod, a body brushed up to my other side, an arm going around my shoulders. Startled, I turned to see it was Lenny.

"What's happening, and who's this we're talking to?" Lenny's expressive eyes were filled with what I was sure was mischief. And holy hell, with my brain spinning out with having agreed to go to the US, the booze in my system, and Ryan's face like thunder now my gaze had returned to his, I could barely think straight.

"Erm—"

Tallis cut me off, saying, "This is Nate's Ryan."

Was it wrong that I liked the sound of that? I'd always hoped he'd be mine one day, and with the new dynamics settling between us, just maybe that would happen. A guy could wish while equally crapping himself.

"Hey, Ryan." Lenny gave a goofy wave, appearing unaffected by the daggers shooting from my best friend. "I've heard plenty about you." He squeezed my shoulder, and I looked at him through the image of us on the screen. "So, he really is hot, huh!"

I frowned, sure I hadn't said that to Lenny, but… I glanced at Tallis. *He*, I had told. Tallis winced and offered me an apologetic smirk.

Once my gaze was back on the screen and Ryan,

his frown had smoothed out a little. "You want to just call me later?"

I nodded a little numbly, overwhelmed all of a sudden. "I can do that." I'd also need to be making a fast apology. The last thing I wanted was to make him uncomfortable.

"I'll be sure to answer." A small smile tilted his lips, and he looked at the two guys on either side of me. "Good to meet you both. Be sure he gets home safe, yeah?"

Tallis nodded. "Absolutely."

Ryan's gaze connected with mine once again, a softness there I liked to think was reserved just for me. "Call me." The call then ended, and I was left a little shaken and aware that the room seemed a lot louder than a few minutes ago.

THE NEXT AFTERNOON, I SAT OUT ON A BLANKET IN THE garden with Amber and Ivy. The flowers on the frangipanis had begun to fall, yet it didn't prevent their sweet fragrance from reaching us in the light autumn breeze.

I'd already told Amber all about my night. She listened intently between tickling her daughter's feet and trying to stop her from reaching out to the blades of grass so she could ram them into her mouth.

"So, did you score?"

I shook my head at her.

"Seriously, Nate, give me something. At least tell me about the hot guys who were there."

I relented with a snort. "There were all sorts of men there. A fair few women too. The blokes I was with were up for a good night."

She bounced her brows up and down. "They were, huh?"

"Piss off. I mean, we had a laugh, talked shit."

"But you hooked up?"

My cheeks heated, and she chuckled. There may have been a couple of guys who'd offered to take me home with them. I didn't plan on telling her that, though.

"You did, didn't you. Nice." She dragged the word out.

"I didn't, not really," I admitted, not wanting her to get far-fetched ideas of me hooking up with anyone.

A frown creased her forehead. "Why not? You're hot and single."

"You saying I'm hot makes me want to gag a little." She simply stared at me in expectation. "I could have gone home with someone if I wanted to."

It should have felt weirder that I was having these talks with Amber, but we spent so much time with each other that it seemed natural to overshare with her.

Amber's brown gaze narrowed. "Is this about my brother?"

The heat in my cheeks dialed up a degree or fifteen. A few years back, I'd admitted to Amber how I'd crushed on her brother. This was after far too many beers one night and a moment of weakness. I shouldn't have been surprised that she'd figured as much. The woman was too observant for her own good. Even when she was much younger.

"I've actually sort of made up my mind to head over for a visit, watch his last game of the season and take a holiday there before he comes home for a visit."

Her brows shot high, and I was silently proud of myself for shocking her.

"Wow, okay, wow." She pursed her lips a moment before they twitched and a smile formed. "I think this is a great idea. It'll do you a world of good to have a break. Plus, I imagine you've got a lot of stuff you need to talk about."

The hammering of my heart filled my ears, so much so I could barely hear my "What do you mean?"

"Well, it's been years since you've really talked, let alone seen each other. A whole lot has changed since you were eighteen. It'll be good for both of you, come to think about it."

I silently agreed, thinking more and more that me visiting him would be the right thing to do, and for once, the right thing for me. I loved my life, my home, but it didn't mean getting away wouldn't be awesome. And the truth was, cutting through the tension between Ryan and me was something I wanted to do. Last night and his reaction to the possibility of me actually visiting had reaffirmed that even more.

The excitement evident in his eagerness, in the flash of emotion in his eyes, may have been good for my ego, but it was more than that. I wanted to get to know him again. And selfishly, I didn't think I'd get the chance to do that with his family vying for his attention once back home.

"Do you think he's worried about coming home?"

Amber's question pulled me out of my thoughts. "As in, what? Seeing you and Gran?"

"I don't know, maybe. It's just been so long."

"I think he's desperate to see you both and meet his niece. I think he'd come on a plane today if he could. And definitely when Ivy was born. He loves you and misses you."

She tilted her head. "I think he loves and misses you too."

My laugh was awkward. Not knowing how to respond, I fidgeted and then picked up Ivy, needing the distraction. With a kiss on her cheek, I made a face at her, choosing to ignore Amber's loud huff.

Thinking about Ryan that way couldn't lead to any good. At least not until I knew where his head was. As rightness settled in my chest while certainty clicked into place, I smiled. Heading to the US to spend time with the guy was definitely what I wanted to do.

***

A HITCH IN MY BREATH WAS A DEAD GIVEAWAY, BUT I couldn't stop it. "So yeah, I'll come out for the week before you return here, then." I forced myself to pause, the desire to ramble and overexplain riding me.

The quiet down the line seemed to drag a beat too long before Ryan's exhale reached me. "You will, definitely?"

Disbelief edged his words, making them rough and a little throaty. Hell, based on how I was feeling, maybe there was some emotion there too. "Definitely. I'll look into flights tomorrow."

"I can get that sorted."

"No, honestly, it's good." He'd offered before, but it felt all kinds of weird to take him up on it. I managed to pay myself a decent salary at the store, and it wasn't like I spent a lot of cash on myself, so my savings were good.

"Don't you remember what you made me promise, though?"

The mere reminder was all it took for the flash of memory to hit me. I chuckled. "Not so much a promise. More of my arsehole self taking the piss." I leaned back against my propped pillows and smiled. "God, it feels like a million years ago."

"Right. I sometimes wonder where the years have gone." The rustle of a packet caught my ears. "We're only twenty-six, but sometimes I feel a hell of a lot older, especially today."

"Yeah, why's that?" Concern had me frowning.

"My ankle—"

"The one you hurt in the Cats game?"

"Yeah. It's twinging and not feeling quite right, you know?"

"What's the doctors or whoever say?"

The sound of the opening and closing of a door preceded him saying, "I'm working with the trainers at strengthening it without pushing it. Doing lots of hot and cold, keeping it strapped." He hissed. "Fuck."

"You all right?"

"Ice packs," he grunted. "You'd think I'd be used to them by now." He chuckled lightly. "But I'll be fine. They're not too concerned. It shouldn't impact Tuesday's game."

I swallowed hard and released a heavy breath, not realizing how much his words had worried me. "Well, that's something."

"Uh-huh, but back to you coming out here...." His words trailed off, and another rustle followed. When he spoke again, his tone was quieter, a little more tentative. "I can't wait for you to be here. Finally watch a game."

I closed my eyes, not having to ask what he was referring to. It wasn't like I thought too hard or often about our millions of past conversations or anything. I rolled my eyes at myself. "Me too. So," I started, wanting to pull away from the past, "LA for a few days, then back to Minnesota."

"Yeah." Somehow I knew he smiled as he spoke. "We'll hang out, do some sightseeing, then head here for the last couple or so days. Obviously we'll have to fly back to LA to get our flight to Brisbane. It'll be a ball ache. Maybe I should figure out a way so we don't have to come back here?"

"No," I said quickly. "I want to see your place, where you've called home for the past few years."

"Yeah?"

"Definitely."

"A whistle-stop tour… I can make that happen."

"Holy shit, Broadwater, you've learned how to whistle. Your balls have finally dropped. Give me a moment while I wipe my tears of pride away."

Laughter burst down the line. "Fuck off, Griffin. And what the hell does whistling have to do with balls?" I made to speak, but he added, "Scrap that, I don't think I even want to know."

I snickered and relaxed even more against my mattress, loving this… how we could banter and talk shit. While we'd never forget how things had changed or that we'd had so much time apart, you couldn't destroy the connection we had. The certainty of my thoughts took me by surprise. Six months ago, I wouldn't have believed that was possible. Yet here we were.

"I'm sure whatever you decide are the must-see places to see, it'll be great." I pushed sincerity into my tone.

"This vacation is gonna kick ass." Ryan's enthusiasm was addictive. It flowed over me with familiarity and warmth I'd thought long disappeared.

"Damn straight it is." The sound of Ivy's cries

filtered toward me. "Shit, your niece is awake. I'll go and see to her, as Amber said she had a headache earlier. I'll talk to you soon."

"Okay." Before I could end the call, Ryan saying my name stopped me.

"Yeah?"

"Thanks for making this happen. It means a lot."

I stood, smiling, my heart doing a little flip at his gentle tone. "No worries, mate. I can't wait."

CHAPTER 8
RYAN

MAY

With my cap pulled low and my shades blocking a decent portion of my face, I angled my head down, only allowing myself brief glances around the busy terminal. Steel walls filled my periphery, framing large, curved glass windows filtering in the spring morning light.

That Nate was arriving on such an early flight was a relief. It meant the crowds were yet to swell to capacity, so I hoped to stay incognito. It was always risky being out in the open like this, so I worked hard at blending in as much as humanly possible. The positive was, being in LA meant I wasn't on my own turf, where my team's fans would much more likely spot me.

A quick glance at the time told me barely a minute had passed since the last time I'd checked. Nate should be heading through security by now, perhaps clearing customs. His flight landed almost thirty-five minutes ago.

I paid no mind to the few groups standing around me, too focused on evening my breaths and willing my heart to slow. Shit, was feeling giddy like this really a thing? The last time I'd been this hyped up was when waiting for the draft announcements, but something about this moment seemed different, bigger, and wasn't that a mindfuck.

There was little doubt in my mind that Nate's hold on me was as strong as it always was, but now, after the past four months or so of conversation—of late- and early-night calls, video chats, and texts—that hold seemed more significant.

With no chance of convincing myself it was just the excitement of seeing my childhood friend again, I didn't even bullshit myself. What was the point?

My initial flipping out when I first saw that photo on Instagram last year told me my overreaction was more than me being a protective big brother. It was all about Nate and just how fucking gorgeous he was. The guy had me wanting things I was too terrified to dream about.

But that was then.

Now, at this moment, with this visit, everything seemed possible.

Two more minutes passed by, and a low hum buzzed through me as passengers tugging luggage, looking tired from their flight from Brisbane, poured through the automatic doorway.

I held my breath, flexing my fingers before scrunching them together, the vibrations in my fingers freaking me out.

And then he was there.

Nate was taller than most around him but a few inches shorter than my frame, all bright-eyed, with a grinning face, and making a beeline toward me.

My plan of a smile and a bro hug flew out of the window when he was in touching distance. My large limbs wrapped him up, held him tight, and like the desperate man I was, I buried my head against his neck and inhaled. I didn't let go, didn't ease up, and with Nate's strong arms gripping me just as tightly, he didn't seem in any rush either.

The sounds of voices close by, the increased foot traffic around us, and a slight nudge as someone rushed past me cut through the moment and the reality of the situation. I needed to get him in the car I'd organized and back to the hotel.

I eased out of Nate's embrace, raking my gaze over him, wanting to have my fill of every single inch of the man. Unable to do so, I cleared my throat, struggling to contain the smile of happiness stretching my mouth wide. "You got everything?"

"Yeah." He nodded, indicating his small bag at his feet and backpack on his shoulder. "We should get out of here, right? There's only so long I expect you can blend in for, yeah?"

I snorted and bumped his shoulder with mine before leading him away. I'd organized a car with the hotel the team was staying at. As the driver took Nate's bags off him, I was relieved I'd planned ahead. Driving when I couldn't take my eyes off the man at my side would have been catastrophic.

"The drive should take us about half an hour," I said to him once settled. I strapped in, legs open and breath hitching when his thigh brushed my own. He didn't move away, nor did I. "Your flight okay?"

"Yeah… and business class?" He quirked a brow at me, but since he didn't look too pissed off by the upgrade I'd surprised him with, I gave a one-shoulder shrug.

"Did it mean you slept so we don't waste our day together?" I challenged, a little sass and gruffness to my voice. I'd arrived at LA early after negotiating with my coach to do so. I still had training to do today, but I had plans for Nate to join me with that, so I really did hope he'd managed to sleep.

"I did, really well actually, and thank you. You didn't have to, but I appreciate that you did."

I grinned, pleased he'd managed to get a decent rest. "In that case, we have a busy day ahead of us. I hope you're up for it."

"Anything, yeah, sure. When's your team arrive?"

I smirked, loving the nonchalance with the question, especially that it was absolutely legit. There was no stargazing or fanboying. Nate was one of the most down-to-earth blokes I knew, and time hadn't changed that.

All time had done was make it almost impossible to keep my hands off him.

Restraint was a fuck of a thing, especially when there was so much unsaid between us.

"Did you say tomorrow?" he prompted, since I'd zoned out, wondering why I hadn't figured how I felt about Nate much sooner.

"Yeah. They'll be here by midday, with the game the following night."

"Last game, huh?"

"Yeah, the Comets are high up in the Conference standings, and while we're not ranking high, we need the points in our division. It'll put the team in a better standing next year, especially when it comes to trades and drafting. We're not in for playoffs this season." I shrugged. While it was gutting, considering the injuries from a few players this year, we hadn't done so badly. Plus my ankle still wasn't quite right. There wasn't a chance I'd be letting a slight twinge hold me back in my last game, though. Not with Nate finally here.

"And you were okay getting me a ticket?"

I chuckled. I had access to tickets whenever I wanted. I usually ended up giving them away to my teammates who were chasing some. This was the first time ever I was using a ticket for someone I cared for, someone here just for me. "Yeah. Other than I think Marv, who deals with all ticket handling for the team, just about had a heart attack with shock when I asked him to make sure you had a good seat."

Nate didn't respond with more than a small smile before looking out the window at the passing cars.

Before long, we arrived at the hotel and headed up to the suite I'd secured. I led Nate in, showed him his room, and handed him a key card. "Coffee?"

"Yeah, that'd be great. I could do with a shower too."

I left him to it, trying not to think about everything I wanted to discuss with him. Today, or any day before my final game, wasn't a good idea. My focus needed to be on the court, not on my heart or my dick. Instead, today and tomorrow morning, I'd concentrate on having a good time with an old friend while building in some training. Everything else would have to wait.

Since I tended to play guard when on the court and knowing the Comets and their go-to strategies, Nate and I were hot and ridiculously sweaty on the small court I'd managed to source for a couple of hours practicing my defensive plays.

Over an hour and a half in, Nate was bent over, hands on his knees and huffing heavily.

"I swear to Christ, I'm gonna throw up." He peered up at me, still managing to shoot me a stink eye while panting so fast I was sure he would hyperventilate.

I snorted despite the twinge of concern in my gut.

Nate was a lot fitter than I expected for a guy who I figured spent most of his time working in his family store. His frame was thicker than the last time we'd played one-on-one together, a given since over eight years had passed by. But underneath his shorts and tee, he still appeared to be in decent shape, though I'd noticed a sliver or two of softer flesh when his top had risen. I liked it. A lot.

Being surrounded by athletic bodies, all hard lines and taut, defined muscles for sure was nice to look at.

But to rub against, to grip and take comfort in, not so much.

Not that I had any experience with that, really. Certainly none since going pro.

"You ready to stop? We can."

He glanced at the clock on the wall and shook his head. "You've still got thirty minutes to go. What can I do, bar sitting out, that isn't going to kill me but will be useful to you?" He heaved himself up to stand and wiped his sweaty brow.

The guy looked shattered and still all levels of appealing.

I racked my brain for what we could do to make him feel involved but without destroying him. "How about we just shoot some hoops?"

"Seriously?"

I shrugged. "It's okay to wind down, and I can always do with the practice."

Nate didn't look so convinced.

"Perhaps we can make it interesting," I offered, not quite sure where I was going with this.

"I'm listening."

I snorted. "Okay, that was as far as I got, since drinking games are so not an option, at least for the next few days."

The roll of his eyes sent a shot of longing straight to my heart. The familiarity of the gesture, something he did so often when we were kids when I came up with half-assed plans, was immediate.

I wished so badly I hadn't fucked up so spectacularly.

"You all right?" Nate took a couple of steps in my direction, and I smoothed out my frown, ignoring the heavy pounding of my heart. Regrets were the worst. I needed to find a way to move on.

"Yeah. That's my thinking face."

Even though he snorted, the disbelief in his eyes was easy to read. Our tells were front and center, and rather than latching on to the ache they created, I snatched hard and fast to the comfort of it, of him.

"Okay, so no drinking games. How about first dibs on places to visit or food to eat?"

I scrunched my nose up at that. "Shit, are we old? We got old, right? When the fuck did that happen?"

Nate's laughter burst loudly into the empty court. I grinned at the sound. "We're not even thirty, so no, we're not fucking old. Hell, I finally believe that forty isn't old anymore. Not now I can see it creeping up on us so quickly."

"Okay, so not old, just dags, since I can't think of a decent wager or whatever."

"Sounds about right." Shifting to stand before me, he took the ball from my hands. "How about we just shoot, and you can—" He cut off midsentence, a flash of amusement filling his eyes, and I winced, knowing that whatever he'd thought of would take daggy to a whole new level.

"Okay, to make it fair since you're the pro who gets paid the big bucks, every hoop I get two points, you get one. First to thirty. The loser has to find a bar or club or something and dance the 'Nutbush.'"

I waited for a beat to see if he was kidding before I widened my eyes and snorted out a laugh.

"'Nutbush,' the dance? Are you serious?" Hell, I'd last done that at our Year Twelve formal. There was nothing quite like a graduating party to break out our moves.

"Yeah. It'll help you prepare for your trip back home… just in case."

"Just in case?" I asked.

"Well, you know there's bound to be a time a deejay plays the damn thing if we head out, especially if it's a cheesy bar, and you're going to be called out if you can't remember your moves. They're gonna pull your Aussie card for sure." The glint in his eyes was pure fun and teasing.

"And obviously if I win"—'cause I expected that was the way it would go—"you'll stand up and dance to it?" I tilted my head to drink in his reaction. Nate had never been one for the spotlight. Sure, he was up for having a laugh, but he was happier when others took the lead.

"Yeah, straight up, I will."

I grinned and reached out my hand. "Deal," I said as his palm connected with mine, and we shook on it.

We took it in turns, each shot from the three-point line. With each successful shot he made, surprise flicked to life in my gut. I'd forgotten what a good shot he was. "How are you still so good at this?" I asked, angling toward him and quirking my brow.

His shrug was nonchalant, but I wasn't buying it.

"Spill."

"I have a hoop at home, plus I put one up at your gran's a while back. What can I say? I like taking the ball out every now and then."

My brows rose in surprise. "You do? But you pretty much hated the game when we were kids."

His shrug was a little less nonchalant this time. "I may have stuck with it after you left. I stopped playing for the Sunny Coast." I didn't miss the sadness in his eyes before he glanced away, bouncing the basketball at his feet and showing a little too much interest in it. He cleared his throat before continuing. "I just needed a link still."

I swallowed hard, a flash of pain hitting my chest. "To me?" I asked quietly, both heartbroken and crazily touched if that was the case.

"Yeah." Nate's gaze found mine. "It's been hard, was stupid hard for a while when you left. I just felt… I don't know. It's ridiculous."

I shook my head and shuffled my feet, though I refused to look away. When we were kids, we'd been close and shared almost every thought and feeling with each other. But this sharing right now, as grown-ass adults, pushed my discomfort into overdrive.

But I couldn't pull away. I needed Nate's words, his truth.

"It's not ridiculous. Tell me. Please."

"Even at uni I played around with a basketball almost every day. It was my half-arsed attempt to stay connected to you." He shook his head, just once, a soft smile tilting his lips a fraction. "You leaving, then you ghosting me, fuck, Ryan, it all but destroyed me."

Instantly, my throat constricted, and sadness slammed into me thick and fast. "I'm so fucking sorry."

He bobbed his head, eyes still on me despite the wetness evident in their depths. "I know you are. Are you going to tell me why? I know you shared some stuff with me, but there's more."

"There is?" I was full of it, and we both knew it, but I couldn't do this now.

Nate's lips pulled tight, and he arched a brow at me, calling me out.

"When the season's over, okay?" I didn't elaborate, but I didn't need to. Not with Nate.

"Fair enough." There was a slight rise in his chest, and I felt the action as if it were my own: that need for a deep breath to pull myself together. "I score the next two, you're screwed and are going to be asking for Tina Turner." While his smile was a little tighter, I accepted the shift.

I gave a one-shoulder shrug. "Tina Turner's 'Nutbush' will find a new lease of life in the States if that's the case." I wriggled my brows, and Nate snorted out a laugh.

"Whatever you say, Broadwater. I'm looking forward to it."

Four minutes later, Nate was laughing his head off, and I was already considering the quietest, most remote bar I could think of when we headed back to Minnesota that I could take him to. The fewer people to witness my god-awful dance moves, the better.

"Okay, calm your farm, Nate. Next time your ass is mine."

He quirked his brows and laughed even louder when heat whipped around my body, scalding my face so fast, it was like taking a visit to the sun or some shit.

"Whatever." I rolled my eyes and smirked. I wasn't ready for that conversation yet. "Shower, and then we can head out for food?"

His laughter eased off, and he nodded. "Sounds good."

"You still doing okay; not jet-lagged?"

"All good. That bed made all the difference."

"Good," I answered. "I'll still need an earlyish night, though. I have to head out for a run in the morning."

"The gym?"

"Nah, can't stand running machines. If I can avoid them, I will every time. I think there's a few parks nearby, so I'll head out there. You can join with if you want."

Nate's scrunched nose was adorable.

"I'll take that as a no."

"You can take that as a hell no."

"You know, exercise makes you sweat, and there's nothing sexier than a naked, sweaty body." The words fell out of my mouth unbidden, and heat hit my cheeks. It was something Jayden said regularly, and I'd always laughed it off, but with Nate, even the idea of him naked had me almost swallowing my tongue at the image that evoked.

Wide-eyed, he stared at me a beat before grinning.

"Yeah, I've heard that about exercise. But you know what?"

"What?" I asked, willing my cheeks to cool.

"So does whisky."

His grin was wide, and I was still so caught up with the possibility of Nate naked that it took me a moment to hear and understand his words. My laughter bubbled over. "Fair enough. As long as with that doesn't come whisky dick, I'm sure you're golden." I grinned as we collected our things and started the few blocks' walk back to the hotel.

We strolled in companionable silence for a block before Nate asked, "I was kind of expecting you to be battling fans chasing you and cameras and stuff. Is this normal? You wandering around and things like this with no one bothering you?"

I shrugged and took a surreptitious glance around. I'd done so as soon as we left the court and multiple times since. That Nate hadn't noticed meant I was excelling at my sneaky, incognito skills. "I stay out of the papers and gossip mags as much as I can. Honestly, I rarely head out. I think it means that fans and paps and such aren't actively looking, or at least they never expect to see me out and about."

"It must be crazy."

"It can be, but I've worked hard at trying to live as normally as possible."

Nate glanced at me, no doubt taking in how I'd pulled my nondescript cap down just so, or the regular-Joe clothes I wore. "It sounds like you're a hermit. Not sure that's normal." There was no barb in his tone. If anything, a hint of sadness wrapped around his words. "You loved going out, causing chaos, getting attention when we were younger."

Nostalgia, as well as a pang of longing for a simpler time, awoke in my chest. It stretched a little too uncomfortably as it brushed against my heart.

"It sounds lonely."

I swallowed and worked hard to concentrate on the pavement without becoming overly emotional at the impact of his words. All I could do was shrug, and when I was sure my voice wouldn't come out shaky, I said, "Being on the court is as amazing today as it was eight or even four years ago. The rest… it seems like a small price to pay for playing in the League." This time I didn't risk side-eyeing him, worried at what emotion I may see reflected in his turned face.

After a beat, he thankfully changed the subject, giving me a reprieve. "You say the team's getting in at midday tomorrow, right?"

I bobbed my head.

"You need for me to make myself scarce?"

"No," I answered immediately. We had such little

time with each other that I wanted every moment I could have with Nate. "Coach and some of the guys know you're here. Jayden and Sutton will give me shit if they don't meet you straightaway." I rolled my eyes and smirked, working hard to ignore the flip in my stomach at the idea of them all meeting.

Since that moment a few weeks back when Sutton had made his impromptu speech about gay players, there hadn't been another incident. Thank Christ. But it made me all levels of nervous.

They knew Nate was important to me, but I had no idea if seeing us together would raise questions. Overthinking this all was doing my nut in, but my attraction to Nate hovered beneath my skin, danced in my stomach, and set those fluttering wings alive in my chest whenever I looked at the guy. And when I was close, or when he laughed and that sweat trickled down his face that I wanted to lick off, I didn't know how good of a job I was doing at hiding my attraction.

For eight years or so, I'd had practice at playing it straight. While it hurt to do, it had become second nature. But around Nate, with my renewed feelings for the guy running rampant, the fear that my friends would know fed into my worry.

"They both have another year's contract, right?"

I nodded in response, giving myself a moment to

get my thoughts back on track. "Yeah, and at the moment, I think they're both hoping for another couple of years." As soon as I spoke, I grimaced, not wanting to open up a discussion about contracts.

But it was out there, and immediately after came Nate's question: "And what about you?"

I side-glanced him as we continued down the block. "I haven't decided yet." I looked away.

"No? And that means…?"

"It means I haven't decided if I want to stay, trade, or maybe even come home." It was the first time I'd said those words aloud. The world didn't stop turning, the pavement didn't crack open beneath my feet, and a hundred paps didn't jump out at me. I smiled inwardly, reminding myself that really, no one gave a shit about whether I played or not. There'd always be more great players coming up in the drafts. The idea was as liberating as it was shocking.

I'd taken a couple of steps before I realized Nate had stopped dead in his tracks. I turned to face him.

Wide-eyed, he stared up at me, his mouth parted ever so slightly, and a flush of color from his previously cooling cheeks sat high on the sides of his face. "You might come home? Back to Australia? Queensland?"

My gaze roamed his before dipping lower. His

chest expanded as though taking a deep breath. Returning my focus on his eyes, I nodded. "I might. I've got a lot to figure out."

"But you love basketball."

"I do."

"Don't forget there's basketball in Australia." His stare was unwavering, searching. Still silent, he nodded before moving forward again, indicating for us to continue. "Another conversation for after?" he asked quietly.

My chuckle was light. "Yeah, definitely."

CHAPTER 9
NATE

IT WAS A STRUGGLE TO KEEP MY BUTT IN THE SEAT AND from shouting like I was hyped up on sugar, but other than a handful of times when I couldn't contain myself and had jumped up shouting or cheering, I'd done a decent job of being the supportive friend. The last thing I wanted to do was draw attention to myself, which was totally me overthinking.

Though the one time he was shoved and I saw him go down, a twinge of panic had roared to life when he stood and seemed wobbly on his sore ankle. That moment I hadn't held back my thoughts of the player who'd made it happen or my extra loud cheers when number twelve fouled Ryan.

The whole game Ryan was on fire.

While it was the first pro game I'd watched in the flesh, I'd viewed every single one of his games since

January and had read the basic stats on Ryan before that. And this game right here, he was phenomenal. While the stakes weren't as high for the home team, I knew Ryan's team had a fair bit hanging on it, and considering the stakes, the whole team played like this was the playoffs.

With my gaze rooted to the court and all but going cross-eyed trying to keep one eye on Ryan and the other on the play, my heart beat loudly in my ears, drowning out the huge crowd filling the courtside.

Overtime was a hell of a thing watching from a TV screen, but from the sidelines, I could barely contain myself. With each pass, each bounce, my heart flipped and did a triple beat, and each time Ryan laid his hands on the ball, I held my breath. Fuck, I was going to hyperventilate at this rate.

The countdown was on, the buzzer set to go off any second when Sutton passed the ball to Ryan. I sprang to my feet, wide-eyed and focused on every move Ryan made as he released the ball from near midcourt. The ball hit the backboard, slipping into the basket just as the buzzer sounded, and that was it. Pandemonium. The best kind. The yellow-jersey supporters screamed and hollered while Ryan jumped in the air, fist-pumping, his gaze landing on me before his team swarmed him.

With my heart in my throat, I gulped in a breath, reveling in the oxygen and the win.

Minnesota had won, epically so, and with a buzzer beater like that….

I clapped loudly, joining in with the hollers. The whole time, pride, joyous and so fucking pure, filled my chest.

Ryan was born to do this.

Just as the thought entered my brain, my smile slipped.

He was considering giving it all up. He was magic on the court, and him not doing this for as long as he was able seemed like complete madness.

I shook off my frown when I realized Ryan's focus was intently on mine, and he indicated for me to take the two steps needed to enter the court. I grinned, more than happy to oblige.

I all but bounced down the steps, renewed happiness for Ryan buzzing in my veins. Once before him, I made no qualms in hauling him into a hug, patting his back, and whispering, "You were fucking spectacular." Another back pat, and I pulled out of his sweaty embrace.

"Yeah?"

I rolled my eyes, giving him a shove. "Yeah! Amazing, seriously. Congrats, mate."

Ryan's smile was as wide as my own. The shout

of his name had him turning. Sutton was calling him over, a bunch of press waiting just off to the side.

"You go."

He glanced back at me and nodded. "Use your pass and meet me out back. I'll be as quick as I can. You still good to go out with the guys tonight?"

I bobbed my head. "Definitely. This needs to be celebrated."

A flash of a grin was directed my way before he hightailed it toward Sutton, his coach, and the reporters waiting for his words. I looked on, wondering if anyone else noticed how he favored his left foot.

It took about fifteen minutes for Ryan to head to the locker room and another twenty minutes after that for him to reappear. With damp hair and stopping close enough to me that I could smell his deodorant, the man looked delectable.

My boundaries were slipping dangerously fast. From the casual flirting over the past couple of months and the sweet smiles and comfort over the past two days since being here, the struggle to hide my attraction was real. But I wouldn't waver, especially when in public.

If, and it was a big *if*, Ryan wasn't straight, that meant he was obviously in the closet, and I thought I understood the reason why that would be.

Outing the guy was not an option, and no chance would I put him in that position.

Three hours later, I was a little fuzzy, but not so hammered I wouldn't remember every single moment of not only today but this exact second.

Ryan, as well as four other players, were full-on doing—or perhaps attempting was a better word for it—the classic line dance that pretty much every Australian knew, to Tina Turner's "Nutbush City Limits."

With my hands clutching my stomach, holding in the joyous pain from laughing so much, I snorted when Jayden got into it even more with his hands on his hips and throwing in extra gyrations for good measure.

The guys were lapping it up, and so were a heap more people who were in the bar.

"You not joining them?"

A quick glance to my left, and I smiled at Sutton. "Nah. Ryan owes me this one. He's paying up. I need to appreciate the moment."

Sutton huffed out a snort and cradled his beer as he stood at my side, the two of us leaning against the waist-high wall splitting the main room from the small dance floor. "You know, we call this the Hucklebuck."

I grinned over at him and laughed. "I did wonder

why after just a few moves so many people were able to join in." My gaze returned to Ryan, still on the dance floor and going for it, making all the moves hilarious. Even over the music, I could hear his loud laughter.

"So I hear you're stealing him away from us."

My brows dipped, and I glanced over to Sutton. I would love to steal Ryan away and keep him forever, but after today's game, the thought of doing so made me uneasy. "What?" I asked, needing clarity as my thoughts were spiraling.

"For a few weeks this summer, right?"

"Oh, right, yeah, well, our winter. It's been a long time since Ryan was home. His gran and sister have missed him like crazy."

"And you?" His question startled me, made my breathing falter while my heart beat loudly in my ears. When I didn't answer and looked at him, my brows low, he clarified, "You grew up together, right? Ryan's your best friend?"

I nodded and exhaled deeply. "We did. He was."

"Was?"

I shrugged and returned my focus to Ryan, my smile reforming quickly. "A lot has happened in the past eight or so years, but we're reconnecting." It would have been easy to gush and overshare, and I thanked Christ I hadn't drunk so much that I'd gotten loose lips, which was what had happened with Tallis a while back.

Sutton grinned, and I noticed that smile turned a little into a lazy smirk. "I think as far as Ryan is concerned, that BFF status is still intact."

"BFF?" I quirked a brow at him. "Really?"

He snorted out a laugh and gave a half-arsed shrug. "Yup, BFF status. It's totally a thing. Jayden insists on it."

The few of Ryan's friends on the team I'd met and hung out a little with yesterday, I liked. When they'd told a few tales about Ryan, there'd been a mixture of envy that I'd missed out on so much combined with relief that he seemed to have genuine people here who cared about him.

While Ryan and I still had plenty to talk about, he'd apologized for flaking on our friendship, and his family to some extent. I knew there was more to the story. My anger had long since passed. Maybe a bit of frustration at missing out on so much bubbled under the surface, but it was more than that. My heart ached for the man and how much he'd missed out on.

He'd left us all, everyone who loved and cared about him.

I hoped soon I'd understand the reasons why

better, but knowing he'd been without his family and me for eight years ached.

"I think it will do him good, going home," Sutton said.

I remained tight-lipped, wondering if he was going to continue. His focus moved to the dance floor, and he grinned. I followed his line of sight, my heart kicking up a notch when my gaze connected with Ryan's. He shot me a wink before laughing at something one of his basketball buddies said to him.

"He seems happier since you guys got back in touch."

I cast a quick glance at Sutton, whose attention remained on his dancing colleagues.

"But I don't know… there's something else too." With his words, he angled to look at me.

Discomfort battled it out with my curiosity. It didn't feel quite right talking about Ryan like this. Not that Sutton was saying anything bad, but it just felt odd. But my curiosity was absolutely piqued. Missing out on eight years left a lot of gaping holes in knowledge. "What do you mean?" My question escaped, despite the fizzle of guilt in prying for information.

Sutton's gaze searched mine, making me still at the intensity I saw in its depths. I had no idea what he was looking for or seeing, but I was sure he saw too much of… everything.

"It's true that he seems happier. He's been laughing more and, I don't know… I hear about people 'lighting up' or some shit. I don't even know what that really means, but he definitely does that when he's texting or talking to you."

Lighting up? I willed my eyes not to close with thoughts of the possibility, willed my expression to remain neutral.

"But he also seems, I don't know… lost, empty." He shrugged, pulling his gaze from me and taking a swig of his beer. When he snorted a laugh, I frowned. "But what the fuck do I know? Fuck, I'm drunk, and I need a piss. You good here?"

I nodded despite the rush of confusion in my head.

"Great. If Ryan asks, I didn't abandon you. I made sure you were good and not left by yourself and shit?"

I quirked my brow. "Do I wanna know?"

Sutton's grin was wide, and he swayed a little on his feet. "He made a few of us promise to have your back and make sure you're not alone." He patted my shoulder and bobbed his head. "Though since the guy's barely taken his eyes off you, I can't see what the fuss is about." He squinted a little. I would have sworn just fifteen minutes ago he didn't seem this drunk.

"No leaving and making him freak out," he ended with, followed by a belch that had him laughing as he walked away.

I stared after him, my brain struggling to process everything Sutton had shared. I didn't have time to think before a new body appeared at my side. I angled to take a look, expecting it to be one of Ryan's teammates who I recognized. My eyes widened in surprise, taking in a man unfamiliar to me.

His smile was wide but seemed natural, friendly even. He was a little shorter than me, maybe by an inch, and was likely in his late forties. What was distinctive about the guy above anything was how polished he seemed.

He didn't look like he'd been knocking them back and seemed a little too dressy for this place. The bar was far from a dump, too friendly and a little too well-kept for that. But it didn't quite seem the place this bloke would hang out.

His voice lifted as he spoke over the last few chords of Tina's "Nutbush City Limits," a distinctive twang that was all-American, but beyond that, I had no idea what accent it was. "You're Nate, right? Ryan's friend from Australia?"

"Yeah, mate, and you are?" I angled my head a

little closer to hear him as the volume on the small dance floor rose with laughter.

He reached out his hand, saying, "Micky, Ryan's agent."

Surprise had my brows shooting high. Ryan had said a thing or two over the last few months about his agent, which of course I'd ribbed him about. As, hello, *agent*! The dude had an agent, for crying out loud. It was still hard to think of Ryan in the big leagues, especially when I flicked my gaze in his direction and watched him line dancing with his thumbs in his belt loops.

The only things he'd shared really were that Micky was an okay bloke, a bit straight—in the not breaking the rules sense, though looking at the guy I expected the other way too—and he left Ryan to it, which was the way my friend liked it.

Micky being here was unexpected. Though what did I know? It was Ryan's last game of the season, but I imagined he had other clients too.

"G'day." I shook his hand and offered a friendly smile. Even if I couldn't get a read on the man, he looked after Ryan and made sure he was paid well.

"How's your visit?"

"Yeah, great. Crazy the last couple of days, but looking forward to heading out of LA and seeing where Ryan's put down some roots."

"That's good. I'll only need to steal him away for a couple of things when he heads to Minnesota. One's taking place near the Duluth Aerial Lift Bridge. Make sure you come along to take it in. Whenever I head over, it's a good spot to see."

"Sounds good, thanks. I think that place is on my list."

"Let me give you my card with my number on it in case you come unstuck while you're here, okay." A small card was passed over, thick and embossed.

"Cheers." I took it off him and shoved it in my pocket.

"And here's the man himself." Micky's attention shifted, the same friendly smile on his face. I followed his gaze, grinning when Ryan appeared.

Sweat covered Ryan's forehead, and a wide grin stretched his face. In the few strides it took to reach us, his eyes were locked to mine.

I had no idea if Ryan knew what he did to me, the power in that one look, that smile of his. But if he did, he was an arsehole, because it made me wish for things I didn't know were possible or not.

The worst thing, though, I expected I was too chicken to find out.

Bouncing brows joined his words. "Dead set legend, right?" A wide, bright smile followed, the genuine joy radiating from the man easy to bask in.

The words took me back to another time, long before this day had arrived.

He'd done it, made it, set out to do everything he'd intended to.

Somehow, I kept my feet planted rather than leaning into him, trying to absorb some of the joy for myself.

"Definitely. You nailed it."

He stopped less than a meter away from me and cast his attention to Micky. "G'day, Micky. If I'd known you were here, I would've dragged your ass up."

Micky chuckled. "I would have liked to see you try, and… 'g'day?' You've only been with Nate here for a couple of days, and already your accent is coming back."

"It's true," I added, having noticed on the phone a few subtle differences from what I thought to be a bit of an American accent to something a little more like mine.

"Trying to get ready for heading back home. Don't wanna stand out like a sore thumb," he jested. Ryan reached past me and picked up his beer, which I'd been guarding.

"For your vacation, right? A short trip before you come back and we seriously start talking about next year and you being a free agent."

My focus moved to Ryan, wondering if he'd been avoiding this discussion. His brows furrowed slightly, head tilting. I knew this reaction. Knew full well this was him holding back from rolling his eyes and sighing.

"Yeah, I know. We'll talk."

Part of me felt like I should step away, but the quick snap of Ryan's attention to me before he refocused on Micky told me he didn't want me going anywhere.

Micky's tone remained the same as every other word he'd spoken in the last few minutes. "I know we've only just finished this season, and there's a whole other season to go, but we need to start looking for the best deal for you."

"I get it, Micky. Thanks." Ryan's voice was tight. It was clear that he didn't want to be thinking about so far into the future, and based on the bombshell he'd dropped when I'd first arrived, I understood it.

"You know I'm just looking out for you." Micky's tone changed a little, this time appearing so much more genuine. "That ankle of yours, ice it, and perhaps take your weight off it for a while."

Guilt slammed into me. After beers and riding on the high of the win and celebrating the end of their season, the last thing I'd considered was Ryan's ankle. "Shit, he's right. Is it hurting?" I grimaced and eyed his covered ankle.

"I'm okay," he answered, glancing at me. I bit my lip to stop myself from calling bullshit. I expected it was the booze in his system making it feel okay. That and the high of the game.

"Remember we're staying in LA for an extra day before we head back."

"Got it." Micky nodded. "I'll email you anything you need to know for when you get to Minnesota so you can wrap things up as quickly as possible ready for your flight next week. Just promise me you'll look after that ankle, okay?"

He offered Micky a head lift. "Will do. We're heading to the hotel."

That was something at least. I said goodbye to Micky and waved off a few of the players, all while wondering why Ryan perhaps wasn't being honest with his agent. I was pretty sure over the past few years he'd looked out for Ryan and done right by him.

Once in the cab, and a little blinded by the camera flashes that had taken me by surprise, I focused on the bright city lights and the overwhelming amount of traffic. "Have you been to LA much?" I cast Ryan a quick glance before turning my attention to the sights. While he seemed more together than a few minutes ago, he'd gone quiet. A sure sign he was lost in thought, probably overthinking.

"Only once that wasn't linked to work."

I chuckled.

"What?"

"Nothing really, it's just *work*. Can you believe your job is playing professional basketball?" I angled toward him as much as the seat belt would allow. "I always knew you could do it, but seeing you today…." I shook my head, awe and emotion sweeping through me at just how spectacular he'd been on the court. Shit, I'd had far too much to drink if I was close to weeping with pride over the man.

My gaze snagged Ryan's before dropping to the soft smile on his mouth. "Sometimes I pinch myself," he admitted, lowering his voice.

"I bet you do." I stopped speaking when the car pulled over, and I figured we'd arrived at the hotel. "This us?" I peered out the window at the bustling street and finally saw the hotel's sign. "Yep."

I looked on as Ryan handed the guy a few bills and stepped out, shaking my head. When he joined me, I said, "I keep forgetting about the whole tipping thing." Tipping was alien to me, something we didn't really do in Australia.

Ryan grunted as his hand latched on to my arm, leading me out of the path of a rowdy group. He started saying something about tipping, but it took everything in me just to remember to breathe, let alone pay attention to his words or our surroundings. My whole focus was on his warm fingers on my arm. And if that wasn't a cue to remind me just how much trouble I could get in being here with Ryan, then I didn't know what else could be more obvious.

"Huh?" We'd made it inside the foyer and stopped short.

"Beer or jet lag finally kicking in?" His mouth twitched.

It would be easy to blame the booze, but in all honesty, my buzz had mellowed considerably. And my jet lag had seriously been nonexistent, courtesy of my upgrade. Rather than bullshitting him, I answered, "Just overwhelmed by being here, finally seeing you play, spending time with you."

As I spoke, his gaze roamed my face, alternating between my eyes before continuing their journey. There was a moment's hesitation before Ryan said, "I was asking if you wanted a beer at the bar, but I think we should head to the suite instead."

I bobbed my head, up for anything he wanted to do. Being alone with him after a full-on day and surrounded by so many people was a decision I happily got on board with. "Sounds good."

His gaze dipped again, this time the movement

making my heart stop before punching wildly in my chest. Biology may not have been my best subject in school, but I knew the exact positioning of every part of my body, and Ryan's focus on my lips was as clear to me as the twinge in my pants. And that flare in his eyes that followed... suck me hard and make me blow, but Ryan Broadwater was *interested*, as in eyeballing my mouth and looking like he was ready to pounce.

While I knew exactly what I wanted to do with that, the question was, should I?

CHAPTER 10
RYAN

Between the booze buzzing through my system, being reminded about my future, and the constant thrum of need burning me since Nate arrived, I was close to combusting. That, or I would make a tit out of myself, since all I wanted to do was lean into him and steal a kiss.

That thought had played on my mind for weeks, even before seeing him in the flesh. When he'd stepped off the plane, my attraction had solidified. Since then, the need had grown enough to make me antsy.

But neither truly sealed the deal of whether or not I should go for it.

No, that had happened the moment I'd made tonight's winning shot and immediately sought him out. Nate's gaze had already been on me when I located him in the jumping, cheering crowd. My breath had caught, and that warm, awe-filled smile directed at me, the sheer joy on his face, was it.

It was the moment I'd decided that as soon as we were alone, I was going to kiss the shit out of him, go all in, and deal with the fallout should there be any.

"You okay?" Nate asked as we stood side by side in the elevator, heading to the suite.

I bobbed my head and offered a short "Yep," not confident I could manage anything else without taking what I wanted.

Heat flushed through me when we were just one floor away.

This was it. Fuck, I was nervous, though the wave of excitement, the tingle of possibility, sat right there alongside my dry mouth.

When the ping sounded, the doors slid open, and I stepped out, Nate close behind me.

My breaths were heavy, seeming too loud in the quiet corridor. Soft-footed steps sounded behind me, each movement sending a fresh shiver through me.

He felt something. I was sure of it. I'd heard it in the calls, had seen it in his soft smile in our video calls, and every second since we'd finally been together.

Being wrong was a possibility, but I hoped to God I wasn't.

We stepped into the room in silence, nothing but the hammering of my heart and my too-loud breaths filling my head. Nate stepped past me once the door was closed and headed to the high stool alongside a bench in the small kitchen space. He sat and kicked off his shoes, eyes on the task, and quite possibly avoiding me since I'd made the last five minutes super weird. "Sit down and let me grab some ice for your ankle."

Ignoring him, I took a step in his direction and reached out and took his hand in my own. The sound of his shoe hitting the floor punctuated the movement. Brushing my left thumb over his palm, I was tempted to close my eyes and absorb the moment, but I was sure that would be weird as fuck and make him wonder what the hell I was doing.

A quick inhale, and I darted my gaze to him. His eyes were fixed on our hands, a soft pink obvious on his cheeks. It felt like an age before I could release a breath and work out what my next move was.

That he hadn't pushed me away was one thing, but with my thumb still stroking his hand, his own breathing changing pace was all I needed to know.

"Nate, I—" My words were stolen by Nate as he brushed his lips against mine, ripping a gasp from me. His hands were on my waist, hauling me close, his thighs spreading wide to accommodate me. I'd barely found my feet before he held me tight and fused his mouth with mine.

He was bold and brave and so fucking beautiful. And everything I wanted. And that he'd made the first move after my fumbling and my overthinking…? Nate could take the lead any time he wanted.

My head swirled with the intensity of the kiss, the rightness of it. The spark flaring between us was almost unbearable. Energy buzzed through my veins, my limbs, forcing me to grip the back of his shirt, hold on tight, and deepen our kiss even further.

Never, as in, honest to God ever, had I ever reacted this way to anyone before. Desire pulsed through every inch of my body. Need for Nate licked at my skin. *Only Nate.* It felt as if the whole of my life was leading up to this, and I didn't even have the will to roll my eyes at that overly romantic bullshit. Because it was true, and wasn't that a heartfuck.

The notion brought me back momentarily to reality. I almost scoffed at how ridiculous I was being. Yes, Nate was an amazing kisser, everything I'd imagined and so much more, but the idea of us being cosmically linked, soul mates of some sort….

Not realizing that I'd actually stopped kissing Nate, I became aware of his concerned gaze. A slight frown played across his brow, making me want to reach out and remove all traces of worry and doubt.

"I can stop if you want me to. I just thought this was—"

Hell to the no.

I didn't give Nate the chance to finish. I angled and kissed his sexy-as-sin mouth, deep and hard. He growled lightly in response, urging me on. I locked my fingers behind his neck and tugged him closer.

After a second, almost primal growl, my breath rushed out of me when he wrapped his legs around my thighs. My control slipped when he deepened our kiss. I couldn't contain my need. As our kiss deepened, my body took over, almost to the point of desperation.

This right here was what I'd been missing. Nate's mouth, his touch, this complete connection.

I caressed his back and moved to unbutton his shirt with a shaky hand. I kissed his neck and traced hot kisses down to his chest to his nipple. Nate moaned when I lapped at his pink peak, and I bit down gently. He pushed himself closer to me as he rubbed against my groin.

Fuck, I was going to come in my pants.

My muscles became impossibly taut, my orgasm dangerously close to the surface as my desire peaked far beyond anything I'd ever experienced.

I needed him.

Here.

Now.

Consequences be damned.

Angling away, I unbuttoned his jeans, my palms sweaty, hands still shaky, but fuck I wanted this to happen. Wanted to taste and savor him. Wanted to finally bring just one of so many of my fantasies to actualization.

Wordlessly, he shifted his hips, the movement enough for me to risk making eye contact.

I shouldn't have.

With his top teeth buried in his bottom lip, his cheeks pink, and his eyes connected with mine, my breath caught, and I paused, forgetting what my hands were doing, too caught up in the intensity in his gaze.

When he released his bottom lip, he raised his palm and stroked my cheek. The shake of his hand helped me to breathe, remember to take in air and exhale.

"You okay?" His voice was deep, breathy, and tinged with a tremble. "Your foot—"

"Fuck my foot."

He laughed abruptly, and I smirked.

I took a deep breath and answered more quietly, "I'm okay." His gaze dropped to his pants and my hand half inside his jeans. His cock twitched against my fingers, and I huffed out a laugh, ending in a smile.

"I think you're more than okay too." His own smile was easy, immediate, reaching his eyes and—

The loud bang on the door made me jump, startling the crap out of me. Reacting without thought, my body locked up, hands clenching on instinct.

"Ouch, fuck, shit."

Alarmed, I cringed and released his cock, having gripped without thinking and far too fucking hard. "Shit, I'm sorry. You okay?"

He grunted and held his junk, brows furrowed. "Uh-huh, yep." The strain in his voice did nothing to reassure me that I hadn't broken his dick.

The door banged again, and I jerked my head in the direction, half expecting someone to break it down.

"I'm just gonna...." He trailed off. "Why don't you deal with that?" Nate indicated toward the door, and I eased away from him. With my cock already deflating, my heart pounded in concern, wondering who was at the door, I nodded.

Nate stood and moved toward his room, and I took a calming breath before making my way to the door. Opening it, I groaned.

Jayden and Sutton stood in my doorway, Jayden

barely managing to hold himself up and Sutton eyeing me from head to toe. He was the one who spoke first with a lazy grin. "Not disturbing anything, are we?"

I clenched my molars and forced a smile. "No. Just about to head to bed, though." I should have known better than to think that would have been a deterrent for my friends.

Jayden pushed past me, reeking of booze. "How'd you get such a good room?"

"Come on in." I rolled my eyes, and Sutton stepped in too, patting my shoulder as he walked past me.

"Seriously. You have a kitchen and a lounge." Jayden swayed, looking around the space with squinty eyes. "Why are there so many doors? Sutton," he hollered, making me cringe. "Am I seeing double, or are there more doors?"

I sighed and headed to the lounge area, actively avoiding looking at the small kitchen area and the high stool where I'd finally had my mouth on Nate's. "It's a suite, and I organized it because of Nate." I plopped down on the sofa, eyeing both of the men as they followed suit.

"Oh yeah. Where is Natey boy?" Jayden asked, kicking his feet up and stretching out. Sutton knocked Jayden's feet off his lap, causing Jayden to start grumbling.

"Bed, I think," I answered, hoping like hell I sounded casual.

"Huh. It's early." Jayden grinned and bounced his eyebrows up and down. "Has he got someone with him? He's into dudes, right? I saw a couple of guys flirting with him at the bar. Is he checking out the American wildlife?" Jayden laughed at himself while I froze all over.

I didn't even know where to start with any of that. Nate was out, even though we'd only skimmed the surface of that conversation, but his sexuality was nothing to do with anyone. Then was the fact that he'd been flirted with. When the fuck did that happen, and how did I not notice? I didn't like that thought one bit.

"It's almost midnight," I snapped, going with the only response I could handle. "It's not early," I added a little lamely, the heat disappearing from my words.

"What's wrong with you?" Sutton narrowed his assessing eyes at me. I swore to God the man was far too perceptive for his own good. "You're all wired, on edge or something." His gaze widened a second later. "Shit, *has* Nate brought someone back with him?" A frown followed, and I didn't have the chance to respond before he continued, "Nah, no chance of that. Not when he was eye-fucking you all night."

Blood rushed into my head. The pulse in my temples beat so fast and loud, it took all my ability to think straight, let alone take a breath.

"Fuck." Jayden cut through the loud noise in my brain. "He looks like he's going to pass out."

"What?" The voice didn't sound like my own. "I'm fine, and you're full of shit."

Jayden seemed a lot more sober when he sat upright, his concerned gaze settling on me. "Full of shit about what?"

I pursed my lips, not knowing how to answer.

"Nate's definitely into you, but the question is…" He angled his head, examining me.

I wanted to bolt, to get the hell out of this room, rewind five minutes and go back to my hand on Nate's cock and not answering the door. I could be kissing his dick right now rather than dealing with a racing heart and deliberating what to do, say, or how to react.

"…are you into him?"

I huffed out a panicked laugh and brought my hand to my mouth, bit the nail of my thumb, and shook my head. The forced smile on my face was painful. "The fuck you talking about? Course not. He's just Nate. He's just being friendly. Just because he's into guys doesn't mean he wants to fuck every man he's nice to."

"No shit, Broadwater. I'm not a dickhead and don't think that either."

"Good, 'cause he's not like that. He's a good guy."

Jayden bobbed his head, and I flicked a glance at Sutton, who remained eerily quiet at his side. "You know if you're interested in him, that's okay, right?" Jayden continued.

My stomach bottomed out, and I felt the color drain from my face. Wasn't this everything I hoped to hear, wanted to know from my friends that I had their support? I gaped at them, willing the words to spill out, desperate to share my truth with them. "I —" I snapped my mouth shut, nausea swirling in my gut.

I couldn't be out. I couldn't be at the center of so much fucking attention that would come my way.

I shook my head and straightened. It wasn't the time. My courage evaded me, ran, and dodged my grasp. "No. You're being ridiculous. Nate's my friend, and that's all he'll ever be." The words tasted bitter in my mouth.

Sutton's gaze shifting caught my attention. I didn't want to follow, didn't want to see what I already expected to find. Pain punctured through my heart when I looked. Nate's expression was shuttered, his attention on me for the barest of moments before he tore it away, focusing on Sutton.

"Hey." The tight smile was unnatural, forced, and shit if that didn't have my knees shaking and wanting to stand up, beg him to listen.

I swallowed back the desire to do just that, knowing the fact I would be asking him to listen rather than taking my words back meant I didn't deserve a single thing from Nate.

"I was just coming to say goodnight and remind you to ice your ankle... so, night." He gave a chin lift and went back to his room.

The sound of the lock engaging hit hard. My teeth clamped the inside of my cheeks.

"Shit, sorry, Broadwater, you think he heard us? I didn't mean anything by it." Jayden's voice was finally low, genuine concern evident.

"I'm sure he's fine, just tired," I lied. "Why are you guys here anyway?"

"Was just going to see if you wanted to meet for breakfast in the morning." Jayden shrugged. "Seems stupid as shit now."

I sighed. "You think? Your cell not working?"

He shrugged again.

"We're going to head off." Sutton stood and dragged Jayden up with him. "We'll text you about breakfast." They headed toward the door and opened it. Before Sutton pulled it closed, he turned to me, his lips pressing together. "Listen, I'm sorry if we fucked anything up, but we both have your back. Just remember that, okay?"

Surprising the heck out of me, Sutton reached out and hauled me into a tight, brief hug. I hugged him back, pissed at myself that I believed him yet still didn't share what was in my heart.

When he eased away, he ruffled my hair a little, like the dickhead I was used to. "When you go back home, just spend proper time with Nate and your family. Figure out what you want and what's good for your heart, okay?"

I couldn't do anything but nod as I clamped down on my lips, too afraid my emotions would spill out and life would irrevocably change.

I wished I was ready for that, but faced with the reality, I just wasn't quite sure when or if that would ever happen.

CHAPTER 11
NATE

For three hours I'd tossed and turned before finally settling into a fitful sleep. Seven o'clock was too damn early to be awake after the shitshow of how my night had ended, but I was awake, showered, dressed, and on my second cup of coffee by the time Ryan showed his face.

While seeing him this morning was inevitable, that didn't do a thing to slow my racing heart battering against my chest. It was already bruised and hurt from what I'd overheard, so what were a few thumps for good measure?

I was bombarded by if, buts, and maybes, so the last thing I wanted to do was take his words personally, but that didn't stop the hurt. Ryan hadn't even told me that he was into men. Not officially. For all I knew, Ryan could be struggling to accept what could be a new discovery. Or our kiss could have been a tipsy experiment. Or perhaps he even knew he was gay, was into me, but didn't want to come out at that moment to his drunk work colleagues.

Those possibilities had kept me awake most of the night, and my "Morning" sounded wooden, despite practicing how to greet him, but the word was out there. Determined to stick to my plan, I indicated the pot of coffee. "My coffee attempt is better than yesterday's. It's safe to drink." There was no follow-up chuckle, though. I didn't have it in me to play casual that much.

Ryan stood a few steps from his door, gaze on me, his hesitation clear. *That* I wasn't going to fix. If pressed, I wouldn't lie and say what he said was okay and didn't hurt, but for now, my plan was to get through the next few days before we headed back to Australia.

"Yeah, thanks." His response was cautious, and rather than offering him false platitudes, I bobbed my head and went back to my phone and checking my emails. Unfortunately, little in my emails needed my attention, so I closed my phone and took another gulp of coffee.

"How's your ankle?"

"A bit tender. I'll just keep it strapped, and it'll be fine."

I hummed in response, not sure if his version of fine was the same as mine or his physio's. "What are your plans for today? Have you got meetings or anything?" I asked, despite already being sort of aware of the answer. At this point, I wanted a safe topic. Plans seemed like the logical option.

The rake of his gaze over my face froze the breath in my lungs. It was clear what he was searching for, but I was tired, too exhausted to control my features, keep the hurt from my eyes.

Ryan rubbed a palm over his face, his own exhaustion evident before he pulled his hand away and took a step forward, so only the small kitchen bar separated us. "You heard me last night… talking to the guys."

The statement was out there, and I waited for him to continue.

"It was a shit thing to say, to talk about you like that, Nate. I'm sorry." Truth bled into his words, complete with so much hurt that my heart ached afresh.

I swallowed hard, my mind snagging on his words. "Are you sorry for saying it or for me hearing?" My voice was rougher than I would have liked. I exhaled, wishing my half-arsed plan of staying casual and leaving this conversation for another time could have played out.

Why the hell now did Ryan decide to be open and talk this out? Sure, it was the Ryan I knew from my youth, but considering his history of running and cutting me from his life, I'd relied on that, expected him to ignore the giant elephant in the room.

"Both." A tremble was evident in that one word, but while my whole being ached for him, I couldn't give him the answers or make any of this okay.

I took another sip of coffee, working hard at controlling my breathing.

This whole thing was screwed.

Yesterday was incredible, and that kiss, my legs wrapped around him, his hand on my cock… was beyond anything I imagined.

Unable to help myself, I asked, "Do you regret yesterday?"

He shook his head and drew in one side of his bottom lip, gnawing on the flesh there. "The kiss was amazing."

My heart flipped at his words, liking them far too much, but the anguish in his eyes snatched at my heart and chained it back. "And you're not out," I stated, needing the words out there.

"No." His voice was quiet, the rasp speaking of probably less sleep than I'd had.

"And do you plan to change that at all?"

He winced, guilt blazing in his eyes. "No, I can't."

His voice pitched, and I couldn't simply sit back and let so much hurt spill out unchecked.

"Hey." I angled forward and reached out, clasping his forearm. "I think I get it, and no one but you should be deciding if and how or when you come out. Is it the work thing?" While my words were simple, I didn't intend them to be flippant. More than distance separated Ryan's life from my own. He was a professional athlete, and with that came outside pressure I couldn't even begin to comprehend.

"The work thing," he said with a nod, "the whole attention shit. It's all of it."

I racked my brain, wondering if there were any out players in the pro basketball league, but honestly, I hadn't a clue. I'd only followed Ryan's games over the years and more recently watched them like the hard-core fan I was.

"This is going to sound really dickish, but I need context here." I smiled when his shoulders relaxed a little and he stopped gnawing on his lip, his mouth twitching. "You being out with your job, would it be like it is in movies and books and stuff?"

The mouth twitch turned into a small smile, though sadness remained on his features. "I suppose it all depends on what movies you've been watching or books you've been reading."

I rolled my eyes as the relief that he was joking helped to settle my heart rate.

"You know that dream where you show up at school naked, and you're in front of the class, and everyone is staring and pointing? Hell, let's throw in some idiots shouting insults at you while you're standing there, maybe a few people then following you around, writing about and photographing your every move."

"All while I'm still naked?" Now I was being flippant, but fuck, his tone had started out light, but as he continued, the waver was there, the stress edging his words.

"Naked," he confirmed, attempting a smile that looked as uncomfortable as it was odd.

"And they wouldn't be talking about how impressive my dick was, right?"

Once again, his mouth twitched.

"Okay, so perhaps it's not that bad. There are some out players in hockey and football, and it's not like fans in the stadium can get away with chanting slurs or anything. I know club and league policies are supportive, and they come down harshly on homophobia." He sighed and rubbed a hand over his face. "In all honesty, this is about me. Who'd have thought I don't like the spotlight, right?" A humorless laugh escaped him. "I just don't want the focus on my personal life at all. Don't get me wrong, on the court, me playing ball is a different story altogether. I can moonwalk like the best of them if I have a shit-hot game." He shrugged. "I know it wouldn't be the worst thing in the world, coming out. I know that. Other pro players have done so and have survived and are playing, but when I think of being that person, that player, I struggle to breathe."

My expression turned solemn. "I hear what you're saying. I even get it." I hesitated and clamped down on words I wasn't sure would do any good. Because I honestly did understand where he was coming from, but then why the fuck had he kissed me yesterday to only brush me aside when I still felt the heat of his hand on my dick... and I wasn't referring to the painful squeeze either.

His gaze tracked my face, searching. "I know I should be sorry for kissing you, especially because of the shit thing I said afterward." I swallowed hard, not sure if I was pissed off or impressed Ryan could read me so damn well. "I'd be so fucking lucky if you were ever more than a friend to me."

My eyes sprang wide open. Where the hell was all this honesty coming from? It was freaking me out while turning me on and putting pressure on the organ in my chest, threatening more damage.

"I have one more year before I'm a free agent.

And I don't have it in me to come out while playing. It's cowardly as shit." I pressed my lips together, wanting to interrupt. Maybe seeing my struggle, he shook his head. "I am. I'm not brave enough to live in the spotlight being a gay man. One more year, and maybe things will be different."

It wasn't the first time he'd mentioned his contract coming to an end, but thinking of the possibility was just too much, and it was so far away. Anything could happen between now and then.

When he didn't say anything for a beat or two, I chose my words carefully. "Is that the first time you've said you're gay?"

Ryan cleared his throat. "Yeah, well, to anyone else."

"And you're gay, not bi, or pan or—"

"Gay."

"I think telling me makes you brave."

"My tongue in your mouth yesterday kinda gave that away though, right?"

I snorted. "Yeah, just a little, and a few things we talked about since getting back in touch." I had so many questions, which I was sure would take months to answer. Keeping that thought tucked away, I refocused, figuring out how to continue.

First and foremost, Ryan was my friend, and he was terrified and so sad that it burnt through my anger and hurt with a ferocity that surprised me. Those embers of my emotions remained, but for now, I'd dig deep, so fucking deep I'd strain myself if necessary, to push them aside and focus on what my visit was meant to be about.

Reconnecting with my friend and taking a much-needed break.

That, I could do.

There'd be time enough for deeper talk, which was probably best left till we were back home. Ryan would be able to disappear from the attention and microscopic lens he lived under here to the normality of the Sunny Coast. Sure there were Aussies who followed pro basketball, but with him being so out of media attention, it was less likely he'd be recognized.

"We have a lot to talk about," I started, "and I think you have stuff you need to figure out too, but that can wait till we're back home, yeah?"

His gaze was searching. "Okay."

"But," I said, the words already forming in my brain, the last things I wanted to share, but I had to, "what happened yesterday can't happen again. I'm your friend. You need to keep to those boundaries." Each word was just as much for me, but it wouldn't help either of us to admit that. "Let's just enjoy the next few days, okay?"

"I can do that." His reaction was so easy to read,

his relief visceral, but it weighed heavily on the dejection he struggled to shutter.

"So, plans?"

He bobbed his head once, and the resolve seemed to sweep over him, something I understood all too well. It was the only way I'd be able to survive the next few days in the States.

RYAN'S FRIENDS SEEMED TO TAKE THEIR CUE FROM RYAN. Not a word was mentioned about what happened, which was more than okay with me. It was proving difficult enough to shrug everything aside, so I latched on to each meaningless although entertaining conversation I could.

Jayden finished off his omelet with a belch. Sutton reacted immediately by smacking him in the gut.

"Jesus, manners. Let your momma hear that coming from you." Sutton rolled his eyes, and I laughed at the pair of them, tempted to call him out on his own belch yesterday, but the more I thought about it, the less convinced I was that he'd been actually drunk.

"Shit, man, don't play the mom card." Jayden rubbed at his stomach.

"You know she likes me better than you, so just keep acting like a pig."

"You two been friends for long?" I asked. Their friendship and how they interacted were different from how they interacted with Ryan. Sure, they were all friendly, but Sutton and Jayden seemed tight.

"This fool?" Sutton quirked his brow in Jayden's direction. "He ain't my friend. He's too much of a pain in the ass for that."

Wide-eyed, Jayden slammed his hand against his chest. "You wound me, asshole. Don't listen to Gale here," he directed at me, and my mouth twitched at Sutton's sneer when Jayden said his first name. "*Gale* here is a big softie, especially when it comes to his love for me."

"Their bromance is legendary," Ryan added, eyeing his two friends with a smirk.

"You see, legendary." Jayden nodded, apparently pleased by the description from the self-satisfied grin and puff of his chest. "But to answer your question, Nate, Sutton here and I go way back. Met at basketball camp when we were fourteen. Sutton now kinda stalks me."

I expected Sutton to interject, but when I glanced his way, he was side-eyeing Jayden with the barest of smirks and offering an eye roll.

"We kept in touch and ended up playing for the

Leopards out west for a couple of years, and a few years back, we landed here. Well, not LA, but Minnesota."

"What Jayden here failed to mention was I got contracted first for Minnesota. He puts in special requests with his agent to make sure we're on the same team or at least close by."

I grinned at how deadpan Sutton was and quickly followed up with a chuckle at Jayden as he went off on some sort of diatribe.

Ryan's soft "Hey" pulled my attention away.

I raised my brows at him, my smile still in place. The slip happened almost instantly, however, before I could control it. The hurt and memory of the kiss slammed in unbidden, though, as soon as my gaze caught on his.

Fuck, I was a fool and had all but set myself up for this gigantic fall. That said, I couldn't regret last night's kiss or just how hot it was. While there were no regrets, it didn't stop me from wishing things were different.

The only tell he gave that he may have seen my reaction was the slight hesitation before he said, "We have to head off to a short team meeting before the guys head back. You okay with coming with me? It should only take an hour, then we can do something."

It took more effort than I thought to get control of myself and bundle away my hurt enough to try to let go—or at least bury it down for a few more days. "I can wait, but I think we then need to head to one of the theme parks."

Biting hard on my cheek was the only way to school my features. The arsehole wasn't a fan of theme parks when we were kids, but I loved a good roller-coaster ride.

"We'd only have this afternoon." His words were careful, eyes examining as he spoke.

I shrugged. "That's okay."

"What are you guys talking about?" Sutton asked, drawing my attention his way. From the corner of my eye, Ryan's focus seemed to still be on me.

"We're going to head to one of the theme parks this afternoon as soon as you guys are done." This time my shit-eating grin appeared, and I side-eyed Ryan, maybe loving a little too much that his gaze was narrowed on me.

A ridiculous glee unfurled in my gut, knowing I was being a bit of a cock, but I did genuinely want to go to a theme park. Not only that, but with the obvious tension between us, this was the relief I thought we both needed.

"For real?" Surprise lifted Sutton's words. His

"Huh" pulled my attention toward him. "I thought Ryan here hated theme parks."

With my smile still in place and very real, I shrugged and paid attention to the man at my side. Ryan stared at me for a beat before huffing out a defeated breath.

"Nate here loves the damn things." He lifted one shoulder in a "what you gonna do?" gesture.

"That'd be cool. Maybe we could stay, watch Ryan squeal like a baby pig." Jayden chuckled and earned a flipped middle finger from Ryan.

"Nope." Sutton shook his head, and I didn't know if I was relieved or disappointed they wouldn't be coming. "You promised your cousin you'd be at their house tonight for dinner."

Jayden groaned, and I couldn't help but think they behaved like an old married couple at times. "I could say the flight was canceled."

"You've canceled the last three times. Just suck it up and go."

The grumble that followed was enough to get us all laughing. "Fine, but if I'm going, so are you."

"And it's time to go," Ryan said quickly, standing and slotting some cash in the folded bill that had arrived a few minutes back.

A few hours later, I was grinning like a fool, high on sugar and having a blast. At my side, though,

Ryan was looking a little peaky. "Seriously, you don't have to go on the ride with me."

Ryan's focus was solely on the monstrosity before us. The roller coaster looked epic. It was all loops and twists and set so damn high, I imagined you could all but touch the clouds.

Not that there were any in the sky. There was only vivid blue holding together the bright sun up above. The humidity wasn't all that bad either. It was mild compared to spring back home. My hair, though, was plastered to my head underneath the baseball cap I'd swiped from Ryan, courtesy of the rapids that drenched us.

The man at my side didn't seem to be coping as well.

Sweat coated every visible inch of his skin, and his shirt stuck to him in such a way, my attention was constantly drawn to it.

"You hot or just shitting yourself?" I asked, aware he still hadn't answered me.

Finally, he tore his gaze away from the 450-feet-high beast. "Both."

I laughed at his honesty and clapped him on the shoulder.

"You going soft in this heat? Has the Australian been whipped out of you with all of the air con you're used to, mate?" I ribbed.

Ryan quirked his brow, sending me the stink eye, and I was so glad we'd done this. Messing around at the theme park effectively cut through all the tension. It made it easier to file away the conversation we needed to have for another day.

"Minnesota is as cold as a polar bear's asshole in winter. I may have acclimatized a little."

"It's a good job that when we get home, it's the end of autumn at least. A nice twenty-seven degrees Celsius should sort you out."

"Fuck, that's what, almost ninety degrees Fahrenheit or something?"

I laughed at how shocked he looked.

"Laugh now. When I left Minnesota a few days back, it was just about sixty degrees Fahrenheit."

My smile slipped. "At night?"

The bastard laughed. "Those are the highs." I did the maths in my head, figuring out that was about seventeen degrees Celsius or something. "Shit, I didn't bring a coat. Why didn't you tell me how cold it still was?"

His laughter continued to ring out. "Nate, that is so not cold."

"Yeah, it bloody well is for my Queenslander blood."

"I'll hook you up with warm clothes. We won't be there long anyway before we head to Australia."

I quirked my brow at him. "Do you have team jackets, like they have in the movies?" Seriously, the idea of wearing his sports jacket sounded fun and dreamy and seriously hot to me. Dangerously so.

I was playing with fire, but fuck if I hadn't been ruined by years' worth of watching teen and college romances. I was a sucker for teen drama, one of my few guilty pleasures. And the bastard grinning widely at me knew that too.

"You want to wear my sports jacket with my name and number on it, Nate?" The teasing in his voice was overshadowed by the intensity in his eyes.

Warning bells went off loud and clear. The thought of wearing anything of his was the subject of too many of my fantasies.

I cleared my throat. Today was about getting back to where we used to be. "So, you in or what?" For several beats his gaze roamed mine. I worked hard at offering nothing but a friendly, teasing smile. Anything more would mean I was a glutton for punishment.

"I've got your back, Nate."

Unable to resist, I shouted, "No take backs," and legged it to the VIP queue, which I was so on board with, knowing Ryan would be on my tail.

CHAPTER 12

RYAN

Vomit not only reeked, but it did its job of easing things between Nate and me.

Somehow I'd managed to hold back on the roller coaster itself, but almost as soon as my feet had touched concrete, Nate had yanked me to the most secluded spot he could find, just in time for me to throw my guts up in the bushes.

While he'd rubbed my back and kept an eye open for witnesses, the ass had been practically bent double in laughter. We'd since recovered from a mostly fun day, made the flight back to Minnesota, and were pulling up to my place.

"Oh wow."

I cast a quick glance at Nate, curious about his reaction.

There was no denying the place looked impressive with its manicured landscaping and square footage. But it was just a nice place. While I called it home, it never really felt like it.

"Cheers." I threw Nate a smile before we stepped out of the chauffeured car. We gathered the bags, and I gave the driver a generous tip and my thanks.

Nate's gaze was glued to the view. The lake glistened in the midday sun, and as soon as the car pulled away, nothing but the sounds of nature filled the space between us.

"I didn't expect you to be so isolated." Nate turned to look at me, his brow raised in question.

I shrugged and returned my focus to the familiar lake, luxuriating in the serenity of the view.

"My job's loud," I admitted. "I used to have an apartment close to the stadium, but there was just no escaping, you know?" In my peripheral vision, I saw him bob his head. "The guys rib me for being here by myself, but honestly, I like it. It's not home but…."

"What do you mean?"

I gnawed on the inside of my cheek and glanced at him. "It's a long way from the Sunny Coast."

A soft smile tilted his lips. "Now that I get. This is beautiful, idyllic even, but yeah, it's not home." Nate's gaze didn't waver from mine, and all I wanted to do was step close and try out that kissing thing we did.

Since it had happened, my thoughts barely strayed far from him or the feel of Nate in my hand. No one was more aware than I that making that happen would be an asshole move. That didn't make me want Nate any less. But he deserved more than a man who was packed up tight in the closet. I needed to tell him as much too, more than aware of the lack of discussion since I'd shoved my tongue in his mouth.

In three days, we'd be on home soil. Once I was home and out of the spotlight, I'd pull my head out of my ass, make my apologies, and talk out the shit in my head. In the meantime, it was my mission to make sure Nate enjoyed his visit. "Come on. Let's get inside and settled. We can explore this afternoon. I've then got that work thing tomorrow."

"Then I get to steal you away." His words were followed by his brows bouncing up and down, ridiculously so. I laughed.

Grabbing our bags, we headed inside. I gave a quick tour before suggesting we go for lunch. I drove away from the city, knowing Nate wouldn't mind the forty-five minute drive. He was a country boy through and through, so he was all about commuting and not making a big deal out of distances.

"This place has the best Juicy Lucys." I grinned at his puzzled look.

"A juicy what now?"

"You're in for a treat. Let me order some, and we can head to the pond to eat if you want?" I wasn't hassled for long whenever I came here, but I wanted Nate all to myself. Not having to worry about anyone eavesdropping if we sat on one of the benches outside instead was a big draw.

"Sounds good. I'm game for the whole USA experience."

We ducked inside, and I made our order to go, only having to sign a couple of autographs, which still blew my mind. There was no getting away from my accent, though, and it didn't take folks long to figure out who I was.

Nate smirked at me, his eyes bright and directed my way.

As I signed a young kid's cap, I blushed when my gaze connected with Nate's. "Here you go. You make sure you keep cheering next season, okay," I said to the kid, dragging my gaze away from the intensity of Nate's focus.

"Will do, Mr. Broadwater. Thanks a lot."

The kid was cute. I ruffled his hair, then shook hands with the boy's dad. They called my order, and I all but dragged Nate out of there. I was never really comfortable with attention off the court, but under the added scrutiny of Nate, discomfort prickled my skin.

Once out in the fresh air, I took a deep breath.

"You doing okay over there?" Concern lifted his words.

I glanced at him, grinning at the hoodie he wore. He hadn't been kidding about his reaction to the seventy-degree temperature. It hadn't taken me long to acclimatize to the real seasons they had out here. For Nate, he'd be feeling it.

Seventy was a fairly cool winter's day on the Sunshine Coast.

"Yeah," I answered, taking him in and embracing the feeling of how good it felt to be around Nate again.

"You hate the whole celebrity thing, huh?"

I bobbed my head and led him off to one of the park benches.

"I know you said it made you uncomfortable, but it's not all bad, is it?" He gestured toward the bench, and I nodded, taking a seat next to him.

"No, it's not all bad. Kids like that are great. I love that they're fans. Ones who adore the game. It's just the gossip rag attention that can be grueling." It was hard to look away with his focus on me, especially as he seemed to listen so carefully to every word I said.

"I've seen a few shots and articles of you over the years." The pink in his cheeks, right alongside his words, had me pausing from unwrapping my burger.

Embarrassment flickered to life in my chest, and I cleared my throat. "You have?" It had been a long time since I'd googled myself. Yeah, I was on Insta again, but that was as far as social media went.

"Yeah." The pink turned a darker shade. I latched on to his reaction and tried to shake off my discomfort. This was Nate, my oldest friend. This was the kind of shit we would have taken the piss out of each other about when we were younger. I longed for that past so much. Fucking yearned for it.

I relaxed my shoulders, a small smile tilting my lips. "You been googling me, Griffin?"

This time his lips kicked up into a smirk. "I may have done a time or two."

I quirked my brow at him. As far as I was aware, there weren't any dodgy images of me floating around.

"You discover anything interesting?"

There was a brief pause before he responded. "Not especially. Mainly action shots of you on the court, a few pics of you at events with a gorgeous woman on your arm." Curiosity colored his words.

While this wasn't the place to discuss anything

significant, I offered, "There are some events where bringing a date is expected."

Nate nodded. "They made you look good," he teased.

I snorted. "Whatever. Eat your damn Juicy Lucy before it goes cold, smartass."

"Arse," he said, nudging me with his shoulder.

"Smart*arse*," I emphasized with a roll of my eyes.

We ate and chatted about stupid shit, figuring each other out all over again. By the time we threw our rubbish away, I was laughing my ass off when he told me about Gran's reaction to my sister's first date.

"She was scary as hell, seriously."

I snorted again, unable to stifle my amusement. "I bet. I can imagine Gran threatening someone with a broom."

"Not just threatened," Nate said, wide-eyed. "She got a good hit on the kid's backside before chasing him off."

I sobered at the fresh reminder of all I'd missed by staying away. "Her threatening idiots away didn't make a difference to my sister, though," I said quietly.

Nate winced. "Amber is a force of nature and her own person."

I bobbed my head, knowing that.

"She's also an excellent mum and is doing so well on her online course."

My heart squeezed at the pride in Nate's voice. "I don't think I'll ever be able to thank you enough, Nate, for being there for Amber and Gran, and now Ivy." Those thoughts had plagued me for years, truth be told, but since I became an uncle, Nate had been incredible. He'd gone above and beyond for my sister. Plus, he'd been helping to take care of Gran. I was all too aware of how difficult Gran could be, especially when she felt vulnerable.

"Nah, don't be an idiot. You know they're my family too."

Unable to resist, I reached out and squeezed his forearm, craving the contact. His self-deprecating smile softened, his gentle gaze roaming over mine. When it landed on my mouth, I swallowed hard and pulled away, standing.

"Okay, next up, let's head back, and we'll get cleaned up before we go tonight." I planned to show him some cool spots where I liked to hang out with the guys. "We'll go the long way back, though, and take in a few sights." I risked a glance at him, catching the disappointment in his eyes before he locked down his expression.

The thing was, Nate hadn't changed all that much. Yeah, he was broader, a little softer around the edges, his voice deeper. But I could read his tells loud and clear. Knowing I was hurting him sat like a boulder in my gut as we headed back to my car.

But short of having my cake and goddamn devouring it, which I couldn't do, I had to remember to keep my hands to myself.

Fuck, it was proving so damn difficult to keep my hands to myself.

We'd had a blast this afternoon. I'd shown Nate an out-of-the-way ball court where a few locals played and I occasionally hung out, and I even talked Nate into going on some hoke paddleboats on one of the larger lakes not too far from where I lived. Once we'd got home and freshened up, we'd headed into the city for dinner at a quieter bar the guys and I sometimes hung out at, and that led to me foolishly answering a call from Jayden.

For the past two hours, we'd been at this club. It wasn't my scene, and from our texts and calls over recent months, I knew it wasn't Nate's either. Yet my friend was tearing up the dance floor, looking so fucking hot as he moved his hips in a way that made me think far too intently about sex. He was dancing with Jayden and a couple of women who'd latched on.

Admittedly, when that had first happened, I'd tensed and wanted to drag him away and take him home, but the bastard had thrown me a wink, which I'd easily spotted over the distance since I'd barely taken my eyes off him.

Since then, I jumped between smiling at the good time he was having and being envious that he could dance so freely with a woman. While I knew a gay club would fix that right up, I hadn't tried to visit one since the last time I'd freaked out.

"Come on. Get your ass on the dance floor with me. This is ridiculous."

"Huh?" I whipped my head around, startled by Sutton.

When his response was to roll his eyes, latch on to my arm, and haul me to the dance floor, I was rendered speechless for a beat. "You never dance," I called over the music. While that wasn't technically true, since Jayden had dragged Sutton up a time or two, usually making a spectacle of the pair of them, he never voluntarily hit the dance floor.

He angled a look at me, once again rolling his eyes.

"What did I do?"

Sutton stopped abruptly and turned to face me. "You're shit company and should be out here dancing with your friend."

With no idea how to respond, I gaped.

"You're impossible. Just come on."

The beat of my heart picked up speed as I allowed Sutton to haul me toward Jayden and Nate. Sutton was a good guy, but fuck if he didn't freak me out a little. The man's power of observation was next-level scary, and I had no idea what to do about that.

Perhaps this would be easier and less of a big deal if I wasn't stone-cold sober. But since I was driving, I'd had one beer with dinner and nothing but Pepsi since.

Strobe lights lit the dance floor, moving in time with a dance track I didn't know. Occasional spurts of fog rolled over the area, and there were just enough gyrating bodies to make me not feel like I was on show, but not so many I felt like a canned sardine.

"Hey, hey, hey." Jayden all but launched himself at Sutton, latching on to the man, grabbing him and dancing provocatively against him.

A wide grin stretched his face, and Sutton laughed loudly at something he said. Jayden then latched on to the arm of the woman he'd been dancing with, making himself the center of a pretty interesting sandwich.

Meanwhile, I stood there like an idiot, watching the show before casting a wary glance around me. No one paid them any mind. Well, no one other than me and Nate, who smirked at them before his gaze traveled to mine.

The asshole tilted his head in invitation, and I wondered how much he'd had to drink. Since I'd had my hand on his dick and I'd shut us down, there'd been a not-so-subtle shift between us. We'd both been trying to ensure we were in the friend zone, but Nate's teasing smile had trouble written all over it.

Jayden's holler caught my attention. "Nate, show our boy how to be a filling in a hot sandwich."

There was no fight in me as a pretty brunette was latched on to my front and Nate's warm body pressed against my back in the next breath.

The likelihood of me surviving on the dance floor intact, or at least without getting a stiffy, was not something I'd bet money on. When Nate's hand gripped my waist, I focused intently on the woman, forcing a smile and winking.

The three of us danced, up close and indecently personal. When I was spun around, my gaze lowering and latching on to Nate, I knew gut deep this was what I wanted, who I wanted, and how I wanted to be.

Nothing was ever going to be the same again.

CHAPTER 13

NATE

IT DIDN'T TAKE ME LONG TO RECOGNIZE I WAS FOOLING myself and doing a shit job at it.

Beneath the strobe lighting and heavy beats of the music, pressing against Ryan destroyed all levels of pretense. The connection, his body against mine, and the intensity in his eyes when ours finally connected eviscerated my sense of self-preservation.

I needed Ryan so badly and would take him however I could get him. With his stiffy brushing against mine as we moved to the beat, the rough denim rubbing in a not-so-soft caress, I was willing to play dirty to get him.

"Did you have anything else to drink, or are you good to drive?" I asked, leaning in closer to speak into his ear.

The shudder that rippled through him had me

gripping his waist even tighter. He angled his head away and peered the few inches down to make eye contact. "I'm good to drive now."

I bobbed my head, not looking away from the intensity directed my way. "I think we should leave." A flick of my chin to his shoulder reminded me we weren't dancing alone. When I returned my attention to Ryan, understanding registered as he peered back at me. "You tell Jayden; I'll deal here."

Our gazes lingered, and my heart flipped when a small smile tilted his lips. It was hard to pull away, difficult to lose sight of the man, but with a wave of certainty, I knew this was where I was meant to be—with Ryan.

We'd missed out on too many years already. There wasn't a chance I could continue to ignore our connection.

Turning to Lizzie, the woman I'd been happily dancing with, I smiled and leaned in. "Thanks for keeping me company. I have an early start tomorrow, so I need to get out of here."

She simply nodded, planted a kiss on my cheek, and kept on dancing. Grateful that she was so chill, I winked, telling her to have fun before I searched for Ryan. I didn't have to look far. Jayden was saying something to him, while Sutton's stare was on the two of them. With a deep exhale, needing to keep myself together, I headed on over.

"…ass back here," Jayden said, his focus turning to me. "And you, you Aussie fucker, get your ass over here and say goodbye properly."

A bubble of emotion formed in my chest, taking me by surprise. I barely knew these blokes, yet they'd been nothing but great. Plus they'd had Ryan's back the last few years. Knowing that made it feel like more than a few days since meeting them. I was tugged into Jayden's arms with an "oomph."

"You keep an eye on my Aussie friend, you hear me?"

I patted Jayden's back. "There's no worries about that. He'll be all good."

Sutton appeared at my side and grabbed me up in a firm hug. "You be patient with him, okay?"

I angled away to see his face and swallowed hard at the intensity of his stare. The question died on my lips. I knew exactly what he was talking about. Nerves burst to life in my gut, and I shot a glance at Ryan. He was caught up in whatever Jayden was saying.

Whether Sutton suspected or not, I wouldn't be confirming anything, certainly not with words. Instead, I gave a barely there nod, saying, "He's still my best friend…." I trailed off, knowing if I said more, the emotion in my voice would make it clear that Ryan Broadwater was so much more to me than that.

After finally getting out of the private club and with only a couple of camera flashes once we stepped outside, we were soon settled in Ryan's car.

I snorted as a memory popped into my head, tearing through the quiet car.

"What?" he asked, and I realized it was the first thing either of us had said since the dance floor.

Angling to look at Ryan's profile, I smiled at him. "Just thinking about Davey's party."

Ryan chuckled and shook his head. "You mean when Linda vomited on the roof of your dad's car, and we spent three fucking hours hosing the damn thing off the next morning?"

"Right. I know it was a hot night, but that sick stuck like tar."

A louder laugh spilled out of Ryan. "Do you even remember why she was on the roof in the first place?"

I shook my head, amusement lighting me up. "We had some good times, right?"

After a beat of silence, Ryan glanced over, a small smile directed my way. "The best." When he refocused on the road, I watched his Adam's apple bob, and he flicked out his tongue, wetting his lips.

"Just ask," I said, more than aware something was on his mind with those tells.

His gaze darted at me, albeit briefly. "When did you know?"

There was no need to ask for clarity; the reference was clear, and this whole conversation was long overdue. "I suppose deep down forever, but more certain when we were fourteen or fifteen."

Unspeaking, Ryan nodded.

"I told my folks when I was in my first year at uni. Your gran and sister not long after." A humorless laugh escaped me before I said, "I downed five shots of tequila before I did."

Ryan's grimace was understandable. Since the time we'd both got trashed on tequila when we were seventeen at a friend's party, I'd sworn never to drink the stuff again, but that visit home from uni had called for desperate measures. Tequila had done the trick.

"How'd your folks react?"

Warmth enveloped me just thinking about how great my parents were. They'd reacted exactly as I'd hoped and expected, but that hadn't made my fear any less palpable. "They both hugged me, told me they loved me. Dad was a bit weird when I brought a guy around for the first time." Out of the corner of my eye, I spotted Ryan grip the wheel a little tighter.

The spark his reaction created pushed out my chest, and I smiled, liking the idea he was a little jealous. Seriously, I could write a playbook on his tells.

Ryan cleared his throat. "How was he weird?"

I chuckled at the memory. "Was just a bit odd, distant. I called him out after Tony left, thinking his acceptance had all been a front."

"And it wasn't?"

"Nope, you know what Dad's like. He told me that Tony wouldn't know a cow's tit from a bull's dick, and the guy wasn't good enough for me."

Laughing loudly, Ryan glanced my way. "Your dad's always had an unhealthy obsession with farming."

I nodded. "True, but he was also right about Tony. It didn't take me long to figure that out."

Ryan side-eyed me as he pulled off a larger road to one that was dark, windy, and I thought familiar. I didn't think we were too far away from his place. "And boyfriends?"

A heavy pause settled between us. I waited him out. While it was apparent Ryan was struggling, he had to do some of the legwork.

"You've only had *boyfriends*, right, and you don't have one now?"

Just as my heart panged at his uncertainty, a wave of happiness unfurled in me. The direction the conversation took was significant, or at least I hoped that was the case.

There wasn't a chance I'd misread what had happened on the dance floor. Even if we hadn't shared a kiss, the chemistry between us had been close to combusting. Seriously, a kiss and the right word were all that had been needed to make us spark. As far as I was concerned, it was the whole reason we'd left the club like our arses were on fire.

"Only boyfriends," I confirmed. He knew about my failed dating attempts at high school, so there was no need to go there. "And no boyfriend for some time now."

The questions I wanted to ask burned on my lips, but my attention caught on street lighting penetrating the otherwise dark road. We were back. Immediately, awareness kick-started my heart, my pulse going wild.

We remained silent as we pulled into the garage and still didn't speak as we entered the house. With still so much left unsaid, it felt like it was up to me to be sensible and talk this out.

I followed Ryan into the kitchen, my focus on his backside despite telling myself to be a grown-up, but then he turned when he reached the counter. Wide-eyed and breathing heavily, Ryan stared at me, his cheeks flushed, his pupils blown.

And hell if he didn't look every bit gorgeous and needy.

My feet had a mind of their own as they led me straight to him. I didn't even blink once before I was in his space. Somehow, I kept my hands to myself. I just needed to know one thing. I had to be sure. If not, I'd be darting to the shower quick smart.

I swallowed the lump in my throat before asking, "Do you want this?"

He searched my gaze, his voice quiet when he said, "I want you."

The words registered and found their mark. My mouth connected with his in the next instant. We stumbled a little with the force, his butt hitting the kitchen counter. We didn't pull apart, our lips bruising and perfect in intensity. I groaned into his mouth, my synapses misfiring as his tongue brushed against mine.

Our mouths molded together, and I leaned further into him, chasing closeness, chasing his heat and everything he had to offer.

When his hands moved to my backside, I almost came undone, savoring the rub, the pressure on my dick. He gripped tighter when I moaned, the sound needy, but I didn't give a flying fuck. He could have every single one of my breathy groans.

A thrill of relief hit me when he tugged me hard

against him, and a grin spilled across my mouth when his moan rivaled my own.

He angled his head back, eyes raking over me and a smile quickly forming. "What?"

I shook my head and leaned in, catching his bottom lip between my teeth. I nibbled gently, following up with a soft kiss. This whole time, my cock all but screamed at me to hurry up. But I could not get enough of Ryan's sweetness. There wasn't a chance I was rushing this. Not with him.

I eased away after dropping kisses on Ryan's mouth. This time, my movement earned me a disgruntled sigh. "You keep stopping."

I couldn't stop smiling. How could I when Ryan was so perfectly beautiful and my mind kept replaying his three sweet-as-hell words of wanting me?

"I want to suck you off."

From the startled look on Ryan's face, he hadn't expected those words.

I chuckled. "That okay?"

He launched himself at me, his arms wrapping around my waist, all strength and muscle. I barely kept my balance as he walked me backward, his mouth alternating between devouring mine and traveling across my cheek and along my neck. More than okay with him leading the way, I did my best to not fall and spiral out of control.

But hell if it wasn't difficult.

Ryan's kisses were hungry and desperate, each pass of his lips and swipe of his tongue snatching my ability to think.

"Thank fuck," I finally muttered when my legs hit the end of his mattress. We went down in a tangle of arms and legs, our mouths connected, our breaths nothing but needy gasps. When Ryan pulled out of this kiss, his heavy, hard body still fused to mine, I chased his mouth. After one more brush of his lips, he paused. I dropped my head back to the mattress, too far down to hit the pillow.

Desire and heat flashed in his eyes when they captured mine. The corner of his mouth lifted. I smiled and raised my hand to his cheek. The way he leaned into my touch eased the pounding in my heart. The beats calmed even as wings took flight in my stomach.

Certainty shone in his gaze, and everything about this moment settled every fear and doubt I had about the two of us reaching this point. The reality existing outside this room was trapped in a concern for another time.

With his whole focus on me, he shifted, trailing warm fingers down my body, up my shirt, touching my skin, and making me hum with pleasure. A lick of delicious heat traced each kiss he dotted on my stomach and then my chest when he encouraged me to take off my shirt.

My groan was unrestricted and loud in the quiet room as he lapped at my nipple while he got to work on my zipper. In the moonlit room with the additional patio lighting filtering through the external doors, I had the perfect view of Ryan. A determined focus cast on his features.

"Fuck, you can multitask. You know how hot that is?" I said with a soft chuckle, followed quickly by a groan as he finally gripped my dick.

He smirked around my nipple and gently squeezed my bare cock, then angled up to peer down at me. Amusement and heat played out on his features, and I smiled up at him, sure my grin was sappy. For years I'd dreamed of the chance to have his heated gaze on me. Now it was happening while the dimple on his left cheek popped with his smirk.

The wait, the absence, it all seemed worth it.

"I think I've enough proof that when it comes to balls, I can multitask with the best of them."

I snorted a laugh, which he quickly captured in his mouth. All amusement left me as he jerked me off with soft strokes in time with his tongue plundering my mouth.

Needing more, I grappled with getting his pants off, our mouths still fused, desperately wanting to feel the total weight of him and the full effect of his naked body.

And fuck, taste him.

With a gasp, I broke the kiss. "Pants off."

There was no time to laugh at how quickly Ryan sprang into action. Before I'd even tugged my socks off, he was naked and swiping my jeans off me, boxers coming down at the same time.

Gloriously naked before me, Ryan was on his knees, his gaze roaming every inch of my body. A flash of color just visible at the top of his shoulder snagged my attention. But before I could ask if it was a tattoo and how I didn't know about it, I shivered under his scrutiny, watching emotion flicker over his face.

Whatever he was thinking, I wanted it all.

When he zeroed in on my aching dick, it twitched against my stomach. My cock was needy and wanted all the damn attention. Ryan licked his lips and scooted down, settling between my knees.

"No fucking chance," I said with a roughness I'd never heard before.

Startled, Ryan paused, his hands on my thighs, eyes wide as they connected with mine. "No?"

"No fucking chance unless your cock's in my mouth."

A hot-as-hell groan spilled from him before he pounced on me, his mouth once more connecting with mine. I smiled into the kiss, loving his reaction, lapping up this affection, his own need and desperation.

"Cock," I mumbled as soon as I could get air. "Mouth."

In the light, his brown irises seemed to bleed black. His blown eyes searched mine for the barest of seconds before he nodded, his smirk reforming.

"I want you to fuck my mouth."

Surprise joined with my lust. "Fuck, just give it to me." I was practically moving him around before I finished speaking. He chuckled as he spun on top of me, and as soon as I had access, I grabbed on to his cheek with one hand, his cock with my other, and I glided him into my mouth. I wanted to fucking growl at how abruptly his chuckle cut off.

There was no preamble. No licks, no kisses, no soft caresses. I sucked Ryan hard and fast. His garbled grunt, his loud "Fuck me" spurring me on.

I moved both hands to his hips, directing his thrusts, encouraging his movements. He felt so good, tasted so incredible, and he filled my mouth just so.

And then my world imploded as wet heat engulfed my erection.

For a second, I forgot my own name, let alone what I was doing, as Ryan sucked me down with one long pull. I attempted a groan, which was pretty damn impossible with a mouthful. The sound or perhaps the vibrations made him jerk and dragged my focus away from how Ryan's mouth on me became the center of my universe.

The need for him to come spurred me on. The desire to taste him, feel him spill in my mouth, drove me to suck harder. Meanwhile, my hips bucked, and I trusted Ryan to control just how far he could take me. There wasn't a chance I could do more than jerk my hips, suck his dick, and hold on to his hips with a bruising grip.

I hung on by a thread, and from Ryan's shaking thighs and the tightening of his balls that periodically slapped against my face, he was just as close.

Wanting his load and needing to explode, I shifted my index finger to between his cheeks. Ryan tensed, shook, and garbled around me as he released, my own cock pulsed, my toes curling, my whole body shuddering. I barely had the presence of mind to hold on and keep swallowing.

Ryan stilled, his body no longer jerking. I pulled off him with a pop, taking a big gasping breath. A similar pop followed, and I groaned when he released me.

"Get your arse off me and get up here," I panted. As much as I loved Ryan's weight, he was a heavy fucker with all that muscle. And as much as I liked the idea of his dick in my face, I wanted his mouth on mine. But more than that, I needed to see his eyes.

With an exaggerated sigh, he shifted, the light through the uncovered doors spilling across his face as he did so. Eyes glazed, he looked debauched—a combination of blissed-out, happy, and exhausted. Together, we scooted up to the mattress properly, heads going to the fluffy pillows while tugging up the soft cotton sheet over our naked forms. When he reached for me, my pulse plateaued into a wonderful, easy, and gentle hum.

He wasn't shying away from my touch. Wasn't shying away from me.

My smile was instant, as was me cupping his slightly bristly cheek. "Hey," I offered lamely.

"Hey back." He shuffled closer, our legs brushing, the heat from Ryan's body pressing against me.

Even though his blissed-out look reassured me, I asked, "You good?" It would have been great to navigate what had just happened with effortless ease. That was impossible.

He searched my expression before saying, "No take backs."

My heart flipped over, and a huff of air escaped my lungs with my soft laugh. "I think it's too late for that."

He quirked his brow, and I brushed my thumb over his cheek.

"And there's no chance I want to take any of this back."

Seeming satisfied, he snuggled up impossibly, perfectly close, and dotted a kiss against my mouth before mumbling, "Sleep now. I've got that thing tomorrow, then we need to prepare to head home." His eyes were already closed, the exhaustion of the season I imagined finally catching up with him.

Home.

For four whole weeks Ryan would be mine. Sure, Gran and Amber had dibs too, but I was determined to spend as much time with my Ryan as possible. I refused to think about what would happen after. Instead, I latched on to his words and smiled as I closed my eyes.

I couldn't ever imagine wanting to take back a single moment I spent with this man.

CHAPTER 14

RYAN

Micky wasn't as annoyed as I expected when I'd blown him off. Between waking up spooning Nate and the man in my arms being uncomfortable joining me for the meeting and the appearance my agent had organized today, canceling was a no-brainer.

I didn't want Nate hating his last full day in the US, and honestly, the appearance was more for Micky parading his pro basketball player. It wasn't a sponsorship or anything, which I still avoided like the plague.

Micky was a good agent, especially how he left me alone and allowed me to fly under the radar. And at the club, I knew he'd been making a point, reminding me we needed to talk about the end of next season and my plans.

I just wasn't ready to think that far ahead.

"You sure you won't get into shit?"

Nate was tucked into my side, his one leg resting on my thighs, as he stroked the skin on my chest. With every sweep of his hand, goose bumps popped up. I angled over and pressed a kiss against his head, sure this level of comfort should feel strange. That was so far from the familiarity I felt at being so close to Nate, though.

His scent mixed with my shower gel, reaching my nose, and I took a deep inhale before answering him. "Don't sweat it, honest. Micky expected me to cancel. He knows I'm heading back to Brisbane, so I have shit to organize."

Admittedly, all that was really needed was to pack my case and touch base with Joan, a local woman who kept up with housekeeping and stuff for me.

Nate peered up at me, his gaze assessing. After a beat, he nodded, his smile flirty. "In that case, what's the plan for the day?" I shifted a little, making Nate grumble as I dislodged him. He soon stopped when he realized I was scooting down to get face-to-face with him. "Breakfast. Then I thought we could take a drive. There are a couple more places I want you to see while you're here."

I refused to think about what came after my visit back home, choosing to focus on the present and the man who I still couldn't quite believe was in my arms.

That smile of his morphed before he asked, "You're going to feed me?"

My brows clipped low. "Isn't that what I just said?"

That same smile remained, and my heart flipped over when I got an inkling of what his smile meant. How he managed to tease and flirt and capture unspoken promises in a single smile was beyond me. There wasn't a chance I'd question it, though.

"You want me to feed you something other than breakfast?" I barely recognized my voice. It was low and gravelly with awakening need.

"I wouldn't say no to an extra hit of protein this morning." His lips twitched, amusement brightening him.

My laughter was abrupt and felt so incredible that we could do this. Be together this way.

"Protein, huh?" I managed around a huge smirk. "As long as I get a shot of the good stuff, I'm more than up for this plan."

My whole body vibrated, so fucking happy and horny. I shifted slowly, stopping abruptly when Nate snagged hold of my arm. "What?"

Wide-eyed, he sat quickly, almost head-butting me with his urgency. Confusion had me frowning.

And then he was at my side, shifting further still, so he was behind me. Silently, a tentative finger touched my shoulder blade, and I closed my eyes, realizing what he'd discovered.

"Is this—?" His question cut off with a hitch of his breath.

Angling my head so I could see him, I let my gaze roam his face, searching for his reaction. "A griffin," I said quietly, his fingers still tracing the colored ink I'd had in memory of the man who I'd never been able to forget.

"Holy shit," he said breathily. "Is this…" He swallowed hard, his eyes flashing to mine. "Is this for me?"

I bobbed my head once.

"I didn't know. How didn't I know you had tattoos?"

"I never get photographed with my shirt off. I got that one just last year, and this and the others have always been hidden beneath clothes."

Nate's brows almost touched his hairline. "And it was for me?"

I understood his confusion. Back then, we weren't in touch. "You, a memory of you, was worth marking my skin for," I answered honestly.

Emotion shimmered in his eyes. "It's beautiful." When he leaned down and kissed my tattoo, my heart went wild in my chest. When he lifted back up, he smiled at me, all sweet and gentle. "I think there's only one way to show you how seeing this, knowing it's for me, makes me feel." The huskiness in his voice took an all-time depth. I turned, snagging him with an arm and tugging him close.

Nate then proceeded to blow my mind, and I held on to every second of these moments I could, knowing they couldn't last forever.

When I'd been scouted for college, my life had changed, incredibly so, but this, what we were doing, how we were connecting, fuck if I didn't see a whole new possible future laid out before me.

So much for living in the present.

THE NERVES SWARMING ME FELT DIFFERENT FROM WHEN I'd collected Nate from the airport. They were less intense, but sweat still covered my palms as we entered Black Mountain. While I'd never visited the house I'd bought for my gran and sister, I'd seen the photos and knew the small area well enough that in probably less than a minute, I'd be seeing my family.

"You okay?" Nate hadn't let go of my hand the whole drive from Brisbane airport. He accepted my palm with a smile after we'd left the parking lot and had offered the physical comfort the entire journey.

"Yeah," I answered, fully aware our joined hands were hot and damp. Like the good guy he was, though, he didn't mention it.

"I know I should have perhaps asked earlier," he said, drawing my attention away from the gum trees. The familiarity of them made me smile. "But how do you want to play this, with me, with your family?" Nate clamped his mouth shut, and I thought he had more to say. But that one question alone was one hell of a start.

The truth was, I'd considered this periodically on our flight and the drive home. Refusing him in any way would be a shit of a move, but that didn't prevent the lump from forming in my throat.

"Hey." The squeeze of my hand pulled my attention to Nate. "We can do whatever you want, okay?"

I cut a glance to him. Nothing but sincerity filled his expression before he flicked his focus back to the road. Nate was too fucking good for me. It hadn't just been the last week I'd figured that out, but his understanding cemented that knowledge.

Before I could answer and unjumble my brain, Nate said, "We're here."

The Park brake wasn't even engaged before the fly-screen door was opening. Nate's words floated over me, my ability to hear hampered by the heavy thud of my pulse.

Gran stood in the doorway, her gaze unyielding. My breath caught as I took in the wrinkles around her eyes, her laughter lines deep around her mouth. And then I was out of the car and in her arms. The strength of her hug drew my smile. Despite her years and the time I'd wasted keeping my distance, she could still make me feel safe and loved just by the magic of her hugs.

"Boy," she said close to my ear, "never again, you hear."

I nodded against her neck, stooped over but not willing to break the connection just yet.

"You think about keeping your distance again, you'll find me on your doorstep or in the middle of a blasted ball game, getting ready to tan your hide and drag your butt back home. Got it?"

I snorted out a laugh, basking in the warmth of her tone and the fresh squeeze she gave me before she eased away. I peered down at her. She looked healthy and strong, much more than I'd expected. While we'd spoken on video calls, even more so over the past five months, I hadn't quite believed she was getting better from her fall and her dizzy spells.

"You look good, Gran."

She quirked her brow at me. "Of course I do.

You're lucky you've got my genes so you don't look like you've been beaten with the ugly stick."

"Gee, Gran, say it how it is."

Nate's warm voice at my side startled me, and goose bumps broke out on my flesh. Just hours ago before we left for the airport, his voice had sounded so much gruffer when I'd sucked him off. I cleared my throat, trying to shake the visual before looking at him.

"Come here and give me a hug. You get an extra brownie tonight since you brought the wanderer home."

I smiled as Nate hugged Gran before the sound of the screen door caught my attention.

Like a punch to the gut, I struggled to take a breath again. It didn't matter how many photos or video calls we made. Nothing could have prepared me for the tight squeeze of my heart at seeing my sister all grown. And a mom to boot.

Ivy was on Amber's hip. With the sun shining down on what looked like whisper-soft hair, Ivy all but glowed. My heart melted in an instant, and I couldn't take my eyes off my niece.

Finally in front of my sister, I refocused on her. "Hey," I offered lamely.

Amber's bright eyes, the same shade as my own,

raked over me. "You look older in the flesh," she deadpanned, "more haggard." Her lips twitched.

I took her sass and that one tell as all the invitation I needed. I angled around to hug her without squashing Ivy, who wriggled between us, babbling. I grinned at the sound and eased back, staring at the pretty baby in my sister's arms. Curiosity filled her eyes, and my heart stuttered. "She looks so much like you."

"Thank God, right." Amber tickled her daughter under the chin. A giggle of delight followed.

"And where's my little hoodlum?" The sound of Nate at my side eased muscles I hadn't realized had tensed. I wasn't the only one affected by him. Ivy's head whipped in Nate's direction, and she all but lurched out of my sister's arms to get to him.

I smirked and held back my chuckle. *Me too, kid. I totally understand the draw.*

Once in Nate's arms, my niece cooed and jabbered on in the cutest of ways as he smothered her with kisses. When he pulled back, he side-hugged Amber and planted a brotherly kiss on top of her head.

The whole reunion between them was natural. A pang of longing hit me hard. It didn't matter that I understood why or was responsible for the distance.

The emotion was there, raising its jealous head and making me feel crap.

I had to look away, my gaze settling back on Gran, whose unwavering focus was on me.

"Come on. Let's go in and get some tea on the go." She took my arm, and I smiled, my forehead smoothing out. I needed to get over myself and enjoy every moment I could get with my family, and most definitely Nate.

Already I could see my month home racing by too quickly. No chance would I waste that by wishing things were different.

It was no hardship sprawling on the soft rug next to Ivy. She was adorable and into everything and did this whole cute push-up thing.

The only time I took my eyes off her was when I couldn't resist a glance at Nate.

For the past couple of hours, we'd been talking about Nate's visit, omitting the obvious. That didn't stop me from thinking about all the time we'd spent together, though, or the soft touches and fierce kisses.

I'd never been so grateful to be able to afford business-class tickets before. Between snoozing and murmuring to each other on the flight to Brisbane, I'd captured as many kisses as possible.

There was freedom being back in Australia. Here I wasn't anybody noteworthy—not really. The status of grandson, brother, and uncle was pretty much it. I couldn't even consider what label I'd put on Nate and me.

It was early afternoon, and both Gran and Amber were taking it easy on me for some reason. Twice I'd caught a shared look between Amber and Nate, but if he was the reason they weren't littering me with questions, or worse, giving me the telling off I deserved, I was grateful. I had no issue with Nate running interference.

"What do you think, Ryan?" Gran's voice pulled me away from my thoughts and the bunny I danced in front of Ivy.

"Huh? Sorry, I missed whatever you said."

Gran smiled. "Nate needs to head and see his folks." My heart constricted, hating the thought of missing out on a moment of his time. Not only that, but Nate leaving meant I was open to interrogation.

"Goodness me, Ryan, you're wearing the same look you had when I grounded you for a week for skipping off school that one time." Gran rolled her eyes, and heat filled my cheeks. "Nate's still staying here a while, unless the plan's changed?" She eyed Nate, whose gaze darted from me to Gran.

"No plans to move back to my place yet," he answered quickly. The news did the trick, loosening my chest and helping me breathe easier.

"Good." Gran nodded and refocused on me. "You see. He'll be back, so you don't have to arrange an escape or have Nate try to climb the veranda to your room or anything. We all know how that worked out last time."

I chuckled at the memory, more than aware this was a very different house, but the visual remained.

Nate's laughter joined mine. "In my defense," Nate started, capturing my attention fully, "my sneaking in when Ryan was grounded would have gone totally unnoticed if it hadn't been for that possum."

At the memory and with the laughter surrounding me, all the tension eased out of me.

"Is this that cute possum Gran used to feed that used to hang out in the veranda?" Amber asked.

She'd have been too young to remember most things about my teenage years, but she was right. The possum had been cute and ridiculously friendly.

"When it's pitch-black and the damn thing screams in your face, it's not that damn cute," Nate mumbled, his lips twitching.

"You're just lucky the bush broke your fall," I teased.

Nate quirked his brow at me. "I don't think thorns in my butt are exactly lucky."

I smirked, my sordid brain dragging me merrily in the direction of thinking about a prick in his ass. And when Nate's eyes widened, his cheeks changing color, it was clear he knew exactly where my thoughts led me.

"So—" He cleared his throat. "I told Dad I'd stop in, then I'll go and see Mum. You need me to pick anything up for dinner?" He spoke to Gran, seeming to deliberately avoid making eye contact with me.

"We're all good. I put something in the slow cooker this morning. It kept me busy while waiting for a wandering grandchild of mine to arrive." Tenderness lit her words, and my heart filled with warmth. Nate wasn't the only person I owed a real explanation to. I knew that. But despite those conversations being needed, I was so glad to be home.

Nate standing and grabbing his keys and wallet snagged my attention. The desire to kiss him goodbye was challenging to ignore, but we hadn't managed to finish the conversation in the car.

Looking worried, Nate stood near the hall doorway, his brows drawn low.

"I'll see you soon," I offered, smiling.

He searched my face before nodding. "See you in a couple or three hours."

And then he was gone, and I was left alone with the three women in my life. Amber appeared to be struggling to hold back while Gran relaxed in her chair, quietly observing, and Ivy had plastic keys in her mouth and was gnawing happily.

Knowing this was way overdue, I exhaled, kissed my niece on the cheek, and then sat up. "Questions or my apology first?" Beating around the bush wasn't a viable option. While I'd missed out on so many years with my sister, and we had a lot of catching up to do, her personality remained the same now as it was when she was seven. Stubborn, determined, and armed with an impressive bullshit radar.

Surprising me, Amber looked at Gran first. I glanced in Gran's direction, saw her pursed lips, and wondered at their silent conversation.

"I think we've had enough of apologies since Christmas, kiddo."

Startled, I stared at her, wide-eyed, feeling unbelievably like a kid again.

"We know you're sorry and are sure you had your reasons, as foolish as perhaps they seem now that you're back home."

I swore she was a bloody witch or maybe a mind

reader. More than likely, I had a shit ability at forming a neutral expression, but only where Gran and Nate were concerned. My ability to be unreadable was part of the reason I'd lasted so long in the closet for all these years.

Amber shifting and picking up her daughter caught my focus. Once Ivy was in her arms, she glanced at me. "I have millions of questions, but honestly, none of them seem important right now."

Confused as hell, I gaped, wondered what on earth was happening and if robots or clones had something to do with whatever this was.

"You know, if the wind changes, you'll stick like it!"

I slammed my mouth shut at Gran's words. A quick look at Amber, and I wasn't convinced she was legit being so chill about everything. Her smile was a little satisfied.

"What gives?" I couldn't take it anymore.

"Huh?" I definitely wasn't buying Amber's wide-eyed innocence. No chance.

"Don't *huh* me. Seriously, you two never keep your thoughts or your emotions to yourself."

"Perhaps I've matured, you know, now I'm a responsible adult, a mum no less." Sass filled her tone.

"Uhm, nope."

Amber rolled her eyes at me and focused on organizing herself to breastfeed Ivy.

My attention moved to Gran. I stared at her, willing her to give me something.

"We're just happy that you're home, Ryan." Her smile was kind. "Right, I really could do with a walk around the block, get my exercise in. You can come with me, kiddo."

With neither of them giving me anything, I sighed and gave up. I expected I'd find out what their game was eventually. For now, I'd enjoy the reprieve and try not to let my guard down. These women were too scheming for that.

CHAPTER 15

NATE

I SIPPED AT THE COFFEE I'D BROUGHT WITH ME WHEN I'D headed to the store. For the past ten minutes I'd been telling Dad and Patrick a little about my visit to the States. Still in awe of watching Ryan's final game of the season, it was easy to waffle on about the whole experience and just how shit-hot Ryan was on the court.

"And his team didn't make it to the playoffs?"

I shook my head at Dad's question. "Honestly, I'm still not a hundred percent sure how the playoffs, let alone things like drafting, work, but I know his team didn't do especially well over the year. He said a heap of injuries or something didn't help. But the game I watched, I swear, Dad, he was magic." Just thinking about the injuries, though, reminded me Ryan still limped. It wasn't as noticeable as after the game—or the night of dancing—but it still wasn't completely healed.

Dad bobbed his head. "Maybe with things how they are now, your mum and I can take a trip out there the next season. Take in a game."

My smile was swift. "Yeah, I think he'd love that." I swallowed back the rush of emotion, aware that in four short weeks he'd be leaving again.

This time would be different, though. The last couple of days pretty much confirmed that. Sure, it would be awful when he returned to Minnesota after everything we'd shared, but Ryan Broadwater belonged on the court.

"How's everything been here?" I cast a cursory glance around the store, wanting to focus on something else. Everything looked exactly as I'd left it. I grinned, sure Dad would have itched to change a couple of things back to how they were when he'd run the place. It seemed like he'd held himself back, though.

"All good. I've already told your mum I'll be working more over the next month too." He eyed me speculatively, and heat hit my cheeks.

Dad knowing I'd be eager for as much time as possible with Ryan shouldn't have been surprising. If anything, I was grateful he'd anticipated my request and was confident that once Ryan and I were back together again, we'd be inseparable.

I wondered if I'd ever get the opportunity to say Ryan and I were more than friends. Fuck, I hoped so, but for the time being, I'd be patient.

"Thanks, Dad. I was going to talk to you about that today but wasn't sure if I'd be pushing my luck or not."

"Pfft. As if. Just enjoy him being here."

I nodded and concentrated on my coffee as if it was the most interesting drink in the world. After the last couple of days, I worried I wouldn't be able to hide my feelings for Ryan anymore.

"You want to sit down now and sort out a schedule with me before you head to see your mum?"

"Yeah, that'd be great, thanks."

"Come on then, kiddo. Let's get you sorted so you can get back to that hotshot friend of yours."

I smirked as I followed Dad into my office, thinking how just last year I'd easily considered Ryan to be a hotshot with the ego to match. Almost six months on, I knew different and figured the past eight years hadn't always been easy for my friend. It was crap that was the case. The knowledge sat heavily on my chest. Regardless, happiness vied for attention that we'd reconnected in a way I'd spent countless years dreaming about.

After catching up with Dad and then Mum, I was sent to Gran's with cake and a message for Ryan and Gran that we were expected at a barbie around their place on Saturday afternoon.

Mum had gushed over the photos I'd shown her from my visit. On the flight over, I'd spent time putting all the holiday photos in an album on my phone, carefully filing away the few pictures of me and Ryan that would tell everyone that he was much more to me than my old best friend.

We sat around the table eating the chili Gran had made, chuckling about being kids and some events Ryan had missed out on. The slight tension in Ryan's shoulders that had been there this morning had entirely disappeared since I'd returned. At ease, he laughed, joked, and spent time fussing over his niece.

We sat opposite each other, and despite the temptation to reach out and play footsy, I held myself back. Already there'd been too many lingering looks between us. At least till bedtime, I could wait, relieved I was still staying with Amber and Gran.

"Next time you go to that bar with the drag queen night, I'm so there."

Amber's statement pulled my wide-eyed stare at her. "Uhm, okay," I said, not risking a look at Ryan.

When Ryan and I did go, I'd hoped it would be a safe place for us to be together. I swallowed my disappointment, knowing that Amber needed some time out too, and I expected going to a queer bar would offer her a safe place away from being hit on by blokes. Not only that, the drag nights at Bar QK were legit entertaining.

"I thought Ryan and I would perhaps head there this Friday night."

The last time we'd danced was before everything between us had changed. The heat had been explosive, and I wanted the opportunity to do so again. This time without the restraints of watchful eyes.

Ryan's gaze was full of heat when I peered at him. I flicked my attention away, saying to Amber, "There's no drag show this weekend." I'd already checked when I'd started planning some of my and Ryan's time together. "The weekend after, on Saturday, Lady Bra Ga is on."

The grin Amber shot my way was a relief. It meant she wasn't put out by the lack of invite this weekend.

"Awesome. You said she's great, right?" she asked.

"She's funny as hell and was fun to watch when I saw her perform." Aware Ryan had kept quiet, I turned to him. "That all sound okay?"

His nod came quickly. "Definitely, especially if I get to meet your friends."

The people I'd met via Tallis were still new friends, but time meant nothing when you connected. And that's how I felt about the group I'd met at Bar QK.

"You guys mind helping Gran with the dishes while I put Ivy to bed?" Standing, Amber reached over to her daughter, who appeared super tired. A quick glance at Gran showed she didn't look much more awake.

Before I could respond, Ryan stood and started collecting the bowls. "Nate and I have got this. Gran, thanks for the meal. Why don't you go and chill?"

Gran had been suspiciously quiet during the latter half of the meal. Earlier, she'd implied she'd been excited about her grandson's return. No doubt that meant she'd barely had any sleep.

"We've definitely got this, and honestly, I expect I'll be heading to bed straight after." While jet lag hadn't hit hard again, courtesy of awesome beds in business class, we'd had virtually a whole day of traveling with the two flights, plus the car journeys.

I was beat. I was also desperate for a moment alone with Ryan.

"Thanks, boys. I think I'll get ready for bed and turn in, if that's the case." Ryan's gran stood, said goodnight to us all, making a fuss of Ryan in the process, which was super sweet, and then headed off. Amber followed after a hug from us both, and finally, after a whole day, Ryan and I were alone.

I gathered the glasses, side-eyeing him. I smiled softly when I realized he was doing the same thing. He followed me to the kitchen, stepping directly behind me when I stopped at the sink. His chest brushed my back as he leaned around me and placed the bowls down.

The air seemed to suck from the room, making it hard to breathe.

"I've missed you." The quiet rasp of his voice next to my ear caused goose bumps to erupt on my skin. Air finally rushed into my lungs when his lips pressed against my neck. A groan quickly followed. "It's been so ridiculously hard not to touch you too. Fucking torturous."

I closed my eyes and sighed as he followed up with another kiss. "I think we need to load this damn dishwasher and take this to my room." Having the guest room at the far side of the house had its merits. While I heard Ivy's loud cries at night, the room was far enough away to offer a semblance of privacy.

"You want me to sneak in at any particular time?"

I turned in Ryan's arms and raised my brows at him. "You think I can wait?" I snorted. "Hell no. Say goodnight again to your sister and get your arse in my room. It'll be quicker for me to tidy the kitchen by myself." I eyed his mouth as I spoke. The temptation to lean up and kiss him was visceral, but stopping would pose one hell of a challenge if I gave in.

Feeling needy, I didn't think I had the willpower to stop and not devour him. "Seriously, go. I can't concentrate while you're so close."

The smirk Ryan shot my way was sinful and filled with so much promise I legit shooed him away. He left with a chuckle, and I raced around the kitchen, ensuring everything was clean and tidied away.

A kiss and hopefully some cock from Ryan was one hell of a motivator.

Fifteen minutes later, after just one glance at Ryan as he stepped out of my room's en suite, I almost swallowed my tongue. The man was perfection personified. All hard muscles, the ridges protruding and perfect for trailing my tongue over. But it was the look in his eyes, the way they roamed over my face, my body, a small smile forming that made my heart beat double time.

With the bedroom door firmly closed behind me, the lock engaged for good measure, I leaned against the hard surface. At my blatant perusal, Ryan's cheeks turned pink. That slight reaction reminded me of one of the many reasons why I'd been attracted to

Ryan in the first place. Sweet, soft edges of personality contrasted endearingly with the confidence he exuded. Both on and off the court.

We remained staring at each other for a beat. While I wanted to commit to memory every inch of this man, I couldn't help but wonder what he thought, what he saw when he looked at me.

The question remained on the tip of my tongue as Ryan shifted his hands to the waistband of his package-hugging boxers. In one swift movement, he tugged them down and stepped out of them.

"Fuck." The word tumbled out of me as a needy groan, earning me a confident smirk.

Ryan's dick bobbed up and down, and he quirked his brow high. My laughter cut through the tension, and I latched on to the sensation rippling across my skin.

I loved I could laugh with this man. Loved how good he made me feel and in so many different ways —whether it was with his cock in my mouth, the words we shared, or the sweet care he offered.

It took but a beat before I stood before him, still smiling. Cupping his face, I swiped his bottom lip with the pad of my thumb. "Kissing you this morning seems like forever ago."

His gaze darted around my face, and he nodded.

"I don't like not being able to touch you whenever I want."

Pursing my lips, I worked hard at not sharing my immediate thoughts. *You don't have to hide.*

When Ryan hesitated, I realized my expression was wide open to interpretation. "You know I can't—"

I couldn't help but cut him off. "You don't owe me any more of an explanation for not being out." When the look in his eyes shifted to uncertainty, I couldn't hold back, trying to ease the expression there. "I'm happy to hear and hope you can confide in me if there's more you want to share, but as to you feeling guilty or however you're feeling, don't. I want you to be happy."

"You don't think I'm a cowa—"

"Hell no, stop right there, and we've already been over this. Being out or not, sharing your story has nothing to do with heroism or bravery. And fuck, this life can be as shitty as it is awesome. It's hard enough, and throw in sexuality and identity into the mix, and we both know there's plenty of hate in the world and people who can't get their heads out of their arses."

He swallowed hard, and it became impossible to not reach out and touch him. Clutching the back of his neck, I stroked my fingers over the skin, dancing across his short hair there.

"You mean that?"

Hurt for Ryan and his fear, the way he possibly saw himself, spread through my chest. Emotion clung to my words when I said, "Since I was fifteen years old, I've wanted you. Even after all this time, you've been this presence in my soul. I couldn't let you go, couldn't shake off this feeling that something was missing in my life.

"I'll be honest and say the thought of keeping this, what could be between us, a secret for a long time hurts, but that's about me and my desire to touch you, kiss you when I want, hold you, and hug you in the street if I feel the need. But that's on me. It's my cross to bear.

"For now, Ryan." I smiled softly at the man who had my heart. "I want to focus on the here and now and see where that takes us. And hopefully the first place will be to my seriously comfy bed."

The chuckle that burst free from him filled the small space between us, relaxing his shoulders and bringing fresh emotion back into his eyes.

"Thank you."

"For dragging you to my bed? Anytime," I teased, wanting to keep hold of the ease to help smooth away the sharp edges of his struggles.

"Well that, but for everything else too."

Not wanting any more distance between us, I stepped into him and brushed my lips against his. That he was naked and I was fully dressed didn't escape my notice. It also gave me wicked ideas.

"Bed." I encouraged him toward the mattress. His steps were willing, his mouth returning to mine as he moved closer. Once his legs connected with the bed, I angled away and peered up. "You want me to suck you off?"

Ryan's nod was instant, his mouth smirk-free as his breath hitched. "Yeah, so much." He gripped his cock, his knuckles pressing against my covered dick as he did so.

"Let me take care of you," I whispered, easing him back, determined to make him pass out with a smile on his face and clear his mind from worrying about our future.

CHAPTER 16
RYAN

EARLY JUNE

Time raced by too quickly, though every moment spent with my family and Nate was everything.

After talking with Nate again about my fear of coming out, some pressure had lifted from my shoulders. That didn't make each day that I couldn't touch him when not alone any less awful, but I felt safe, understood, and so grateful he didn't pressure me.

The days Nate worked, I happily hung out with my sister, niece, and Gran. They still remained weirdly quiet about me staying away. While our conversations were nonstop about our time apart, not a single challenging question was asked, and any discussion about the future was related to the team and our hopes for next year.

The first Friday, we'd headed out of town and stayed in an Airbnb so we could enjoy our night out meeting with Nate's friends. That night I'd been all up in Nate's business. My hands had barely released the man, and my mouth only parted from his for polite conversation. By the time we returned to Gran's, I'd already been mulling over the advantages of coming out to my family.

The ridiculous thing was, they'd be nothing but supportive. I knew this as well as I knew the grass was green. That knowledge didn't stop my heart from slamming against my chest. Nor did it prevent my mouth from drying up like the outback desert. And all that led me to being confused as hell and spending too many hours arguing with myself.

I hated that I talked myself in circles. Detested my heart and head, and every emotion that sprouted legs and left me more confused and frustrated.

"Hey, you okay?" Nate lowered his voice.

I bobbed my head and shot him a reassuring smile. With my sister in the back seat, it was necessary to sit on my hands to stop from reaching out to him. It wasn't that far to the Airbnb we were staying at, with thankfully separate rooms. That didn't mean the thirty-five-minute journey wasn't torturous. Not with my inner turmoil playing on a loop.

"You have been unusually quiet," my sister

offered. "Not that I'm complaining, as every now and then, your accent gets weird."

From over my shoulder, I flipped her off. "Whatever, traffic cone. You just struggle knowing how awesome I am."

Amber snorted. "I haven't missed your ridiculous nicknames. They're lame."

I grinned, easing into the familiarity of arguing with my sister. "Nate was the one who came up with 'flasher.'"

"Hey, don't bring me into this. I'm here, all grown-up and sensible-like, driving us to a bar so you can see your little sister pissed for the first time." Humor laced his words.

I groaned. "Ugh. Don't remind me." I glanced back at a grinning Amber. She was so excited to be going out tonight that I couldn't even be annoyed with her that I had to keep my hands to myself. "You behave. No accepting drinks from anyone but us. No leaving your drinks unattended."

"It's not the first time I've been out drinking," she sassed.

"It's the first time legally," I shot back.

Nate snorted. "Your sister has been known to stumble home after drinking a few ciders with her friends. She's even more mouthy when she's tipsy."

I groaned again, something I expected to be doing a fair bit of tonight. "Just don't drink too much."

Amber snorted. "Yes, *Dad*. I imagine I'll have one cider and that'll be enough. Between pregnancy and breastfeeding, I'll be a serious lightweight."

"Hmm... in that case, make sure if you go to the toilet, you let us know." From the corner of my eye, I saw Nate's shoulders shaking.

"Right...," Amber dragged out. "Maybe I'm wrong here, but I can't imagine too many straight men being there tonight, certainly none on the prowl for women. If any at all. That means I'm only likely to pull women, right, who'll all be using the same bathroom as me, so...."

My sigh was loud and heavy, and both the assholes in the car laughed. "Just—"

"Ryan." Nate stopped me short. "She'll be fine. She's not a kid, and we're both there. Plus it's a nice place. Safe. You saw that for yourself last weekend."

A glance in his direction reassured me that despite the teasing, he was being serious. "Okay. You're right." When his hand twitched on the wheel, my heart rate kicked up, convinced he wanted to reach out to me as much as I wanted to touch him. I subtly sat back on my hands.

It didn't take long before we reached the motel. Once checked in, I regulated my breathing, trying to be as casual as possible about Nate and me sharing a room. Amber didn't even blink when we saw her to her room first. We agreed to meet in an hour, and I had a sneaky suspicion she planned to spend forty-five minutes of that napping.

Every night when Ivy woke, I'd not only heard her loud and clear, but tucked up in Nate's room, I'd held my breath. The situation was far from ideal, but being the selfish git I was, no chance was I prepared to give up my nights with Nate.

Once in our room and with the door locked, I pounced on Nate. I needed his mouth and his touch. "Shower with me?" I asked breathily. We only had an hour, and every minute counted. Nate nodded, his mouth brushing over mine as we stumbled to the bathroom. With our clothes discarded on the way, we were naked by the time our bare feet touched the tiled floor.

"You're not getting farther than a meter from me in the next hour," I muttered, only half serious.

I felt his smile against my mouth before making good on getting my Nate fix. Hopefully it would be enough to get me through the night.

A FEW HOURS LATER, I COULDN'T REMEMBER LAUGHING so hard. My cheeks ached from the first half of the show. Nate had not been exaggerating how epic Lady Bra Ga's performance was.

It was more than that, though.

Amber and I snickered and joked in a way that took me by surprise. With our big age gap, I'd never had the opportunity to consider her more than a slightly annoying kid. Sure, I loved her and had tried to look out for her, even in my absence. But tonight, seeing her in a new light, blew my mind.

"I so did not break your weird CD thingie."

I quirked my brow at Amber. "Uhm, hello, you drawing Dorothy the Dinosaur or whatever all over my DVDs, in biro no less, kinda destroyed them."

The grin on her face reached megawatt level, and she nudged me with her elbow. "Thanks for letting me come hang tonight. I didn't want to rain on your parade or anything and get between you and your mate time."

Since I'd had four beers, rather than tensing, I redirected the conversation. "You're not. I'm surprised you wanted your first night out to be with your old-fart brother, though."

"Your farts do still smell like something crept up your butt and died." She scrunched her face, and I laughed hard.

"Me, fart? I'm too much of a gentleman to do such things."

"Yeah, right. Hell, I lost count of the farting competitions you and Nate had. Thanks for that, by the way." The stink-eye she shot me lost its impact with the twitching of her lips. "One of my earliest memories is of you two idiots running into my room, farting, then not letting me out."

My laughter was loud, raucous enough to draw Nate's attention to me.

Sitting opposite me in the large booth, the seven bodies squeezed in tightly, Nate smiled. "Do I want to know?"

Amber leaned forward. "You two being dickheads and torturing me with farts."

Amusement lit Nate's face, his eyes twinkling in the low lighting and the occasional flashing of lights from the small dance floor. "It was an important learning experience for you," he said.

"What, how boys stink?"

"Yup, and how they can be arseholes." Nate followed up with a wink.

"Ooh, whose arsehole are we talking about, and is it pretty?"

Wide-eyed, I choked on air when Lenny's question came out of nowhere. He wasn't working tonight, so he was one of the seven people in our group.

"Wait," Amber said, her voice carrying loudly over the chuckling group. "Buttholes are pretty? For real?"

Equally amused and mortified, I groaned. "Please don't anyone answer my baby sister."

"Hey, a woman needs to know these things," she grouched.

"No, they don't." I glanced at Nate, silently pleading for help. The bastard laughed, looking far too delectable even when being unhelpful.

"Come on, Ryan, let's head to the bar to save your delicate sensibilities," he offered with a wide grin.

"Whatever, asshole." I stood and eased out of the booth.

"I'll have another cider. I'll be fine here with my new teacher," Amber threw out, high-fiving Lenny.

I shook my head, not-so-secretly happy she was having a great time. My happiness jumped a level or five when Nate led me to the far side of the bar, took hold of my hand, and urged me to the rear courtyard.

Grinning, I followed him eagerly as we wound around the tables and standing bodies. More than one appreciative glance was sent Nate's way. I held on tighter, so damn lucky that we were here together.

As soon as we reached the far wall, Nate turned

and backed toward it, allowing the wooden fence to support him. I stepped into his space without hesitation, not stopping until our bodies were flush and our mouths touched.

The kiss was fierce and all-encompassing and most definitely not appropriate for public viewing. Our tongues brushing against each other's turned my brain to blissful mush. And I loved every single moment of it.

Nate pulled back first, his breathing heavy, pupils blown underneath the scattering of outdoor lighting. "You needed that about as much as I did, huh?" His gaze darted around my face, much like mine was his, drinking in his expression.

"And some," I readily admitted.

Nate reached up and cupped my cheek, remaining silent. I swallowed hard, desperation threatening to crawl out of me. The words spilled out anyway. "How the fuck am I going to leave you in two weeks?"

Tightness appeared around Nate's eyes as he winced. When he spoke, there was a roughness in his voice. "Let's not think about that now."

Emotion bubbled in my chest. "Maybe it would be okay if Amber knew about us." Nate's wide eyes, I was sure, matched my own. "All your friends here know," I continued, conviction and desperation clinging to my words, "and I'm safe here, right, and—"

"Hey." Nate cut off my rushed words. "Breathe, okay."

I gasped and sucked in air, not even realizing I hadn't inhaled for Christ knew how long. Nate studied me, gaze darting between my mouth and my eyes. Once I took a few steadying breaths, a smile touched his lips.

"Amber loves you. When you're ready to tell her, it'll be the right time, but it needs to be for you, and not just because I'm so irresistible you can't stand not touching me." Lightness lifted his last few words, and I smiled, suspecting that was his intention.

"I think me holding back is because telling her and Gran makes everything more real."

Nate's brows drew together as he nodded. "Okay?"

I shook my head. "No, I mean I'm gay, obviously." I attempted a smile but wasn't sure I pulled it off. But I needed him to understand that, like it or not, this… me coming out was everything to do with him, with us.

The right or wrong of that was inconsequential. It simply was.

"My first year at college, five times I packed my bags. Twice I made it to the airport."

Nate's brows shot high, and his breath caught. "You did?"

I nodded. "Two things stopped me. Gran and Amber, and me knowing I had to see college and ball through. You know how broke we were growing up. I needed to see how far I could take basketball to make sure they were okay."

Understanding shone in his stare.

"Then there was you."

"Me?" A fast shake of his head followed.

"As soon as I left, I missed you. I felt it gut deep. And speaking to you made it so fucking hard, made me miss you even more. It took me a while to figure out I wasn't straight, and that part of how I felt for you was more than me missing my best mate." Determination kept my voice steady. Admitting it all, finally, needed to be done. Screw that we were outside in a courtyard. Screw that I heard low rumbles of laughter surrounding us. None of that mattered.

"It was too freaking hard missing you, feeling so much for you, even though I hadn't seen you in the flesh in so long. There wasn't a chance I could tell you. And coming home scared the shit out of me. Plus it was likely you'd kick my ass for quitting, let alone if I attempted some grand declaration or something equally as mortifying."

Soft pants escaped Nate, his eyebrows almost touching his hairline. Tempted to carry on, I instead clamped my mouth shut, giving him time to process.

"That's why you stopped calling, were a dickhead to Amber when she visited." The statement of his words was clear. Then I lost his eyes as he dropped his head.

When he remained quiet, uncertainty raised its ugly head. "Nate, I'm so sorry, but I just couldn't deal. And there was no chance in hell I could handle being out, not only in college but playing professionally." I stopped talking, exhaustion kicking in and draining me of any fire I had left.

"Amber's probably wondering where we are," I said reluctantly. With my heart constricting and with no idea what to say or do, I released a heavy sigh, my feet shifting on the spot.

Nate reaching out and taking hold of my forearms surprised me.

Shaking his head, he finally looked at me. "I don't know how to respond."

Feeling awkward, I twisted my lips and went to speak. Nate caught my words with his mouth. I groaned at the contact, relief firing my synapses and making my head spin. Fire returned in a flash of heat, the flames licking at my skin in the best of ways. My shoulders sagged, rightness slamming into me.

All too soon, Nate angled away. "I think I need to understand more, but not now," he said, his mouth still close to mine. "All that matters is you're here, and I can't even begin to tell you how fucking happy that makes me."

The ache in my chest took me by surprise. My heart twisted and grew and seemed to melt all at the same. Who even knew that was possible?

"Amber," he continued. The mention of my sister forced me to stand up straight and not attach myself to Nate like a stage five clinger.

"Right, Amber." I returned his smile and reached for his hand. Together we walked back inside. When Nate shifted his fingers to pull away, I held tighter and peered over at him. "It's okay," I said, with more confidence than I felt. But Nate was right. I'd worry about the reality of returning to the States in a couple of weeks. For now, I squeezed Nate's hand and grinned, welcoming the happiness he brought into my life.

Once we were through the crowd and before the booth, my gaze connected with my sister's. A shit-eating grin stretched her mouth wide. "Damn, is that what happens when you head to the bar here? They pour a big glass of gay love?"

The table erupted into laughter, while Amber's expression softened as she peered over at me.

"Lenny said the show starts again in five." She indicated for Tallis to let her out. Once before me, she prodded my stomach. "Come on, big brother. Looks like I can't trust you to not get distracted." She prodded Nate too for good measure. "Let's the two of us get drinks," she said to me before leading me away from Nate, who simply chuckled and watched us leave.

I rolled my eyes and hooked my arm over her shoulders as we headed to the bar. Once there, she peered up at me. "Love you." She squeezed my side, and I fought hard not to get sappy and emotional.

"Love you." I punctuated my words with a gentle kiss to her head.

Once we'd ordered, Amber quirked her brows high.

"What?" I asked, wondering what she would tackle first.

"You know on the drive to the motel we were talking about the bar and that it wasn't the type of place I expected straight men to hang out?" She cocked her head, and my eyes grew large in understanding.

"Shit."

"Uh-huh. You didn't even question it. Neither of you did."

My shoulders slumped a little, my mind blown

that I'd been so careless. For near enough a decade, I'd kept a massive part of myself concealed, with only a handful of nameless, barely worth mentioning encounters in all that time.

"You knew?"

Amber tucked a lock of hair behind her ear and shook her head. "Not really. It passed through my mind a couple of times, but I only hoped something was going on between you. Nate's loved you for a long time."

My breath froze in my lungs.

A slight huff escaped her as she took in my reaction. "All I'm saying is the two of you together is awesome, especially if things are serious and it means you come home."

Turning away from me, she smiled at the bartender who passed us our drinks. Meanwhile, my heart thumped loudly, blocking out the sound of the room. The heat of possibility flooded my veins. Trust Amber to come out and say what I'd been too terrified to voice, even before Nate made his visit.

Amongst the loud laughter and the flick of the microphone that burst to life, I followed Amber, drinks in my hands. Could I really give it all up and move back to Australia? To be with Nate? To be with my family? More than that, did I have the courage to follow through if I made the decision?

CHAPTER 17
NATE

No longer did Ryan have to sneak into my room. It helped the week pass by that much sweeter. Gran, as I'd predicted, had listened attentively when Ryan told her he was gay.

My pride for the man burned deep. That didn't mean it didn't sting that we were keeping things on the down-low, nor the fact that he wasn't coming out publicly. I hadn't lied a couple of weeks back when I'd understood his reluctance to be out. But with just a week left of his visit, my uncertainty grew, made worse that he'd finally responded to his agent and was on a video call with him in the bedroom he never used.

"Why are you walking a hole in the carpet, Nate?"

I scrunched my nose in apology and attempted a

smile. Gran's no-bullshit radar, though, was firing strong. Standing, she headed to the kitchen. "Come on. Let's put the kettle on." Gran busied herself making tea while I sat at the large island. "What's going on? This about the call Ryan's making?"

"Maybe a little," I admitted.

She angled to look at me, a frown forming. "Why's that?"

Focusing on my hands, I picked at the edge of an envelope dumped on the granite. "I suppose it makes Ryan leaving more real." The shuffle of Gran's feet caught my attention, followed swiftly by the opening and closing of the fridge door. She remained silent while I gradually destroyed the envelope with small tears.

When a mug of tea was placed before me, I jerked up, startled. "Thanks."

Kind eyes connected with mine as Gran stood at the other side of the counter. "It's been wonderful having him home."

"It has," I agreed.

"Have you spoken to him about his contract? He has just another season left, right?"

My stomach clenched. I hadn't, deliberately so. My whole approach to Ryan leaving was ostrich-head-in-the-sand. The past four weeks had been a whirlwind of kisses while getting to know and fall in love with the man all over again. When I wasn't in a loved-up haze, I pinched myself, still not quite believing my life or Ryan's affection was real.

"I'll take that as a no," Gran said when I remained quiet. "You boys need to talk." She laughed when I blanched. "Come on, now. I know you're not allergic when it comes to being truthful and talking about exciting things like your feelings."

My lips twitched. "I don't know. There's usually red skin and a rash involved."

With a pat to my hand, Gran smirked. "This is time you suck it up and talk. Don't you think enough time has been wasted?"

I huffed out a breath. "Stop being all levelheaded and wise, Gran. You know it freaks me out."

She chuckled. "Come on, let's take these and go and watch some TV while we're waiting."

As I picked up my drink, I thought about Gran's words. The difficulty was, I had no idea what to say. Did I want Ryan to stay? Of course, but that was impossible. Did I want Ryan to give it all up in a year and not chase a contract? That'd be a hell yes. There was no chance I'd ever say that to him, though.

The memory of him on the court slammed into me. Talent like that couldn't be wasted, especially when he was legit living the dream. I knew pro athletes retired young, but not *that* young, right? Or maybe I was wrong, and he was already considered ancient. I sighed as I sank into the comfy sofa. As far as I could see, all I could do was tell Ryan I was proud of him and I'd miss him and perhaps try to book a couple of flights to see him. Beyond that, there was nothing I could do.

A WEIRD TENSION BLANKETED RYAN SINCE HIS PHONE call. When I'd asked if he was okay and if he wanted to talk about it, he'd simply shook his head, kissed my cheek, then went and helped Amber bathe Ivy.

It was now bedtime. Having already washed up, I was in bed with a magazine, one about steel fencing that would earn me a chuckle from Ryan. The bathroom door opening drew my attention to the man in the doorway. Just like every other time, my heart flipped at seeing him like this—in his boxers and nothing else, freshly showered with damp hair. I closed the magazine and gave him my full attention as he moved to what had become his side of the bed.

While the tension from earlier seemed to have eased, something was clearly on his mind. Even as a kid he'd get this way when he was worried or something bugged him. Then, shooting some hoops had been my go-to distraction, breaking him out of his funk and getting him to open up. Somehow, I didn't think that would be the answer today.

Ryan slid between the sheets next to me, shifting in close, his intention as surprising as it was clear. I looped my arms around him as he rested his head on my chest, his hand moving to my stomach.

While we were tactile and made the most of touching whenever we got the chance, this was different. Ryan needing comfort was a hell of a thing. My heart thundered in my chest while my stomach did somersaults. I wanted to be Ryan's everything so much, but his reaction added to my anxiety about him leaving.

More than that, Ryan seeking comfort was an anomaly that worried me.

"What's wrong?" I kept my voice low, attempting not to destroy the peace and comfort I tried to offer. As I stroked my fingers through his hair with one hand, I used the other to dance my fingers across his back.

"Does something have to be wrong?"

I hesitated but didn't have the patience to keep quiet. "You can cuddle me anytime you want, happily so." My lips made purchase with the top of his head. "But you doing this after a call with your agent makes me think everything isn't okay."

A weary sigh escaped him, and he rubbed his hand over his face.

"You don't have to tell me," I said, not sure how convincing my offer was since I really wanted to know. That way, I could at least try to help or just let him vent.

"They're talking about a trade."

Surprise shot through me. "What, trading *you*? To where? Can they do that?"

Nate angled to peer at me. "League contracts and rules are a mindfuck. It's why my agent has a sweet deal to sort all this stuff out for me." He shook his head before resettling on my chest. "They're saying maybe Vegas. And no, I don't have a choice if they want to do a deal. I know the Eagles could probably do with freeing up some cash by trading me."

"Bloody hell, okay, wow, and what did you say?"

"That I was still on vacation for another week, so he needed to get everyone off my back."

Laughter bubbled out of me. "You didn't seriously?"

"Like fuck I didn't. Shit, he knows I'm on vacation. I shouldn't even be traded next season. Life's complicated enough without that bullshit. Plus there's the guys, you know?"

I squeezed him hard. With no idea how these

things worked, my advice wouldn't fly. "Is it possible to ignore this till you get back?"

"No. I'm fully aware I'm being a petulant fuck, so you don't need to point it out to me, okay?"

My lips twitched, despite the seriousness of the conversation, because seriously, his tone was the exact one he'd used when he was eighteen and sulking about not getting the last Tim Tam.

"You want tea and a Tim Tam?" I asked, smiling inside.

Once again, he glanced at me. "Make it a packet and not one, and that'd be awesome. Thanks."

The barest of smiles he gave me was worth it. I dotted a kiss on his mouth, and he grumbled as he moved away so I could get off the bed. "You know a packet will mean at least an extra two-kilometer run tomorrow, right?" I received a pillow in my face as answer. Chucking it back, I legged it out the room, laughing, impressed it made contact with his head.

Three Tim Tams later, I was pathetically chocolated out. Unlike Ryan, I didn't have a massive sweet tooth.

"You got enough sugar in your system to talk?" I asked.

"I said I'd call him back in the morning. Then tomorrow night I need to talk to someone from the team. Not sure if it'll be one of the suits or Coach."

"Can they trade you without you agreeing, you know, since you're not a rookie?"

Ryan shrugged and placed his empty mug on the bedside table. "Yeah. I don't have free agency until the end of next season, and while trades are perhaps rare in the off-season, it's not unheard of." He stopped short and shot me a glance. "I'd started to think about telling a couple of the guys about you and me."

Air escaped me so fast I struggled to think, let alone remember how to inhale again. We'd still not discussed anything about when he left. It looked like that was about to change.

"Jayden and Sutton?" I went with the safe question, amazed my words sounded steady.

"Yeah." His gaze stayed glued to mine. "I think telling them would help me cope with you not being there. Either that or you come with me."

Wide-eyed, I froze, gaping and with no idea what to say. "You serious?"

He shrugged. "You want me to be serious?"

I frowned. "No. You can't do that, say that and put it back on me." My whole body vibrated, a rush of confusing emotions vying for attention.

"Shit, Nate. I just—" He sat up and faced me. "There are things that I know." I raised my brows at him, indicating that I was absolutely paying attention. "I know that leaving you is going to be miserable and hurt like fuck. I know that I do not want to be out in public, but our friends and family... I want them to see how much you mean to me. How amazing you are."

A lump formed in my throat so big, I wondered if I'd be able to dislodge it without breaking down.

"I also know that if we can't be together next season, one year is all I have left in me."

"What do you mean?" My question was whisper soft. While I was sure I understood the meaning, I couldn't quite believe it, nor was I sure I could let it happen.

And fuck if that thought didn't shoot poison into my gut.

"I have one more season left before I'm a free agent. I can take an offer or leave."

"You can't leave," I rushed to say. "You play in the League, for Christ's sake. This is your dream, and you're so fucking good at it."

"But what if my dream's changed?"

Dead. Kaput. Melted. Ryan had officially destroyed me.

Held frozen, I gaped at him. For a man who was the master of struggling to share his emotions, Ryan had nailed it. Hell, he'd blown all declarations in the history of mankind out of the water. Or at least where my heart was concerned.

After closing my gaping mouth, I finally spoke. "I don't know. Is that what you want?"

Everything seemed too much, too soon, despite this moment feeling like it had been fifteen years in the making.

Shifting to his knees, Ryan reached out and touched my face. I melted into his warmth, not quite believing this was all going on now.

"If you say all that you want is me, I swear I'm either going to die or break out in a Mariah Carey tune." The words tumbled out of me, unexpected and unplanned. But apparently, my overstimulated brain didn't give a damn about random thoughts escaping.

For a split second, Ryan paused. Hovering above me, his lips twitched. Then the bastard laughed, full-on belly laughed. He collapsed on top of me, whole-body shakes vibrating through me as the muscled oaf squashed me. Flat on my back and squished, trying to breathe was pointless. Instead, I let Ryan's hysteria sweep over me until I gasped for breath. This time, I wheezed and patted his arms, needing him to move.

Ryan did so immediately, his whole face alight with amusement while I chugged in lungfuls of air. "You trying to kill me?"

His smile still in place, he said, "You're apparently the one who's going to die. Or would you prefer me to turn your playlist on?"

Reaching out to the side, I clamped on to a pillow and smacked it across his head. "Piss off," I grumbled. My heart remained unsteady and still accelerated. While my faux pas made me cringe, it gave us both a slight reprieve from the oversharing.

Ryan leaned on his elbow and peered down at me. Warmth shone in his eyes, and I felt the heat scorching into me, leaving a trail as it maneuvered around me.

The intensity in his gaze sobered me almost instantly. I gnawed on my cheek, building the courage to tell him the truth. After what he'd already shared, he deserved it.

"I love you." I didn't look away as I spoke, didn't fidget despite the flicker of embarrassment sparking to life in my chest. The intensity remained as Ryan stayed freakishly quiet and calm, enough that I worried if, after all that had happened, he'd been pushed over the edge.

Either that or he had a Mariah Carey song stuck on a loop in his head.

"If I tell you I love you, you promise you won't be dead?"

I almost sprained something with my eye roll. "I

promise not to change the ringtone on your phone." I could compromise when the incentive was there.

Ryan's smile was wide and perfect. "I love you."

I laughed out a huff of air, amusement, relief, and full-on happiness mingling.

"Can that be enough for tonight?" I hedged. The multitude of reveals had blown me away. Exhaustion crept into the edges of my vision, and all I wanted were kisses and maybe Ryan's dick in my mouth too.

It seemed only fitting that declarations of love were celebrated with blowjobs.

The man, knowing me so damn well, something I'd have to stop being so surprised by soon, nodded before he leaned in to seal the deal.

CHAPTER 18

RYAN

Waking up in Nate's arms would never get old. Sure, he sometimes did this weird snore thing, but that was more adorable than annoying. But with the dawn sunlight stroking my cheek, I smiled in contentment, basking in the feel of Nate's body pressed against mine.

Last night, it hadn't escaped my notice that my suggestions freaked him out. Springing such things on the man would do that, I supposed.

When he told me how he felt… that he loved me, for more than a beat I'd thought I wasn't hearing him correctly. Rather than him shooting me down, perhaps saying I was insane and rash, and we were moving too fast, I'd received his heart instead.

It was one hell of a thing. Even now, aware I

needed to get up and make a call, everything seemed possible, or at least less *im*possible.

The solutions or the answers remained out of my grasp, though. There'd been no epiphany in my sleep or when I'd blown my load as I'd sucked Nate dry. It didn't matter, though, not this morning.

Resolve beat in my heart, sure that whatever happened, we'd figure this out and be together. How could we not when the best guy I knew loved me! More than that, he'd forgiven me, and we'd moved on together, just like he'd helped me realize so much about myself and who I wanted to be.

Nate stirred at my side. Easing up to my elbow, I peered down at him, a goofy smile on my face. Movement behind his closed lids gave me the warning I needed before he opened them.

"Motherfucker. What the fuck!" He jolted, springing up just enough for his forehead to connect with my nose. Pain sliced through me, and I covered my nose, seeing stars.

"Fuck!" I gasped, my pained groan following.

"Hell, Ryan. You scared the shit out of me."

Through watery eyes, I looked at him. He rubbed his head, breathing heavily, while his other hand rubbed at his chest. I chuckled and winced at the fresh throb of pain. "That's not how it happens in the movies."

Nate squinted at me. "In horror movies that's exactly what should happen. Fuck, I'm sure I've shit myself."

My chuckle turned into full-blown laughter. "Better shitting yourself than having a busted nose." It seriously throbbed.

Nate sat back up, this time making sure he wouldn't hurt me. "It's broken? Let me see?" Concern danced in his eyes, his amusement flagging.

Removing my hand, I attempted to wriggle my nose. I stopped abruptly at the fresh pulse of pain.

"It's not crooked. I'd still do you." Bright-eyed and looking far too entertained, Nate bounced his brows up and down.

"Well, that must mean it's not broken, then, if that's your official diagnosis." I smirked, knowing he wouldn't be teasing if he thought I'd done some serious damage.

"Yep. You're gonna need some ice, though, and there may be some bruising."

"Is your forehead okay?" I eyed the red mark speculatively.

"Yeah, sore, but you know how hardheaded I can be."

I snorted. "Ain't that the truth. I'll go and get an ice pack and get some coffee on the go."

The light in Nate's eyes shifted a little. "What time's your call?"

A quick look at the time, and I answered, "Forty-five minutes."

He nodded, brows dipping. "Okay, I'll get up now too. Remember I have to go into the store today."

My pout earned me an eye roll.

"You'll survive. I'm sure Amber would appreciate having the house to herself so she can work on her assignments."

I'd been thinking the same thing. "Yeah, I might see if Gran wants to come with Ivy and me, and we'll head to Eumundi Market or something." A market was not a place I'd usually suggest going to, but the beach was out, as Gran wasn't great on sand. Plus there'd be plenty to see at the market that would keep my niece entertained.

While the market was a tourist trap, I still felt unbelievably invisible since being home. The luxury of being free to wander a market or head to a restaurant or stroll one of the local beaches was hard to pass by.

Being a pro basketball player had afforded me little in the form of privacy. It was why I was such a homebody, and the guys razzed me for not going out more. But the whole public figure stuff blew my mind, even now. Other than my first year of getting a little carried away with earnings and my ego growing a little uncomfortably, it didn't take me long to remember to be the man Gran raised me to be. And me being a dickhead to my kid sister on her single visit had a lot to do with that wake-up call too, especially when she'd demanded to go home early.

Since then, frugal and private was my middle name, and Jayden and Sutton loved ribbing me for being such a Scrooge. Not only that, but I legit tended to only hang out if going to someone's home.

Nate standing naked before heading to the bathroom cut off all thoughts. Well, apart from the attention I gave his tanned skin and the smattering of hair on his thighs, leading so perfectly to his ass.

"Eyes off and get ice and make coffee," he threw over his shoulder.

I groaned. "You haven't even kissed me."

Nate paused at the open bathroom door, having turned so I got the best view in the world. I made a show of my gaze eating him up.

"And *that* is why there's no chance I can kiss you now without my mouth falling on your dick." He sighed and looked as disgruntled as I felt, especially when his cock hardened. "Seriously, Ryan, eyes off the goods. You're impossible." He stepped away, closing the bathroom door behind him, leaving me chuckling and considering suggesting we stayed at his place tonight.

I loved sucking and jacking him off. It was the best feeling in the world, and when we sixty-nined, it was fucking magic. But having the chance to ride him, something we'd been reluctant to do while being under the same roof as my family, was something I was desperate for.

The prep, the mess, the bite of pain I'd already experienced with the hours of foreplay... I groaned just thinking about his cock. All that would be worth me giving him something I never had given before.

I finally got my butt into gear and got on a call with Micky. For the past hour, it felt like I'd been hit by a steamroller. It was no lie yesterday when I'd told Nate contracts were beyond confusing.

At the end of the day, I didn't have a no-trade clause, and while the team wanted me agreeable to the trade, they didn't need my permission. Saying that, Minnesota was in talks with Vegas, and it wasn't a done deal. Yet.

"I think it would be a really good move for you, Ryan," Micky said for easily the tenth time. "You know they've made it to the playoffs this year, and last year they got through to the conference semifinals."

I nodded into the camera, acknowledging they

were a good, strong team. "And they're thinking of trading O'Hare for me?" I clarified. The more I thought about it, the more it made sense for both teams. O'Hare was a forward with impressive averages. Offensively speaking, the trade would work. And they needed the driving force of a younger guy like him to no doubt free up cash with the trade. While he didn't have as much court time as me, I expected he also wanted the break and the chance to prove himself.

"That's right." Micky paused and sat forward in his chair. "You've got good notice here, and it's not midseason. I've gotta ask, Ryan, why aren't you all over this and as excited as hell?"

I rubbed a weary hand over my face, knowing I should be ecstatic about this. The reality was I couldn't do anything about the trade. Not only that, but Micky was also correct. It was rare to be in the loop so quickly. Plus it was a strong team, making it more likely we could make a real go of it next year.

I exhaled and glanced at Micky. "This is good, Micky. Thanks for the heads-up."

"Yes." He clapped his hands and cheered loudly. "You focus on riding kangaroos or whatever it is you get up to down there."

I rolled my eyes at him but smirked, some of his excitement beginning to rub off on me.

"I'll let you know if the meeting's going ahead in the morning, your tonight, right?"

"Sure, I'll keep my phone on me."

"Turn it up nice and loud, okay, kid? I'll let you know any news as soon as I hear anything. Talk soon." Without preamble, he signed off.

Collapsing back on the chair, I placed my phone on the table. My head buzzed, every part of me over-whelmed with the possibility. A trade seriously messed up any grand plans I considered with Nate, specifically having the support of my friends, but it wasn't all bad, right?

Standing, I headed to find Gran and found her outside on the veranda with Ivy. "Hey, Gran, before we head out, you mind if I borrow the car to go see Nate real quick?"

"The keys are in the pot near the house phone." Pausing from playing with my niece, she peered over at me. "Everything okay?"

"I think so. I'll tell you all about it when I get back. I'll be an hour, tops."

She waved me off. "You'll be fine for a couple of hours, as this sweet girl is ready for a nap."

After kissing Gran's cheek, I grabbed the keys, trying like hell to focus on the drive rather than the trade news filling my head. By the time I arrived at the store, I practically vibrated, and I had no idea why. Beyond that, I needed to see Nate.

"Hey, Mr. G," I greeted, seeing Nate's dad first.

He directed a smile my way. "G'day, Ryan. How's it going?" He reached out and shook my hand.

"Not too bad. You know how it is." I'd caught up with Nate's family a couple of times since being back. Just like Nate, they'd opened up their home to me and happily welcomed me back into the fold.

"Good to hear. If you're looking for Nate, he's just gone to grab us coffees."

"I'll head him off then. I could do with a caffeine hit." Mr. G waved me off, and I reentered the sunlit street.

A couple of folks passed me by, offering a smile and a g'day, and I wondered if this would be what it could be like if I moved back here. Life here was so perfectly simple. There were a bunch of small communities close by, Cooroy included, plenty of beaches and national parks. Plus, the major cities in Australia could be reached easily by flight, and our closest, Brisbane, wasn't that far away.

The biggest pull of all was Nate, who'd just stepped out of the coffee shop with two coffees and a white bag. He was saying something over his shoulder to the person inside, following up with a chuckle.

God, he was handsome, and the way that his laugh wrinkled his eyes just so was sexy as hell.

Pushing away the pang of regret that I'd be leaving soon, I stopped in my tracks, waiting for him to spot me. It didn't take long for his attention to fall on me, and a very different expression formed.

As if on cue, my breath hitched, just like it always did when longing, heat, and joy filled his expression. The emotions were as clear on his face as they were imprinted in my heart. I shook myself out of my Nate-induced haze, something I fell into more and more.

I never expected to be like this, ever, but I didn't regret a single jumble of emotions the man brought out in me.

"Hey, what are you doing here?" Once before me, his arm jerked ever so slightly, and I knew he struggled with not reaching out. Fear and rules sucked. Even more so when I was responsible for both.

Shoving my hands in my pockets, which earned me a soft smile, I indicated toward the paper bag. "Got something good in there?"

He quirked his brow and gripped the bag tighter. "Nothing you need to know about. You missed your run this morning."

A disgruntled moan escaped me. "You're almost as bad as Coach." My stomach flipped at that.

"What's wrong?"

"Well, probably my *former* coach."

Eyes wide, Nate stared at me a beat. "I think you need this more than me." Like the good guy he was, he handed me the bag. A quick look revealed a fresh and thick lamington.

"God, I missed these. You're the best."

Nate snorted. "And don't forget it. Let me drop Dad's coffee off, and then we can head to the park if you want?"

I nodded. "Let me order a coffee."

It didn't take long before we sat on a park bench, and I munched happily on the chocolate, sponge, and coconut-sprinkled lamington. Having told him the basics of the call, I struggled to fix on exactly how I felt, and told him as much.

"It sounds like a great move for you. They'll be lucky to have you." His words were careful, a little too controlled.

"Well, I like to think so." My chuckle tapered off to a soft sigh. "It's just thrown me for a loop."

After finishing off the dregs of his coffee, Nate angled to face me, giving me his full attention. "I'm excited for you, and honestly, proud as hell. Plus, hello… Vegas, baby." This time his voice was much more animated. I appreciated what he was trying to do.

"At least Vegas is so much closer to LAX." I eyed him carefully, waiting for a reaction.

"Just over an hour's flight. Much better than four hours."

Hope awoke inside me, stretching and fluttering. "You've already looked into it?"

Nate rubbed a hand over the back of his neck, color touching his cheeks. "I may have spent some time looking into it this morning."

My spirits soared, the wings taking flight. "Yeah?" Grinning, I briefly stroked his cheek with my thumb before forcing myself to pull away.

I didn't miss the twitch of Nate's lips when he rolled his eyes at me. "You'll miss your friends, though."

His words pulled me up short, dowsing the wings, making them soggy before they plummeted to the pit of my stomach. "I will." Regret sat heavily. "It changes things a lot." While I rationally understood the trade didn't have to change anything about the offer I'd made Nate, there was something about the safety and familiarity of Nate being with me in Minnesota that made everything more feasible. Not having that, not having Sutton and Jayden literally at my back if I needed them, shouldn't have impacted a single thing. But knowing I'd be in a new town, in a new team, with players I didn't have bonds with, all while trying to keep my love for Nate on the down-low, all seemed too much.

"I know."

Fuck, I hated this.

"Listen." The sternness of Nate's tone took me by surprise. "Let's focus on how amazing this is, okay? That's what matters."

I wasn't sure I fully agreed, but I nodded regardless.

"We knew you were leaving after a month. We expected it was going to be crap, but we can't get buried in any of that. Seriously, it's depressing."

A snort escaped me. "True that."

"You need to go spend the day with your gran and your niece. And let's promise to figure something out."

The soggy wings of hope made a valiant effort to shake themselves off. "You think we can? Figure something out, I mean?"

"I love you, so of course we will. Now, I need you to bugger off so I can get on with my day and not give in to the need to kiss you."

Nate managed to draw a grin from me. While he'd always been a miracle worker at getting me to smile, the man I knew was a dead set happiness fiend or a magician or something.

"Love you too," I said as I stood. Leaning into his

space and absolutely playing with fire, I whispered, "Also, just to let you know, tonight we're staying at your house." I edged back and took in the heat in his eyes. "I think it's about time you showed me what other skills you have with your cock."

Red spread like wildfire on his face, and his jaw fell open.

"The earlier you finish your day, the quicker we can get started." And like the bastard I was, I smirked, winked, turned away, and headed to the car. I just hoped the short drive back would give me time to encourage my raging hard-on to calm down.

CHAPTER 19

NATE

Distracted by Ryan and how he'd left our conversation, I mixed up an order. Not just once, but three times. Dad, thank Christ, had come to the rescue. Not a surprise, since I'd returned from coffee dazed.

On top of the order mess, I'd fumbled when shifting some chook food, my brain absolutely focused on thoughts of Ryan riding me. Clearing up the five burst bags was my punishment. Meanwhile, Dad looked on, bemused. He attempted to engage me in conversation, but I'd blundered and stuttered before dashing off like a bloody teenager.

Having hidden in my office for the past fifteen minutes, I looked up when I heard a tap on the door-frame. Standing in the doorway was Dad, still wearing a look of bewilderment. "Hi," I greeted, already feeling heat creep into my cheeks. I needed to get a grip.

"You doing okay in here?"

"Yep."

"Not ordered five hundred kilos of pasture boost rather than fifty?" Dad teased.

"Not yet." I flashed him a slightly mortified smile. "But give me another half an hour, and it could happen."

Amusement filled Dad's features. "Good to know. And probably a good job I've asked your mum to come in and cover for you."

Feeling guilty, I winced. "You shouldn't. I'm fine. You guys have already covered so much for me."

"Nonsense. You're distracted, and I understand why." I held back my snort at that, confident Dad didn't know the thought of Ryan riding me had hounded me all day. "With Ryan leaving soon, it makes sense you'd prefer to be with him than here." Concern marred his previously amused face, while my stomach clenched.

The last thing I wanted to think about was next week, or how Ryan's bold, brave wishes and plan yesterday had been ripped away just when I was giving it some serious thought.

Aware I still hadn't spoken, I gave a half-hearted smile, not quite sure I could form words.

"Listen, Nate, I just want to remind you that me and your mum are here for you, okay?"

With a nod, I swallowed the tight lump in my throat. When Dad hesitated, my gaze sharpened. While Dad wasn't touchy-feely, he was up-front. "What?" Curiosity colored the word.

"It's just... me and your mum were talking." He paused, and I lifted both brows, encouraging him to continue. "Well, this place is just a store, just a building. A business." Shock rippled through me as he continued, "I picked up running the place after my dad retired, gave it my all, and enjoyed it. I just..." He trailed off, his gaze intent and searching.

With the loud pounding of my pulse, I couldn't hear my question as I asked, "Just what?"

"It doesn't have to be your dream. And even if it was, it's okay for dreams to change."

The pounding turned to heavy, fast beats, taking on the pace and volume of a freight train. His words sounded so much like Ryan's, I struggled to fully register them. "You-you want us to sell the store?"

A low sigh fell from Dad before he smiled gently, his eyes filling with patience I recognized. "I'm saying you can do whatever you wish. You don't have to feel tied... trapped—"

"I'm not trapped," I was quick to say. "I've never felt trapped." When Dad arched his brow at me, my shoulders sagged. "Not *trapped*," I emphasized. "Perhaps a little responsible, but never once have I felt forced to take over, or that you wouldn't support me if I'd chosen another path. I love working here and in town and with you." My chest tightened, hating that my parents were so concerned about me.

The creases on Dad's forehead smoothed out, his relief obvious. "That's good, son. I just needed you to know that we'll support you, no matter what."

I huffed out an emotional laugh, completely overwhelmed by my parents and how fucking awesome they were. Rubbing a hand over my face, I shook my head. Today had been jam-packed with revelations. Hell, the past twenty-four hours had been. "Why are you saying this now?" Curiosity wriggled in my belly, despite me having a decent suspicion why.

"We didn't know if you were considering moving with Ryan to America." His words were so matter-of-fact that my heart stumbled, sure that was no longer an option. Ryan felt vulnerable, that much I was sure of. I also expected such a huge move with me there and trying to keep our relationship a secret would be too much for him.

I knew when my expression faltered, my hurt rushing to the surface, because Dad took a step forward, his lips turning down. "What's wrong?"

Twisting my mouth, I tried to buy a few

moments, wondering if I wanted to share with him. Over the past month, Ryan had been my world. I'd damn well orbited him. It meant I hadn't voiced any of my concerns or the beginnings of my likely heartbreak to anyone. And Ryan and I had barely scratched the surface of dealing with the fallout of our separation.

"Ryan's not out."

Dad's brows shot so high I was a little concerned by his level of surprise. "But I thought since being home and him telling you… and the two of you being together, and telling us—"

I shook my head, cutting Dad off. "I can't go to America with him. And Ryan won't be coming out."

"Ever?" This time a deep frown appeared, something akin to disappointment and sadness finding purchase.

I took a breath. "Just while he's playing in the League." *I think.* I shook that errant thought away, knowing my own sadness weaseled its way into my system.

"I see."

But from the look on his face and the tone of his voice, I wasn't sure he did. Hell, I did "see." I understood completely. That didn't mean I didn't resent Ryan's fear or how fucked-up the world was.

I needed to get out of here, away from Dad's pity,

away from talking about shit that impacted me yet I felt I had no control over. "Listen, if you're sure, it's probably best if I do head out."

Dad nodded. "Absolutely," he said, giving me the pass I needed and letting me go.

It didn't take long before I was buckled up in my car. After fifteen minutes of driving and chaos in my head, I indicated and pulled over to the lookout point just a few minutes from Gran's house.

Once parked, I stepped out and took the few steps needed to the barrier. The view from the mountain was stunning. I took it in, hoping the beauty would help center me or at least distract me. Below, a canopy of trees spilled down the mountainside, stretching out to the valley. If I squinted, I could just make out the shine of water from a large dam.

Closing my eyes, I inhaled deeply before exhaling a little shakily. Dad's offer had appeared out of nowhere, throwing me for a loop. Just two days ago, the same offer would have buoyed me, especially knowing Ryan's initial thoughts about Minnesota and having the support system he wanted to come out.

How quickly my world could be turned upside down.

It didn't escape my notice that while I had this freak-out, Ryan waited for me, eager for us to spend the night alone together. Christ, how I wanted that. Hell, at this point, Ryan and his desire for me, his feelings for me, were all I could count on.

With fresh resolve zipping in my veins, I made a dash for the car. The fuck was I thinking, lamenting on the what-ifs and the seemingly no-win situation I was in when I had the man I loved desperate for me to fuck him?

Rather than smacking the upside of my head, I focused on getting to Ryan. The sooner I did, the sooner I could escape in his warmth and comfort.

***

"Oh, wow." With my brows set high, I peered down at the spread Ryan had organized. "Ryan Broadwater being romantic." While the teasing was blatant, I pushed affection into my words.

The truth was, as soon as we'd left Gran's with Ryan carrying a couple of bags and saying we didn't need to go to the store for supplies, I'd been intrigued. And then, when he'd encouraged me to shower while he prepared dinner, I'd left him to it. Curiosity kept me occupied in the shower and when I'd pulled on my sweatpants. Winter had well and truly kicked in. That meant our Queensland days were just on the right side of warm, and the evenings gave me the perfect excuse to cuddle up with Ryan and use him as an extra blanket.

I looked at the feast he'd organized, my pulse galloping at Ryan's sweetness. When I glanced over at him, I melted even more, taking in his pink cheeks. "I love it. Thank you."

"Yeah?"

"Absolutely." I headed over to where Ryan sat on a bunch of pillows on the floor before the coffee table filled with our dinner. I leaned down and captured his mouth. Heat warmed my chest, quickly spreading to my stomach as our kiss deepened. Cupping his cheek, I used the contact as an anchor. While I definitely wanted to get lost in Ryan tonight and drown in his kisses and his body, for now, I needed him to know how much I appreciated him.

After a few more sweeps of our tongues against each other's, my dick became seriously invested. It was time to pull away. I did so breathing heavily, and touched my forehead against Ryan's while I caught my breath. Angling back so I didn't go cross-eyed, I smiled at him. "Thank you."

Skin flushed, lips puffy, Ryan was temptation personified. And for the whole night he was all mine.

Nodding, Ryan tilted his lips. "You want to watch TV or listen to music while we eat?"

"Music's good."

Hitting a button on his phone, Ryan looked thoroughly pleased with himself when David Archuleta's voice came through my Bluetooth stereo.

I chuckled. "I can't believe you remembered this track." Hell, the cheesy goodness of the song had held a much bigger meaning for me when I was sixteen.

"Yeah, right. Like I could forget it. You had it playing on a bloody loop that one summer we went camping with your parents at Carnarvon."

I nudged him, once again touched by the small details. Eyeing the collection of random picnic food, I decided on a cracker with Vegemite and cheese first. It seemed Ryan's nostalgia hadn't stopped with music but included food we devoured when we were kids.

I munched happily on the salty tang of the food. After swallowing, I asked, "So tell me about your day. Did you head to the market?"

While chewing, he bobbed his head. When he'd emptied his mouth and had a drink of water, he said, "Yeah. Ivy loved it. She was knackered by the time we left, taking in everything. Gran was a bit worn out too, but I made sure we took our time and rested loads."

"She's so much better than she was." I offered him a reassuring smile, which he returned. "And I'm glad you had a good time. You get yourself a tie-dyed T-shirt or anything?" I quirked my eyebrow for good measure and bit into a cheerio dripping in tomato sauce. These small sausages were the best of processed goodness.

"Nope, but I'll go back on Saturday and get you one."

I snorted. It was the sort of thing Ryan would do. Even as a kid when he was broke, he would have saved money from his mowing jobs to go and blow it on a crappy T-shirt, just so he could laugh his arse off at me. Because of course I would have worn the damn thing. Now that he was not at all strapped for cash, I dreaded the sort of mischief he could get up to. Not that we'd discussed his whole money situation. Honestly, I didn't want to think too deeply about it. Knowledge of how much he earned and had in the bank made me weirdly uncomfortable.

And that I could probably find out with a quick internet search stirred unease in my gut. It was best not to think about it.

Distracting myself from my warped mind, I scooped up another mini processed sausage and indicated for him to eat it. He did so with a smirk. "We have plans on Saturday that don't involve tie-dye shirts."

"We do, huh?" he asked around his mouthful of food.

"We will do when I think of something," I joked.

We carried on munching, but midbite of a strawberry, I remembered about his call. "Didn't you have another video call tonight?"

Ryan swallowed his own piece of fruit before answering. "Postponed till tomorrow evening for me. Though I expect the call will be canceled, as from the latest message I received, it's pretty much a done deal."

Honestly, that wasn't a surprise. I told him as much. "You're a brilliant player, and I imagine it'll make all sorts of sense to each team for the trade." I didn't know anything about the player he was being traded with. Even though I'd been tempted to search, I wasn't that much a glutton for punishment. "So you'll need to pack up as soon as you get back to Minnesota?"

Shaking his head, he placed his drink back on the table. "It's not crazy fast like it would be if the trade took place in the season. But it's best if I get settled sooner rather than later. It means I can get my fitness up. Burn all the lamingtons off." He grinned.

"What will you do about a place to live?" While Ryan had done this all before, the whole thing was alien to me.

"Micky will help me get something sorted."

As he spoke and continued to tell me about some of the players he knew on the new team, he became increasingly animated. The building excitement in his voice and his expression created fresh warmth to flood my system. He should be excited by the move, and I was relieved he was, now the initial shock had bled away.

With the new eagerness in his eyes when he told me about a player called Joyce, certainty swept over me. Ryan playing with a team with strong stats was how his future should look, especially with retirement not being too far away. Maybe a handful of years or so—if he chose to stay the course.

"Hey." Ryan's quiet voice and his palm on my arm startled me. "You okay? You haven't said anything for a while." Concern dipped his brows.

Immediately I reassured him. "Just listening." I held back the direction of my own thoughts.

"Was I waffling on?" A sheepish look crossed his face.

I smirked. "Nah. You're excited, and I'm glad. You deserve this move."

Pink spots appeared on the apples of his cheeks. "I do, huh?" The drop in his tone caught my attention, and I quirked my brow.

"You cruising for compliments, Broadwater?

Thousands of fans chanting your name not enough for you?" My words were light and flirty.

A flash of heat flared in his eyes before he leaned into me. "There's only one person I ever need to hear chanting my name."

The fluttering of wings returned full force in my abdomen, soon beating frantically, swooping high and hitting my rib cage. "You want me at your games cheering the loudest?" I could barely hear, let alone breathe, as I waited for his answer. While I was flirting and playing along, it didn't stop my need to know.

"Every single fucking game." The force and possession of his words and his tone took me by surprise. I'd barely grabbed a breath before his mouth slammed down on mine. Then everything was fast and frantic as we tore our clothes off, and Ryan all but dragged me to my bedroom.

My shoulder whacked the wall and the door with enough force I was sure to bruise. I didn't care about any of it. My whole focus was on the man whose lips were perfect against mine. On the man whose tongue got me so revved up, I saw stars and leaked precum like my cock had something to prove.

I grunted when my back slammed onto the mattress, then groaned before I could ask a single thing when he slathered my dick with lube and stretched himself. "Fuck." No chance was I missing out on my fingers inside him.

Swiping around for the lube, I smiled in triumph when I took hold of it. A small smile broke free on Ryan's face as he continued to ride his damn fingers while spread over my lap.

"Let me take over." The hoarse dip of my demand had the desired reaction. Once more, want flashed in his eyes, and he scooted forward to straddle my stomach, giving me better access.

Two fingers slipped inside him with such ease, my dick pulsed. I groaned, and he gasped as he bore down on them, leaning forward and pressing his mouth to mine. I captured his groan when I plunged in with three fingers.

"Holy fuck," he gasped. "That... so full."

"Just wait till you're riding me," I said with a grunt, my fingers needy, searching. While I'd explored Ryan before, it had never been like this. And with the heat of him as he sucked my fingers deep and his urgent kisses, I understood why.

"Fuck. I need you on my dick." My words were loud, full of heat. With my fingers pressing against his prostate, Ryan nodded just as he shuddered. His mouth flew open, and I glanced down at his cock. My stomach glistened with his precum, making Ryan picture-fucking-perfect.

"You still okay to go bare?" Just saying the words aloud had my dick straining.

"Yes, definitely."

I nodded, reached for the lube, lathered myself up again, and then encouraged Ryan to settle back on my lap. Taking a calming breath, I rubbed up his thighs, needing a moment to pull myself together. "Remember to go slow and stop if it's too much." I maintained eye contact as we spoke. Just last week we'd had a surprisingly unawkward conversation about me being on PrEP and negative, and Ryan sharing he'd only exchanged BJs and handjobs. Not only that, regular testing confirmed he was negative.

Knowing Ryan had never been penetrated this way before did a hell of a thing to my needy cock, making me desperate for him. With that came a fierce craving to make this good for him. "You ready?" I asked.

"So fucking ready," he said, so breathlessly that my gaze slammed into his.

The expression on his face almost unraveled me. Need, desire, and absolute trust filled his features. Every single emotion was for me.

"I love you."

Ryan bit his bottom lip and nodded as he lifted.

I took hold of my cock, helping it find its mark. Then the fucker did exactly what I told him not to and slammed down, his arsecheeks meeting my flesh and me filling him so completely, my dick and my heart would never be free of his hold.

Both were more than okay with me.

I recovered quicker than Ryan, who froze above me, eyelids closed, bottom lip white from how fiercely he bit down, and breathing in short, fast pants.

Somehow I found my voice. "Christ, Ryan." I grunted at the tight heat wrapped around me and willed myself not to twitch in happiness. "You okay?" Despite the bliss of being buried inside him, worry edged my words.

"Yeah." The strain in his voice matched the wild look in his eyes when he finally peered down at me. "I'll be okay."

"What happened to slow?"

"You ever know me not to go ahead and take what I want when I've made up my mind about something?"

Humor filled me, knowing he was absolutely right. There was something else, though, in his tone, his words, the emotion in his expression. "And you made up your mind convincingly when—" I gasped when he lifted slightly, the motion exploratory.

"When what?" His voice shook and thighs trembled when he lifted again. This second slide down, the lines on his forehead smoothed out.

"When," I started, valiantly rallying my thoughts—no easy task when Ryan eased up and down once more, a steady rhythm being created. "When," I tried again, "you decided you were going to be a pro at riding me."

He barked a chuckle, and both of us groaned.

"Well, that," he said, his breathing picking up. How was he having a rational conversation? True, I'd yet to move, but there wasn't a chance I could stay still for much longer.

"And?"

"I meant what I said about wanting you at every game."

Reacting straightaway, I pushed myself up to sit. Ryan hooked himself to me—whether to steady himself or hold on to the significance of his words, I had no clue. I held him tight, his cock pressed to my belly, my arms a vise around him.

And then I was kissing him while thrusting slowly, pouring every sense of myself into this kiss, into this man who had managed to recapture my heart despite the time and distance.

Our mouths remained connected, sharing breaths, sharing heat, sharing our whispered, incoherent words of lust and love, and then I pushed back, needing to be on top.

Settled between his legs, I held on to his lips and angled away to capture his half-mast stare. "Okay?"

"Yeah."

I smiled before I eased out of his tight sheath and slammed back into him. I lost my smile, groaning at the sensation. My thrusts were fast, becoming more erratic the more Ryan garbled me to fuck him, the requests for "harder" taking me over.

Sparks flashed in my eyes, my legs going numb, toes cramping up as fire coursed through me, quick and fast and so mind-blowing as my orgasm burst free.

I groaned, shouted, shivered, and somehow I found the power to pull out. Hearing Ryan's grumble, I smiled, scooted down, and latched on to his dick.

Flicking my gaze to his, I watched as he fell apart, reveled in how he clung to my head. And when he spilled into my mouth, I sucked and lapped every last drop until his shaking limbs stopped and he was a puddle of bones and muscle.

With my head on his sweat-soaked stomach, I breathed heavily and grinned. Ryan's hand found my head, where he lazily stroked.

"You doing okay?" I asked, trailing my finger up his thighs, curious and still feeling needy.

He wiggled and grunted when my finger brushed against his pucker. Finding him dripping, I groaned. "That's so hot."

"It is?" he asked, still squirming.

"Fuck yes."

The tug on my hair had me glancing up at him. "In that case, shower, power nap, then I'm so doing that to you." A large, sleepy smile was sent my way. God, I could absolutely get used to seeing it there.

According to Ryan, he was going to find a way to make that happen. My heart bounced around in my rib cage. Holy shit, were we really going to do this?

CHAPTER 20
RYAN

Waking up tender and content, I huffed out a happy sigh and clung to Nate like a koala did a gum tree. A wisp of a moan swept over me at contact. His ass rubbed seamlessly against my morning wood.

Last night had been incredible. When he'd fucked me, all gentle and sweet before losing control and absolutely annihilating me with his intensity, right then, the wish for our future I'd shared with him felt a hundred percent right.

Even now, no longer riding the high of lust and orgasms, certainty settled into my chest.

"Morning." Nate's gruff voice made my balls tingle, remembering a similar tone when I'd finally fucked him from behind. Shamelessly, I wedged my dick between his thighs, flush with his buttcheeks, and I kissed his neck.

"Morning."

Nate chuckled as I got myself extra comfortable between his thighs. He peered over his shoulder at me. "You doing all right there?"

I nodded, my gaze connecting with his before I tugged the sheet off and leaned my chest away a little. The view as I looked down, my cock snug and totally content, was a hell of a way to wake and get the day started. "I am now," I muttered gruffly, moving my hips just so, groaning when the sensitive head knocked against his balls, gifting me with his breathy moan. "Best way ever to start the day," I panted, my gentle thrusts continuing. The urge to grab the lube was intense; the rub could be so much sweeter with a smooth glide, but that would require disconnecting.

No chance that was happening.

"Pretty fucking perfect if you ask me." The tease pushed back against me.

My gaze whipped to his, and I smirked at the desire reflected in his dark brown eyes. Somehow my thrusts didn't falter, but when he made a show of licking his fingers and shifting his hand out of view, my steady rhythm stuttered. As soon as I saw his arm move, his muscles strain, I went to town, rutting against him, careless of the dry friction.

Instead, my focus was on the way his thighs and

the crease of his ass gripped my cock. On the way, his small grunts ramped me up. Until finally, and even quicker than last night, my balls drew high, my spine tingled, and after two frantic juts of my hips, I released between his legs with a raspy moan.

The whole of my body shuddered, and I quickly pressed close, looping my arm around Nate. His mouth sought out mine, our tongues clumsily tangling as I reached for his dick. Finding purchase, I spread my fingers over his and helped jack him off.

Nate's grunts were loud and wild, and I eased back out of the kiss, wanting to watch him unravel.

He didn't disappoint.

With a couple more jerks, Nate gasped, his eyes slamming closed, pink touching his cheeks. Warmth spilled onto our joined hands.

"Fuck." I tugged him back. "Want to taste you so bad."

Startled as I nudged him to his back, Nate gazed at me through half-closed lids, his mouth gaping. His mouth fell open even wider when I licked his shaft, lapping up the taste of him.

"Fuck, I'm sensitive," he grumbled as I wrapped my lips around his softening dick.

I grinned but slowed down. When I did so, a happy sigh spilled from Nate. Finishing with a final lick to his stomach, I peered up. "Not quite clean. A shower's needed."

"Your spunk is in crevices I didn't know existed," he sassed, and my laugh tumbled free. "Not sure I can feel my legs yet, though."

My laughter settled and morphed into a broad smile, and I hummed in approval.

Nate quirked his brow at me. "Why do I get the feeling the thought of me numb and fuck-fogged makes you far too happy?"

"Fuck-fogged? Nice. I like making you fuck-fogged. It should be on my to-do list every day possible."

The gaze Nate sent my way was all soft and full of question. "Every day, huh?"

I shrugged, aware my cheeks heated. "Shower, food, then I think we need to figure this out." Determination drove my words.

"*This out* as in our future and what you said yesterday?" While Nate's words were clear, curiosity sparked in his eyes. I also felt the slight tremble of his limbs. I didn't need to ask why that was. We were in this together, both filled with as much love as uncertainty.

Tired of second-guessing and of letting my heart play second fiddle, I bobbed my head. "About our future and making us work, yeah."

When he smiled, a slight shimmer forming in his eyes, my heart leaped so fucking high that not even a buzzer beater could have made me feel so ecstatic or sure I was doing the right thing.

It didn't take long to wash up and prepare breakfast from the bunch of food I'd brought with us yesterday.

Having eaten fruit, cheese, and bread, we took our second mugs of coffee out onto Nate's back porch. While he had neighbors, there were plenty of trees and bushes around to give us complete privacy.

"I'm just going to come out and say all the shit floating around in my mind, okay?"

Despite the gentle smile of reassurance Nate directed my way, he was on edge. Since I'd been a mess of overthinking, I didn't for a moment expect I'd be the only one.

"Okay," he answered. He released a steady breath and indicated for me to continue.

Amongst the quiet rustle of the leaves in the trees, I focused on being as open and as honest with him as I could. If I couldn't manage that, I didn't deserve Nate. A spark of certainty flickered to life as I said, "I'm not yet ready to share with the League, the media, that I'm gay, nor that I'm in love with my best friend."

Emotion flickered in the depths of his eyes, but

Nate carefully controlled his reaction and didn't interrupt.

"I *will* be, but I can't give a timeline. Pressure is shit at the best of times, and a promise beyond loving you and putting you above all else, outside of the commitments of my contract, is a lot. I don't want that hanging over either of us."

I paused for a beat, but he stayed quiet, so I continued. "I want to tell Sutton and Jayden about the two of us, if that's okay. I know we're not on the same team anymore, but they're my friends, and I want them to know." I swallowed thickly. "Honestly, at some point I expect this'll blow up in my face, so I'll—*we'll* need all the support we can get."

Sutton especially had been far from subtle before I'd left the States. The guys had their suspicions; I was sure of it. It felt right, good to share this with them.

Reaching for Nate's hand, I willed my pulse to settle. "Will you move to the States with me? I know it's more complicated than that because of visas, but I love you and want a future with you."

Pink crept up Nate's neck, and his Adam's apple bobbed. His silence was also beginning to freak me out.

"What do you think?" My question dipped low, doubt beginning to sneak in. Plan B was always an option, one I'd share with him regardless. Until I did, I needed a reaction.

"And what am I supposed to do in Vegas when it's no longer the off-season? I have no idea how visas work, but I can't imagine there's a need for someone who knows about farm supplies and can run a store in the middle of the desert." There was no challenge in Nate's question, just genuine curiosity.

"That's something we can work out together, right?" I lifted a shoulder. "I don't have all the answers. I just know I want us to be together."

Rubbing a hand on the back of his neck, Nate stared out into the distance. "And I'd be playing your friend who's moved from Australia to just hang out with you?" While he wasn't quite incredulous, I could see he was struggling. "Shit, Ryan, everything inside me is screaming at me to say screw it and take the risk." Hope flickered to life until he opened his mouth again. "But you can't believe anyone is going to buy we're 'just' friends, unless you plan to keep me locked away in your rental."

The hammering of my heart made it difficult to concentrate. What was worse was I'd thought the exact same things, debated the shit out of it. "Well, I did say I expected it will all blow up."

"No." Nate shook his head, and I froze. *No?* "I don't mean *no* no."

"Fuck," I huffed out on a gasp.

Nate squeezed my hand. "I mean *no*, that can't be how it happens. You need to control the narrative, especially as with no uncertainty me being there, hanging out, and all but being attached to your hip, the truth will come out. Based on what you've said and what I know, you don't want to be outed by the gossip rags, or anyone, in fact. Fuck, no one does."

My breath stuttered, my hands shaking a little. That was exactly what I didn't want.

"What worries me," he continued, this time brushing his thumb against my cheek, "is that you've made it absolutely clear you don't want to be under the microscope any more than you are, and you don't want to be the League's only out queer player. I won't be the reason you become any of those things."

"But I'm willing to for you," I rushed to say —*eventually* went unsaid—but Nate was already shaking his head. I took a breath, frustration clawing its way to the surface.

"Just stop and think," Nate said before I could press on. "You have to do this for you. You do it for me, and one day, if it all goes balls up, you could blame me, resent me." Sadness laced his words.

"I could never resent—"

"You may not think so, but you could. I just want you to spend some real time working this out." He scrunched up his face, saying, "Yesterday, you were riding the high of your first f—"

"Don't you fucking dare." I leaned back and balled my hands into fists. "I'm a grown-ass fucking man and am not just trying to get you to America so I can get a regular fuck." Anger swept through me, thick and fast. A tidal wave of disappointment that he could even say such a thing threatened to take me under.

Nate startled, his color disappearing so quickly, a rush of concern hit me. "I'm sorry, that's not what I— Shit, Ryan, I didn't mean you only wanted me as an easy fuck." A wash of green bled into his white, and for a moment, I thought he was going to hurl. "That's not what I meant." Whisper-soft, his words found their mark. Tension drained from my body, and I closed my eyes. Why the fuck did everything have to be so complicated?

"I'm sorry I jumped all over you," I whispered, flexing my hand, craving his touch. His gaze caught my movement, and he reached out and clutched my hand. "I love you, and I don't know how to do that and be happy, and work, and be who you need me to be. I'm a selfish fuck because I want it all. I'm greedy, and I want the whole fucking cake."

Shit, I was going to cry.

Tears threatened, and I begged them not to fall. I

hadn't cried since the day Nate's dad dropped me at the airport all those years ago. Even then, it was after he'd left me, and I'd raced to the restroom where I could snivel in private. But fuck if I didn't want to bawl my eyes out now.

Nate's finger brushing against my cheek created a damp path. Hell. He kissed me, barely a peck, but enough to remind me he was still here.

When he pulled back, his eyes glistened. "I want you to have it all. You deserve it all."

With a calming breath, I leaned my forehead against his. "I have a second plan."

A soft chuckle passed his lips. "Of course you do."

The warmth in his voice eased some of the aches in my heart.

"You going to tell me about it?"

"I finish my season's contract with Vegas, you visit me once a month to help keep us sane, I'll fly back if my schedule ever allows it. Then I'm done. I'll retire and come back to Australia. Make myself cozy in this house of yours and call your bed ours."

The hitch of Nate's breath grabbed my attention. Unsure what to expect—surprise, perhaps—my brows shot high at the fierce expression forming.

"What?"

"That's a hard fucking hell no."

So startled, I huffed out a short laugh. No lie, I was confused as fuck. "A *hard* no? What sort of agreement do you think we're hashing out here?" Bewildered humor seemed like my only possible response.

"Giving up basketball isn't okay. At least if you're doing it just for me. We've already discussed this."

Tilting my head, I managed a soft smile, despite us still being at an impasse. "I know this isn't the first time I've mentioned to you about coming home," I reminded him. "I mean before yesterday."

With his gaze darting around my face, uncertainty registered.

"Even before I came back, before you made me fall head over heels in love with you"—that one earned me a sweet, pink-cheeked smile—"already I was considering my options." I shook my head, feeling exhausted despite it only being midmorning. "I love basketball, love my job. I'm also not a spring chicken anymore in the League. But I also love you." I shook my head when he opened his mouth as if to speak. "I also love and miss my family. Miss the peace of the Sunny Coast." I rubbed my thumb over his hand, enjoying the sensation. It was a touch I didn't think I'd ever tire of.

"Hell," I chuckled, "I love the anonymity." When I stopped talking, Nate remained staring at me, lips pursed. "I've finished. Your turn."

At my smirk, he rolled his eyes. That simple gesture made me giddy. We'd figure this out. I knew it as surely as I knew Nate was a grower. I'd marveled, almost swallowing my tongue when I'd stared in awe at *that* transformation.

"I know you've mentioned it before," he admitted, "but do you think you'll be satisfied not playing professionally? Especially when you're still doing so well? I'm not yanking your chain just because you give great head. On the court, you're spectacular."

Happiness broke free, and I tugged him toward me, capturing his lips and going to town on his mouth. I swallowed every groan and committed his taste to memory. When I pulled away, Nate's eyes were closed, and he panted.

"I like to think I'm spectacular off the court too."

Nate's lids popped open so fast, my giddiness burst free with a loud, snorting laugh. Despite the narrowing of his eyes, his lips twitched.

"You want me to start adding not so complimentary descriptors to that list, wisearse?"

With a quick shake of my head, I sat back and took him in. "I don't feel like I ever started really living again until we reconnected." The heat of embarrassment rushed to my skin, but I hadn't been lying to myself about sharing all of me with him.

"Fuck, Broadwater. You can't say shit like that and not expect me to give you whatever you want."

Hope, all light and floaty, sparked into existence, and this time it caught fire, refusing to extinguish.

As a kookaburra laughed its noisy ass off from its perch on the fence, I quirked my brow at Nate. "In that case, I'm calling it." I leaned in and paused a hairsbreadth away from capturing his mouth. "No take backs."

CHAPTER 21

NATE

EARLY AUGUST

ONCE AGAIN, NERVES THRUMMED THROUGH ME AS I disembarked the plane. This time a very different level of excitement rode my heels. Under the bright lighting of baggage collection, and accompanied by the heavy rumble of voices while I passed through border control, I could barely contain myself.

Seven long weeks had passed without Ryan's arms being wrapped around me. Forty-nine days since I'd seen in the flesh his smile or heard his voice. Over a thousand hours since I'd woken with him at my side. It was worth it, though.

Once I was out in the bustling crowd of LAX arrivals, the sound of squeals, laughter, and happy reunions greeted me. There was no time to smile or take any of it in, though, not when I searched franti-cally for the man I was desperate for.

I frowned, wondering why there were so many tall people around. While I was far from short, Ryan, who had several inches on me, was usually easy to spot. Not so much in this freakishly tall crowd.

Changing tack, I focused on the walls. I was more than aware that Ryan was a known face here, espe-cially with last month's press surrounding his trade deal. I expected he'd be staying under the radar.

As if my final thought summoned him, my gaze caught on the face I'd missed so much. Hidden under the shadow of his cap, he blended in well. But he couldn't hide from me. For four weeks I'd explored every dip, sharp line, and curve of his body. I'd recognize him anywhere.

Hauling my large wheeled case and my heavy backpack, I picked up my step. The universe decided to be kind, parting the way toward him. He stood straight when I was a couple of meters away, a slight shake to his body. And hell if I couldn't relate. My whole body vibrated, desperate for contact. Finally, I was in his arms, wrapped in a fierce hug and swal-lowing hard.

"I've missed you so much," I mumbled against his neck, risking a small kiss against his warm skin. A shudder racked through him, and he held tighter still before releasing me. I forced myself to step back, stopping at what would be an appropriate distance for two friends greeting each other. Despite the frustration, my smile came quickly when I took my fill. "Hey."

With that one word, heat flooded his expression. My smile stretched into a grin. That he struggled was a hell of a thing and reassuring as fuck.

"Let's get out of here. I've booked us the nicest, closest hotel." His gaze dipped down my body and dropped to my hand. A vibration tingled through my palm, knowing what he wanted.

Clearing my throat, I nodded and grabbed the strap of my backpack. It took all my effort to play by the rules, but we'd both agreed to our compromise. There was no chance I'd screw with that.

With a flex of his fingers, Ryan reached for my large case. "Let me get that."

Warmth settled in my belly. "Thanks."

Indicating for me to follow, Ryan led the way, head down but clearly keeping an eye on the path ahead. We dodged passengers, avoided large groups of people, and made for the exit and the area with waiting cars.

A man stepped out of a large SUV, nodded at Ryan, and opened the back door. Ryan passed him the case and waited for me to hand my bag over before he ushered me in. I scooted over, my focus on Ryan, mildly aware of the blacked-out windows.

Once the door was closed and the bags were stowed, we had a few seconds of privacy. Ryan's eyes dipped to my mouth, and I wet my bottom lip, fresh flutters forming in my belly. And then his mouth touched mine, so damn brief I could have imagined it happened. Only the buzz on my lips, Ryan sitting up straight and repositioning his T-shirt over his shorts, reassured me that for a blissful second, we'd shared a kiss.

The door opening jolted me and made me aware my own pants situation wasn't doing too well. I shifted as subtly as possible, trying to nudge my dick from being strangled behind my denim. Beneath the radio playing and the start of the engine, I didn't miss Ryan's quiet chuckle.

Bastard.

"Piss off," I grumbled quietly, lips twitching despite my discomfort.

Amusement lit his features, though his eyes told a very different story.

"Straight to the hotel, Mr. Broadwater?"

Ryan turned his head toward the driver. "Yeah, that's great, thank you."

"We should be there in under thirty."

"Perfect."

The driver nodded and focused on maneuvering through the crazy LA traffic.

"How was your flight?"

Somehow I held back the shiver at the sound of his voice so close. Meeting his stare, I smiled. "Easy, comfortable. Thanks again."

A soft smile formed when he nodded. "I can be selfish when I want to be."

I bit the insides of my cheeks, recalling all too clearly one of our compromises. During his final few days in Australia, we'd been to-ing and fro-ing through our whole plan. The business- or first-class tickets so I could travel in comfort, but more specifically so I'd be well-rested and ready for more nefarious activities was not something I'd balked at.

My acquiescence had taken Ryan by surprise, as he'd prepared for a battle. I'd laughed, saying, "It's as if you don't know me at all," before pouncing on him and sucking him off. After weeks of not being together, I didn't want to be too exhausted to enjoy every moment of our reunion.

"So," I said, quickly changing the subject, "what did you do yesterday after you flew in?"

The bastard quirked a brow at me and smirked. It was a look I could decipher so bloody easily. The wanker had been, well... wanking, while I'd been traveling.

After a moment of his less-than-subtle leer, he said, "Called up Sutton. He's weirdly super animated on the phone."

I chuckled at the image of a chatty Sutton. Jayden… absolutely, but Sutton was generally quiet, only speaking when he had something of substance to say. My impression of him had been confirmed by Ryan. "Yeah, he okay? Jayden still pining for you?"

Ryan's grin was sexy as hell. "He's stopped being so needy. They're both flying out next week to hang out."

My brows shot up in surprise. "Really?" The knowledge made me happy. One of the first things Ryan had done seven weeks ago when he'd returned to Minnesota was talk to his friends. As predicted, they'd done more than taken it in their stride. They'd said the right things, were supportive, but more than that, they meant it and had Ryan's back. Before Ryan moved to Vegas, they'd interrupted more than a call or two between us. It was a relief to know he had their friendship, especially when I'd be splitting my time between Vegas and the Sunny Coast.

"It'll be good to see them."

"You should be thanking me." I quirked my brow in question. "It took a whole heap of threats to stop them jumping on a flight so they could see you today."

The sentiment was crazy sweet, my smirk quick to form. "In that case, I owe you one." Neither of us planned to do anything beyond being wrapped up in each other for the next week, and selfishly, I didn't want anyone to spoil those plans.

The LA traffic was kind to us. Before we knew it, the bellman gathered my bags, and we took a slight detour to the reception where I stood by, amused at how the young woman flustered over Ryan's request for room service in forty-five minutes.

It took a stern look from a middle-aged receptionist for her to pull herself together. I smirked, understanding the young woman's reaction completely. The desire to pounce on my boyfriend was unwavering, the test of my willpower worthy of a gold star and a BJ.

By the time we got to the room, the tension was thick, our need obvious. Since my bags were already stowed away in our suite, I sighed in relief, knowing there'd be no more disturbances. We had forty-five minutes to make the most of.

In the middle of the opulent suite with the sun spilling through the sheer curtains, Ryan and I made quick work of undressing. Gloriously naked and our bodies flushed against each other, our mouths connected. Heat, desire, and desperation clung to each caress, each parting of lips, and each stroke of tongue.

Beneath it all was a fierce sense of coming home.

I gasped; whether it was with that realization or his grip finding purchase on my dick, I didn't know. All I was sure of was that I was exactly where I was supposed to be.

Letting Ryan take control, I groaned when he laid me out and feasted on my skin. "You want me to fuck you or BJs?" he asked between nips and licks.

"Cocks in mouths. Can't wait for prep." I'd been traveling for hours, so a shower was in order, especially if I wanted Ryan's dick in my arse. Before landing, I'd done a desperate cleanup, wiping over my dick and balls and brushing my teeth. This—I grinned at the thought—was the exact reason why. The likelihood of stopping for anything had been laughable.

"What are you smirking at?" He crawled up my body and hovered over me.

"Me being generous and washing my sac before I got off the plane." Not a shred of embarrassment crept through me. How could it when I talked to Ryan, my best mate, the man who still knew me best after all these years?

His smile stretched wide. "I best get tasting then."

After an all too brief kiss, he clambered around,

kneeing me in the head in his haste. "Hey, knees to yourself." I slapped his bare arse and laughed.

"Fuck," he grunted. "Do that again when my dick's down your throat. I dare you."

Amusement balanced so perfectly with my desire. I loved this man so much. A simple "Uh-huh" escaped me before I licked a long line down his cock. His groan was reward enough, but when his mouth enveloped my rock-hard dick, the prize got a whole lot better.

***

After spending the one night in LA, we'd headed to Vegas. Both of us had been eager to get to his rental, my home for the next eighty-nine days.

The ninety-day visa open to Aussie residents was one of our compromises. Not only had I argued it'd help us fly under the radar—a long visit from a friend was less likely to be gossip column fodder for a start—but it also ensured we'd have time afterward to reevaluate our next step. The latter had been reluctantly agreed to by Ryan.

By the time I returned to Queensland in twelve weeks, the League's season would be starting up for training. It meant I wouldn't be a distraction, and

Ryan would feel less guilty about the hours he needed to pour into preparing.

"You sure you're happy staying in?" Wearing nothing but a pair of tight black boxer briefs, Ryan was a walking wet dream. Heat flashed into my system, and I took a long, slow glance at him.

"You really need to ask?" I raised an eyebrow for good measure.

"You're insatiable." He stepped toward to where I lounged on his huge bed, the distant lights of the strip twinkling. "I like it."

The bastard pounced on me, and the magazine I was browsing flew out of my hand. "Hey," I complained, though I sighed contently when his warm body pressed in at my side.

"What you reading?"

"Just farming equipment reviews." I peered over at him. A gentle smile tilted his lips.

"Were you happy with how you left things?" Interest reflected in his deep brown eyes.

"Yeah." I wrapped my arm around my boyfriend and trailed my fingers over his arm. "Patrick worked his butt off the past few weeks so he can step up as manager. Catherine, who I took on for the admin side of things, is solid. She knows her stuff and will help Patrick when it comes to the more annoying side of running the place."

"That's a relief. I know it's huge, you coming here." The vulnerability in his voice tugged at my heart.

Pausing my strokes, I turned to my side to face him. "You're worth it, and you still have your sister to thank for reminding me I'm allowed to chase my happiness too."

Ryan stroked my jaw, his expression lifting, contentment settling there. "You got the good stuff while I got my ass handed to me." An honest-to-God pout formed on his mouth.

"At least it stopped you freaking out about how calm she was being when you first got back."

A derisive snort left him. "Yeah, giving it to me both barrels, but four weeks delayed, kinda took me by surprise." Amusement laced his words, and I chuckled, thinking about Amber. Admittedly, I'd also felt a little guilty discovering her softly-softly approach was a weird plan of hers to help convince Ryan to move back home for good. If not now, at least when he retired.

When she'd discovered that option had been on the table, which I'd sort of vetoed—we would wait to see how this year panned out—I'd expected her to come gunning for me.

Oh, how wrong I had been.

"Nineteen-year-olds are scary as fuck," he grumbled.

Not sure I could make my voice solemn, as while he was right, it was still funny, I ended up nodding instead.

"I spoke to Micky after you abandoned me earlier," he said, taking me by surprise. I'd managed just over an hour working out in the complex's private gym before I'd worried I'd curl over. I'd waved Ryan off when he offered to come back to the condo with me, aware he usually spent three hours training a day. Me being here wasn't going to change that. While he had time off before the season started, he needed to be in peak physical condition.

Keeping my voice light, I asked, "What did you talk about?"

"Asked that you were here safely and wanted to make sure you were settling in okay. Micky reminded me again to ask you to store his number in your phone, in case you needed to contact him."

I smiled. "That was good of him."

Ryan chuckled. "I think he's super aware that I'm still undecided about next year. Can't blame the guy for making an effort. If I retire, it'll impact him as well, you know?" His smile was tender when he finished speaking.

"I know," I said, "and no decisions yet, remember?" While Ryan retiring after this coming season remained on the table, we were absolutely keeping it on the down-low. I also felt a little guilty about Micky, especially as his agent's reaction had blown my mind. His support had been instant. There'd been no harassment, no pressure, no grumbles of disappointment, simply legit acceptance. Honestly, from the way Ryan described it, he'd expected to hear that Ryan was quitting with no plans to return to America, contract be damned. That he wasn't made him overjoyed, apparently.

"I'll add his number. Not quite sure I can ever imagine a scenario of needing it." The slight shift in Ryan's expression caught my eye. "What are you thinking?" I asked.

"I know our plan is limiting risks of me being outed, but it could happen. And if it did, you'd need to contact him, especially if I'm not around. Micky would be the one to help you."

My pulse picked up, thinking about the possibility of the fallout. I didn't like the pressure Ryan put on himself one bit. I nodded. "I get it. But it'll be fine. We'll be careful and get through this year."

If I said it often enough, just maybe I'd believe it. If Ryan decided to be a free agent and accept a new contract at the end of the season, it would be then that we'd be controlling the narrative.

CHAPTER 22
RYAN

Sitting on the patio with the sun spilling down around us, the umbrellas offering us shade, I subtly pinched myself. Being out in public, even with the few cameras that had been directed our way, was all okay. I didn't doubt that Sutton and Jayden being here took off the pressure.

I'd admitted to Nate that his real introduction to cameras, fans, and any paps would be easier if we weren't alone. The hope was that while the gossip rags would get the scoop of me having a friend from Australia visiting, they'd be more focused on snapping images of me hanging out with my former teammates.

Drinking water like I'd just survived a hike in the Sahara—hell, it was hot—I laughed as Jayden told me about his zany aunt flirting with Sutton.

"He's making it all up." The eye roll from Sutton simply made us all laugh more.

I accepted my chicken salad from the waiter with thanks and sneaked a quick look at Nate's plate to make sure they'd got his order right.

"You going to offer to cut his grilled chicken for him as well?"

I flipped Jayden off, ignoring my embarrassment that I wasn't subtle. "Fuck off."

Jayden reacted with a wide smile. "It's all levels of adorable, you being attentive and shit."

"What the hell! *Adorable*," I scoffed.

"You know, that there screams years' worth of indoctrinated toxic masculinity." Sutton's deadpan words dragged three pairs of eyes in his direction. "What?" he asked, picking up his fork.

"You see what you've started," Jayden complained, his focus on me.

"What did I do?" For a short while, I'd forgotten what life was like with these two as my friends. The conversations they started, the shit and sometimes mayhem they created, forever kept me on my toes.

"You see," Jayden said, pointing his knife at a bemused Nate, "this is why he needs reining in. Ryan just can't help saying shit that gets Sutton all ramped up."

As I grumbled a "Hey," my boyfriend cracked up, finding the attack on my character highly amusing.

"Do you know what Sutton studied at college?" Jayden continued. My brows dipped in confusion, wondering where the hell he was going with this. "Go on, hazard a guess. You both get one try each."

I glanced at Sutton, taking in his huge frame, his ink-black hair and hazel eyes. It was the relaxed expression he sent my way that had me thinking harder. Honestly, I didn't know much beyond knowing Sutton had a large family, his mom moving to the USA from Zimbabwe when she was a kid, and his dad being second-generation Polish-American.

He was kind and intelligent. He also had a killer field goal percentage and, on the court, tried his hardest to get the job done. But his personal history, I knew very little about.

"Anthropology," Nate said from my side.

My brows shot high. Fuck, I was going to go with the standard "communication." Rather than answer straightaway, I rethought my answer while all three men looked at me. No way could I say what I'd been thinking. While Sutton was smart, I'd assumed he'd elected for communication or arts and social science while being on a ball scholarship like most players I knew.

Apparently, I was a dickhead. "Uhm." I racked

my brain. "Economics?" There was no certainty in my selection at all. Sutton scoffed, and I had the good grace to shoot him an apologetic smile.

"Bioethics." A grin stretched Jayden's mouth wide.

"Oh, wow. I have no idea what the hell that is, but it sounds complicated," I said.

"Right. That's what I said when Sutton told me. The point is, don't get him started."

A frown dipped Sutton's brows low, and he angled a look at Jayden. He didn't say a word, simply turned his frown into a challenging stare and a raised eyebrow.

Sutton, to anyone who didn't know him, and honestly even to those who did, could be super intimidating. Not so much to Jayden, though. The guy simply winked at his friend, blew him a kiss, and said, "You know how I like to brag about how smart you are."

When Sutton groaned and dropped his head back, I chuckled and glanced over at Nate. Doing so was always a risk in public, as it was a legit struggle not to touch him, let alone stare at him in a way that wouldn't share with the world that my heart was his.

Nate still appeared bemused, but his attention was sharp, focused as he studied my two friends.

They acted like an old married couple. Everyone

and his dog commented on it. It was something I liked about their relationship. In many ways, I envied their freedom and bravery in being themselves, and without apology. But I supposed that was a luxury two straight men had. They could fawn over and love up all over each other without the fear of being outed, perfectly comfortable in their own skins and sense of selves.

The thought pulled me up short. What the fuck I'd give to be my authentic self. I steadied my breathing, determined not to let Nate clue in to my brain and emotions working overtime.

It would happen at the end of the season for sure.

No excuses. No hesitation. Absolutely no take backs.

THE GUYS' FIVE-DAY VISIT PASSED IN A BIT OF A BLUR. We hit the casinos, took in a show, and did a heap of touristy stuff, most of the time managing to avoid cameras. Admittedly, it was pretty hard to stay incognito with four tall guys, three of whom were well above average, especially when one in particular thought he was a comedian.

Their visit was worth it, though. Not only because of the added freedom it allowed Nate and me, but it was good to be reminded they had my back.

Nate and I said goodbye to them as they headed to Cleveland to watch a soccer game. Despite me being able to get my hands on tickets, Nate agreed he'd prefer to stay incognito a while longer. Considering we'd spent hardly any time alone in the past five days, I was more than okay with that.

What we hadn't banked on was my new coach reaching out to me for a get-together at his house. He'd latched on to my hesitation, even when I explained I had a friend visiting from Australia. But he'd lapped up the idea of another Aussie being around and had followed up with "Your friend will probably make mixing with your new team easier for you, right? Most are bringing their families so have a buffer. Call it good timing." I hadn't been able to refuse.

Felix was a good coach. There were plenty of stories floating around about him being a ballbuster, which I believed after meeting the guy. But I knew enough just from the four times we'd met to know he ran a tight ship, wanted the best out of his players, and also cared about them.

That now included me.

"You're being weird and fidgety," Nate unhelpfully said as I drove us toward Henderson, where Coach Felix lived.

"Joining a new team is always the worst," I complained.

Nate side-eyed me. "Says the man who moved to a whole new country by himself, knowing no one, when he was *eighteen*. Hell, you couldn't even buy booze till you were twenty-one here. Must have sucked knowing I was getting wasted legally."

His words had the desired effect and earned him a grin.

"Holy shit, that's the real reason you stopped calling, right? You couldn't cope with my being an adult before you," he sassed, like the dick he was.

"Piss off, *Griffin*." The sat nav in my car announced we'd arrived, and I pulled over, distracted by the collection of expensive cars outside what looked to be a fairly traditional suburban family home. Yeah, it was big, but it wasn't ostentatious. Taking it in, I relaxed a fraction.

"Nice place," Nate said from beside me.

"Yeah," I agreed.

"We doing this?"

I nodded. "I'll grab the cooler." Nate snorted at the name. I rolled my eyes, saying, "Well, they don't have Eskys here."

We got out of my car, and I opened the trunk—

just one of the many words Nate teased me excessively for when he heard the multitude of Americanisms I'd picked up over the years.

Large cooler in hand, I headed toward the front door, Nate on my heels. After ringing the bell, I worked hard at easing the tension in my shoulders. I needed to make an effort to get to know the team. Them getting used to having Nate around would be ideal too.

Coach answered the door wearing an apron and a smile. "You made it. Come on in." He led us in and straight through to the backyard. A swimming pool took up a fair bit of space. A handful of kids were currently playing volleyball, and Jason Curtis, Vegas's point guard, bobbed around on a giant flamingo.

"Everyone," Coach called out, and I fought hard not to wince at the attention, "Broadwater's here, so be nice and don't scare the man off before the season starts. This here is Nate, his buddy visiting from Australia." My chest warmed a little that he'd remembered Nate's name.

Several of the guys called out, and Phillips, the captain, stood up from a lounger, a toddler on his hip, to greet me. He looked curiously at the large cooler in my hands.

"Beers and soda and lots of ice," I explained.

"Shit, Coach, you expecting us to start bringing drinks with us?" Phillips looked a little wide-eyed, his question genuine rather than him taking the piss.

"Nah," I answered quickly, "it's just an Aussie thing. You don't turn up anywhere without an Esky and beer. You'll get used to it." I grinned, put the cooler on the ground, and shook Phillips's hand.

"Good to know, and good to meet ya. Coach said he'd hoped you'd come along." His grip was firm and friendly.

"Glad for the invite." I indicated toward the girl in his arms. "And who's this princess?"

Phillips grinned. "Less princess and more wildcat, I think. This is Milly, my daughter. It's her first birthday in a couple of weeks. We're actually having a big party. You should come, and Nate here too if he's still visiting." He glanced over at Nate and pumped his hand in a friendly shake.

"I'll still be here," he answered, his tone warm. "I'm making the most of my ninety days."

Phillips bobbed his head. "Nice, though why you'd want three months in Vegas is beyond me," he teased, earning a "Hey, my home city you're cussing there," from Tucker Andrews, another of my new teammates.

With a smile, Phillips rolled his eyes. "Come on,

let me introduce you to everyone. Best grab a beer first. You're going to need it dealing with this lot."

The rest of the afternoon continued with the same level of good-natured shit-talking, three more party invites, and me feeling like this might all just work out after all.

"Did you have a good night?" Reaching out and placing his hand on my thigh once safely in the car, Nate squeezed. "They seem like decent guys."

I covered his hand with mine, relieved to be able to touch him again. "Yeah."

From the corner of my eye, I saw him smile, another sliver of tension that had sat with me since Coach's phone call disappearing. "I was thinking maybe we should head for a week to the beach together soon, before training starts properly. Banksy mentioned he and his girlfriend head to a resort in Mexico. It's pretty exclusive, no paps, apparently a state-of-the-art gym too."

When the shooting guard had mentioned the place to me and suggested it was a good place to escape the craziness of Vegas and perhaps an ideal place to take my friend, I'd initially frozen.

Wasn't that a couples thing to do? Before I could react more or even ask questions, he'd mentioned a few of the guys on the team went too, but with friends, so it wasn't a romantic escape or anything.

When I'd grinned in response and said I'd talk to Nate, he'd laughed, saying, "Seriously, it looks like you need to unwind. Privacy before season starts… you should already be on the phone with your travel agent."

The magic word privacy had pretty much sold me. My condo was great, spacious, but the image of Nate and me chilling on the beach, perhaps getting some surf in, was a visual I liked.

"Oh wow, really?"

I signaled to turn. "Yeah, why not? A week with not having to go to parties." I threw him a quick wink. "Sounds awesome."

"A week on the beach and chilling with you would be brilliant. You think we can get a room at such short notice?"

As I pulled into the underground parking lot, I shrugged. "Not sure, but I'll try my hardest."

CHAPTER 23
NATE

SEPTEMBER

WAKING UP TO THE SOUND OF THE OCEAN, ONLY TO PEER out the large doors to take in the golden sands and shimmering water had become my second-favorite thing. The first stepped naked out of the bathroom, towel-drying his hair.

"You should have woken me. I'd have liked to shower with you." I stretched like a lazy cat, not tearing my gaze away from the smirking man.

"You looked too cute to wake," he said, "especially with the drool."

The pillow I threw smacked him in the face. I didn't even have time to prepare before he was on me, plastering me to the bed and licking across my cheek.

"Gross," I said, between my snickering, trying to buck the arsehole off. "Tongues are for mouths—" I spluttered when he didn't give up. "—or cocks."

That got his attention. The look in his eyes was wicked when he angled above me to properly see my face. "Is that right?" I never tired of his heat, his flirting, or just how happy he made me.

"Yes?" I answered, knowing full well he heard my question.

Heat flared in his gaze. "You thought of another place for my tongue?"

Holy fucking hell. My dick throbbed as my hole legit fluttered. Who the fuck knew it could do that in response to simple words? I may have gaped, struggling to respond, but I liked that idea a lot.

Ryan hummed, grinning with cocky satisfaction. "Let's hold that thought."

"Really?" The word came out sounding far too disappointed, especially as I'd already been planning in my head a quick shower and prep to make the whole experience as fucking sweet and satisfying as possible.

"Yep. Scuba diving, remember? The boat leaves in forty-five minutes."

I did remember. Holding back my disappointment shouldn't have been a hardship. It had been my idea, after all. But yesterday morning I'd been excited with the plan. Now, Ryan's tongue rimming me sounded a million times better.

"Coming?" Taking my palm, he tugged me out of bed.

"No, I'm not. See for yourself," I sassed, looking pointedly at my dick.

"You should have gotten up with me for morning gym time, and I could have worked you over real good in the shower."

"You're not helping," I threw over my shoulder, on my way to wash up. The git simply laughed loudly and set about making us a coffee.

Fortunately, the caffeine stopped my grumpiness, even though it didn't help with my morning wood. It took creative, not-so-pleasant thoughts to make that happen. But on the private charter Ryan had insisted on, putting a hold on our morning plans was worth it.

There were less than a handful of people on board —just the diving instructor, the captain, and us.

It was super peaceful as the vessel cut through the waves. Ryan and I sat together, enjoying the spray. We'd just finished applying sunscreen and managed to keep the application process absolutely PG-13. But rather than feeling disappointed, I pressed my thigh next to his and sighed, perfectly content.

"This holiday's been amazing, thank you."

"Anytime. I think it was good to get away from the noise. I know that's going to be our life now"—my heart rate spiked a little, still getting used to the idea—"but even more reason to escape while we can."

I'd barely got an inkling when we'd reconnected at the beginning of the year about what life was like for Ryan the League player. But phone calls and him telling me stories weren't close to preparing me for the reality. I was sure of it.

When I returned to Australia, it'd be for two months before I returned to Vegas for another three. We hoped that by March, we'd have a clearer idea of where we were at. Though honestly, that was bullshit. Our original plan was completely defunct since we'd both agreed we didn't want to spend so much time apart.

By March, we had to make a decision. Come out at the end of the season as a couple, right alongside a new contract, or take early retirement and start our lives together back home.

The boat slowing caught my attention. It was time to get in the ocean.

Once suited up and instructions had been given for the second time, we entered the warm water. I grinned at Ryan, excitement thrumming through me. Scuba diving was an item to check off my extensive bucket list. I couldn't think of a better person to be experiencing this with than him.

The weather had held off, the rain and winds dropping the second day we'd arrived. With no idea how long that would last, it was lucky we'd chosen today, with the cloudless sky offering a perfect backdrop.

After checking over our equipment once more and ensuring I could breathe properly, I gave the thumbs-up. Ryan quickly followed, the instructor doing the same before signaling for us to dive.

The water was clear and the visibility incredible. It didn't take long to get used to the flippers and swim in the direction Samuel, our instructor, had indicated. The further we swam, the more my awe grew. The whole scene was stunning. Reefs, pristine and colorful, captured my attention, the strength of their colors difficult to look away from.

A school of fish caught my attention, swimming seemingly haphazardly at first, but the formation soon became apparent. As the abundance of fish swam around, I couldn't decide where to look, what image to savor and capture to memory.

Bubbles to my right pulled my gaze. Ryan's focus was on me. Beneath the mask and the breathing apparatus, I was sure he was smiling. Or he would be if it wouldn't make him drown. He signaled, asking if I was okay. A thumbs-up later, he reached for my hand and didn't let go. It was a whole new world down here, and if Ryan wanted to hold my hand, no way would I stop him.

For an hour we swam around the coral, absorbing the beauty of the moment. By the time Samuel indicated it was time to return to the surface, I pushed aside the pang of regret. This was what we should do every year. From the look on Ryan's face when we surfaced and removed our masks, I expected he would agree in an instant.

A few hours later, the ride back to shore was quiet, peaceful. We sat together sipping beer and eating freshly cooked fish. While we were positioned the same distance as when we'd arrived, we held hands, our connection concealed by our thighs.

We'd had two more dives in different areas, making a full day of it. "I think this is one of my favorite days." I squeezed his hand.

"Yeah?" He gave me a quick glance, the pink on his cheeks kinda sweet.

"Definitely."

"Good. The day's not over yet, so I think we keep it going."

Bloody hell, I loved it when he said words like that to me. It touched me in the best and most profound of ways.

"I love you," I whispered, unable to hold the words back.

His focus intensified when he stroked a thumb over my hand. "I love you, and as soon as we're in our cabin, I'm going to show you with my tongue just how much."

Narrowing my eyes at him, I sighed. "You never play fair."

"I disagree. I play to win. Simple as that."

Keeping up the exchange, I lifted my brow. "And what's your prize?"

"My tongue in your ass."

I snorted and pushed him away. He jerked to the side, spilling his beer, releasing my hand and laughing.

"What did I say?" he shot back at me, straightening, still laughing his butt off.

"You're incorrigible."

Ryan's wink made my stomach somersault. There was something annoyingly sexy when he did that. "Just the way you like me."

He wasn't wrong.

Once docked, we kept our dicks in our pants a while longer and went to the bar. While I was eager for him to claim his prize, we were hyped up and buzzing from laughing so hard and the couple of beers we'd had.

We settled at the bar, shooting the shit, attention occasionally flicking to the TV and the soccer highlights they were showing. It was nice being here, sitting so casually like this. It was what it should be like, I thought, being in love with my best friend, hanging out before returning to our sanctuary and sucking each other's brains out.

Rather than sharing that with him, I asked, "So no more plans the next couple of days before we head back?"

"Nope." He popped the *p* and picked up his beer. Noticing it was empty, he asked, "You want another?"

"Sounds good, thanks."

He signaled to the bartender for another round. "If you want to do something, I'm open to ideas," he said after ordering, picking our conversation back up.

My smile felt a little lopsided, my brain pleasantly fuzzy. "Honestly, I'm happy to chill and laze about with you, ogling you behind my sunnies."

Our beers were set in front of us, and as we said thanks, Ryan peered my way. "Behind your sunnies, huh?"

"Yep, it's what gets me through the day."

Loud laughter to the right of the bar caught my attention. A small group gathered, mainly young blokes, but it looked like a couple of young women mixed in with their group. They laughed again, loudly, but there was nothing obnoxious about the sound.

I smiled over in their direction, saying, "Did you have that, a group of friends to go on holidays with?"

"I've been on a couple of weekends away with Sutton and Jayden. At college I was broke, so worked every chance I could get, including holidays."

The thought made me sad. "Do you sometimes wish things were different?" I didn't expand, figuring the implication was there.

He shrugged and leaned his elbows on the bar, picking at the beer label. "There's been more than a time or two I regretted how things played out. But I've finally reached the point where I'm happy. You're the main reason for that."

My heart melted at his words. While sadness hovered just under the surface for Ryan, I chose to hold on to the here and now. "You make me happy too," I said, lowering my voice.

Affection flushed his features. Opening my mouth to suggest we should head back, I slammed it shut when a man appeared at Ryan's side. A large grin was plastered on his face, and he looked ready to pee himself.

The slow turn of Ryan's head in the direction of

the young guy, who seemed barely legal to be in the bar—or at least back in the US—was enough to make the guy's eyes widen. Comically so.

"Oh my goodness. You're him. I'm so sorry to disturb you, Mr. Ryan, uhm... Mr. Broadwater—" Flustered, the bloke stopped abruptly, his face turning crimson.

Rather than releasing my snort, I formed a gentle smile and nudged Ryan.

"Ryan's fine," my man answered, his voice impressively normal. "There something I can do for you?"

The guy nodded, face still red, and I wasn't sure he'd breathed at all since appearing. I willed him to take a breath and almost suggested as much, but thankfully, he gasped, sucking in air.

"It is you. Oh, holy nutballs. It's just, I know you're here relaxing, and I totally shouldn't, but you are freakin' incredible. The last game at the end of the season... I swear, I almost had palpitations. My boyfriend... he's over there"—he waved over his head but didn't pause for anything—"well, he adores you even more. He begged me not to ruin your night, but seriously, you're Ryan freakin' Broadwater."

This guy was pop-you-in-my-pocket adorable.

Ryan remained frozen at my side, quite possibly overwhelmed by the enthusiastic greeting.

"Anyways, I'd love to buy you a beer. You don't have to talk with us or anything." His eyes went wide, and a new flush of red filled his face. "But yeah, a beer, just for being incredible." He finally paused, and there was an eerie quiet before Ryan cleared his throat. "Uhm…"

"We'd love to have a drink with you. But Ryan's buying," I offered helpfully. And that was how we ended up drinking with six twenty-one-year-olds, here celebrating Simone's birthday, courtesy of her very generous parents, apparently.

Dean, the young guy who'd first approached, was not only a hoot, but he wasn't lying about being a hard-core fan. But it was his boyfriend, Kieran, who pink-cheeked admitted to being the real wearer of that mantel.

We'd had a couple more beers, but I'd refused the shots. Honestly, I got handsy when I drank hard liquor. It wouldn't be my drunken escapades that outed Ryan Broadwater to the world. And a drunk grope-y version of me could quite possibly do that.

"How long have you guys been dating?" I asked. Dean and Kieran were a cute couple, and on the surface looked like polar opposites.

"Just over a year now," Dean answered, and I could almost see the love hearts in his eyes. "We met in a study group. Truth is, he was a bit of a dick at first."

Kieran called, "Hey."

"Am I lying?" Dean fired back, all sweetness and sass.

With a roll of his eyes, Kieran admitted, "No," earning a chuckle from the whole group.

"Kieran's on the basketball team," Dean continued, and I couldn't help but side-eye Ryan.

My boyfriend surprised me when he interrupted Dean's story to ask Kieran, "Oh yeah, that's cool, mate. You hoping to be drafted?"

Kieran gave a very audible gulp before shaking his head.

It was Dean's sigh that snagged my attention. Nothing but adoration appeared on his face when he focused on his boyfriend, but his sigh was all frustration.

"Just don't start." Kieran's voice was low.

Something was amiss, and with beer fueling me, I just came out and asked, "What's going on? What's with all the tension?"

Emotion shadowed Kieran's expression. A quick dart of his eyes toward Ryan followed before he cleared his throat. "There're no currently out League players."

His words were a punch to the gut, and I could

only imagine how they impacted my boyfriend.

"Honestly, it's too hard fighting the system, fighting assholes all the time. Especially being so young." He shrugged. "It's just not in the cards for me."

Fuck, his words hurt, his sadness and complete acceptance soured the beer I'd just taken a swig of.

"I've already said—"

"No." Kieran cut Dean off, following with a tender smile.

"But I'd absolutely do it for you. I love you, baby."

Holy hell, this felt like we were intruding on something too personal, and unfortunately, something I could completely relate to. Awkwardness crept into my stomach.

"What will you do for him?"

It took me a moment to register that the quiet, solemn question came from Ryan. Wide-eyed, I stared at my boyfriend, willing him to meet my gaze and wondering why he was digging, despite me doing the exact same thing a moment ago.

Self-preservation had kept me from pushing it, sickeningly sure I knew exactly what the bone of contention was.

"I've said I'll keep our relationship on the down-low until he's ready, or maybe something changes."

Unbidden, I closed my eyelids, selfishly wishing we'd just gone straight back to the cabin rather than being smacked with reality. These poor kids' plight hurt my heart. Weren't they too young to be dealing with such shitty realities? Hell, it would only be a few years until I turned thirty, and I still felt unprepared.

"And I love you for it," Kieran said, drawing my attention back. "But I'm not willing to do that to you… to us. I won't lie about loving you."

It was time to leave. With their sweetness and their pain beating so heavily against me, I couldn't take any more. I took a calming breath and sought out Ryan. His attention was already on me.

And fuck, the look in the depths of his dark, penetrating eyes froze my breath. It stalled my heart, and I had no choice but to cling to the tabletop.

"I'm gay." Ryan's words sliced through the group quicker than slashing rain in a storm. "And one day I'll be marrying Nate Griffin. And anyone who can't handle that can go fuck themselves."

No one spoke.

No one moved.

I wasn't even sure a single soul in our group breathed. And when Ryan stepped around the table, arrowing straight for me, I knew our world was about to unravel.

CHAPTER 24

RYAN

THE ONLY THING GROUNDING ME WAS NATE'S SOFT KISS and the way he clung to me. I didn't want to let go, too afraid he would float away somehow and that my moment of bravery, my moment of being so moved by a kid's story, would disappear with it.

I didn't want to take it back. Not ever.

"I love you," I murmured against Nate's mouth, savoring his smile.

"Is it fucked of me if I demand no take backs?" he whispered, pulling away slightly. His eyes were damp and filled with emotion.

"If you don't say it, I will."

Nate's laughter was everything. It warmed my soul and freed my heart. "No take backs," he said breathily before he pressed his mouth firmly against mine.

When we eased out of the kiss, I was absolutely aware of the stunned silence. A quick peek showed six shell-shocked faces. I did a cursory glance for cells and was relieved when I didn't spot one.

A quick glance over my shoulder confirmed the almost empty bar seemed to be minding their own business. Aware I could have heard a mouse's fart, I cleared my throat, stood by Nate's side, and held his hand. "So, yeah."

Dean was the first to lose the gobsmacked expression. "Holy shit, are you engaged? Was that a proposal? Did that just really happen?" He shot a look at Kieran, whose eyes were as round as saucers. "Kieran, did that just freakin' happen?"

Wordlessly, Kieran nodded while my brain went into an all-out panic. "The what? No. Shit." Alarmed, I also got whiplash at the speed of rotating so I could see Nate. The bastard wore a huge-ass grin, amusement dancing in his gaze.

"No, it wasn't a proposal," he said, rolling his eyes at me.

"Fuck me." I legit held my hand to my chest, hoping to stop my heart from bursting free.

"Hey, who's to say I'd even have said yes?"

"What?" Okay, so that wasn't what I was expecting to hear, especially since a marriage apparently was something I wanted, according to my declaration. I was so not yet ready. But still. "What do you mean? You'd have turned me down?" Hurt rumbled ridiculously to life. Sure, I didn't want a proposal to happen today, but yeah, that was definitely disappointment pouting in my chest. When Nate shot a dangerously high eyebrow my way, I sensed the need to keep my mouth shut. He was wondering what the fuck I was talking about and why I was even debating this.

As if taking pity on me, he leaned in, only hesitating for a moment before brushing his lips against my own. "When we're ready, we'll know." His words made me feel marginally better, but the shifting of a beer bottle across from me reminded me we weren't alone.

And that I'd just come out to strangers.

And that I needed to get a jump on this before someone else did.

Dean, honest to God, lifted his hand, saying, "I've got questions."

I snorted, and Nate squeezed my hand. "You get two, then I need to go and call my agent."

Understanding registered in Dean's eyes, and his whole intensity shifted slightly, softening a little. "I know this can't be public knowledge, 'cause of course we'd know. I promise none of us will breathe a word." He stared pointedly around the table.

I watched as each person offered me a genuine smile and a solemn nod.

"But you *are* coming out?" The question was gentle and kind, perhaps more than I deserved considering I'd been such a selfish prick to the man I professed to love. Thinking about Nate, I peered over at him. He remained at my side, smiling, a steady, confident reminder that he had my back, just as he had my heart.

"Yeah. It's more than time for me to live…" I hesitated, considering the right word. "…authentically." I turned my attention to Kieran, who still hadn't said anything. "Truth is, Nate and I have been best friends since we were kids, but when I moved to America, I was too chickenshit to admit I'd left behind more than my home and family. I'd left my heart behind too."

I returned Nate's tight squeeze to my palm.

"Officially we've been together since May, just this year"—fuck, had it only been four months? I could barely remember my life before he was mine— "but Nate's been the only man for me." This time I glanced at Nate, taking in the emotion directed my way. "Taking you for granted, not being true to either of us was not okay."

He shook his head. "Don't you dare. We decided this together. We had a plan."

While that was true, we both knew it was fucked-up.

"Next question." Dean cut through the onslaught of emotions threatening to bulldoze me. This kid was a force of nature. I wished I could have been more like him growing up. Hell, now… with his sass and fearlessness.

"Shoot," I said.

"Can we get a group selfie, and are you on WhatsApp?"

"You're talking to the app challenged here, Dean," Nate said. "But you can have my details. I'd just appreciate it if you'd keep them to yourself."

An earnest promise later, we grouped together and smiled ridiculously at the phone attached to a selfie stick.

"I do really need to go." Nate stood at my side, and then I found myself hugging all six of them goodbye.

With my arms around Kieran, I spoke quietly. "Thanks, mate. I think I'll remember this meeting probably for the rest of my life." I pulled back and was surprised I was almost eye to eye with him. He seemed so much younger than twenty-one.

"What's your last name?"

Confused, he dipped his brows low. "Kendall."

"Kieran Kendall. Next year I expect to see your name in the draft."

When his eyes welled, I clamped down on the inside of my cheeks hard. "I'll try my hardest." A resolve, one brave as hell, hardened his words.

"I know you will." I patted his back before seeking out Nate, who waited next to Dean for me. "Ready?" I asked.

"Definitely."

"Don't forget what I said about using Insta or something. Throw it on TikTok too for good measure," Dean called out to us as we headed away.

"What was that about?" We followed the path to our secluded cabin, the moonlight guiding our way. With the moon set so high in the sky, I figured it was a lot later than we'd planned to be out for.

"Dean's expert opinion is that social media should be your platform of choice when going public. That's based on countless successes and fails of public figures and other pro athletes coming out apparently." His chuckle was tight. "And I actually agree with him. You've mentioned a couple of times about controlling the narrative. Who better to do that than yourself?"

We let ourselves into our room, and I refused to let my pounding pulse drown out my thoughts. I kicked off my shoes and stripped. The material felt constricting, tight and hot against my skin.

When Nate's concerned expression appeared before me, I startled.

"You can change your mind."

"No, I can't. I won't."

A gentle curve lifted his lips. "I'm so proud of you. Always have been, but in this moment, I'm probably the proudest I've ever been."

"Is that because of my impressive cock?" I joked, already feeling the words fall flat. "Fuck, I'm sorry. I'm nervous as hell."

He bobbed his head. "You want a shower first?"

"Yeah."

I set about undressing Nate. He stood quietly, allowing me to unwrap him like a gift. Naked and before me, Nate was everything I wanted. And I was sure he'd be all I'd ever need.

"After the shower, will you help me?" Vulnerability hung heavy in my request. But since I'd already ascertained Nate deserved it all, I offered him every one of my truths.

***

It took five attempts to get the short twenty-eight-second video recorded. Nate helped me with everything.

We'd headed to the beach before dawn, having already hashed out what I wanted to say. As soon as the morning sunshine reached us, the first rays touching the golden sand under our feet, we'd recorded.

Once finished and still unposted, I'd called Micky. Both Nate and I had almost fallen flat on our butts when he'd not asked me to reconsider or think of my future or anything like that. There'd been no objection, no trying to talk me out of anything, just a request for me to call my new coach and give him the heads-up.

And wasn't that a fun fucking call.

There I'd been, sharing with the man who'd I'd met a handful of times that I was about to come out. I had to give it to the guy; he listened, never cutting in. Asked a few surprising unintrusive questions, asked if I minded sending him a copy of the video before I uploaded, with the promise of watching it so he knew what to expect and that he wouldn't be sharing it.

This was followed by my promise to speak to the team's PR.

At the end of the call, Coach Felix's words had legit made me well up. Nate had looked on, concerned, wondering what he was saying to cause such a reaction. When I'd told him how he'd said he was happy I'd given him the chance to support me, then went on to say how he had faith in our team and the management and that Vegas Stallions were honored to help me through this, Nate had been as choked up as me.

I'd uploaded the video to Instagram yesterday morning with shaky fingers. After that, I'd spoken briefly to management, sent a series of emails to Derek, their PR guy, who promised to support and protect me as much as possible, and Nate reached out to Gran and Amber for me, preparing them for any media attention that may come their way. The last call I'd made was via loudspeaker with Jayden and Sutton, both vocalizing their support.

It was no surprise that after that, we'd switched off our phones, refused to turn on the TV, and spent the day crashed out on our private porch.

But there was no more hiding.

Sitting in the private jet I'd happily shelled out for when Micky talked me through the reality of what would be waiting for me in Vegas, I squeezed Nate's hand. The Strip's lights sparkled and shimmered in the beginnings of dusk.

"You'll be fine." Nate was trying so damn hard, but his nerves shook his voice, strained the syllables of his words.

"This is going to be a nightmare." I whipped my head around to see his face. "I'm so sorry." For so long, I'd managed to dodge the press. I'd spent years being an expert at evading them—not getting too wild, not taking on endorsement deals, never saying anything that could be misconstrued. It was no wonder I'd been struggling with and questioning my life in America.

I'd been exhausted.

Sure, there'd been photos over the years of me with no-strings dates to functions, and yes, there'd been a couple of close calls out of the handful of times I'd sought out a willing mouth. But through it all, I'd stayed out of the limelight as much as possible.

It wasn't unusual to be described as a recluse. It would all change the moment our bubble broke and we stepped into the dry heat of Vegas. Once we did, America would know the real reason for me hiding.

My chest ached, my breathing speeding up.

"Hey."

I dragged in a painful breath but struggled to fill my lungs. Nate then filled my vision. Out of his seat, he kneeled before me, one hand on my chest, the other on my cheek. "Ryan." His voice cut through the ringing in my ears, and his outline came into focus.

"You're going to be okay." There was no shake

this time. No quiver. With an unwavering gaze, he continued, "Just breathe and know you've got this."

Focusing hard on drawing in air, I slowed my breathing, exhaling after a couple of beats. I followed the same pattern, relieved when the pain gripping my lungs eased.

"I need you to listen to me." He waited until I nodded before continuing. "This, all of this, is just noise. You hear me? None of it is real. It doesn't matter what photos are taken, what anyone shouts or prints. It's all just insignificant noise."

God, how I wanted to believe him, but he didn't know the world I lived in. And I'd done a god-awful job at preparing the both of us for this. His gaze narrowed, and I wondered if I'd spoken aloud, but I realized my boyfriend could simply read me too well. The thought was just enough distraction to remind me how lucky I was to have him. To have Nate's heart, his friendship.

"I love you."

Nate twisted his mouth for a beat, but he finally dropped his frown and smiled. "I love you too. And I know you don't believe me, and I also know this is going to be a shitfest and overwhelming, but I want you to answer me truthfully."

Drawing my eyebrows together, I said tentatively, "Okay."

"Could anyone say or do anything to stop you from being gay?"

I rolled my eyes at him.

"You think it's a stupid-as-fuck question?"

"Yes."

"Good. So there's fuck all anyone can say or do that will stop this part of you from existing. Being queer is one important part of what makes Ryan Broadwater so epic." My heart leaped a little at his words, loving just how incredible this man was. "There's also a part of you that is a kick-arse basketball player, a loving brother, uncle, and grandson, a great friend, a man who thinks he's funnier than he really is—"

"Hey," I challenged with a laugh. "I so am too hilarious."

Nate arched a brow at me. "You're so much more than one part of you. You have hundreds of quirks and traits and skills all combined. And nothing that the gossip rags, or Joe Blogs on the street or watching a game, can say will change that. Or do you think otherwise?"

He was right. Of course he was. The truth of his words registered. It didn't mean what happened as soon as we got off the plane wouldn't be exhausting or stressful or absolutely invasive, but only I could dictate and control my reactions and how they impacted me.

"You didn't add how having a smart, sexy boyfriend has reshaped my heart." The words were sappy, and perhaps any other day, I would have cringed or laughed and likely taken the piss. But I meant them. And from the look Nate directed my way, he knew it too.

The voice of the captain filled the cabin, asking us to strap in and take our seats. We did so, once again holding hands.

We were heading to Henderson Airport, where a security team would be greeting us. While I expected some press to be milling about outside the gates, we aimed to keep my arrival quiet.

As the wheels touched the tarmac, my attention drifted once more to Nate. "There's no one else I'd want to do any of this with."

A wry grin transformed his tense features. "Too bloody right. Plus there's the fact that no one else could put up with your weird habits."

"Weird habits? The fuck you talking about?" We taxied down the private runway, but I barely noticed, too focused on Nate.

"You can't be serious?"

"As a bloody heart attack."

Nate chuckled. "You don't think stripping when you do a dump is weird?"

I gaped. "That's not weird, it's—hygienic and comfortable. And it's not like I do it if I'm not at home or in my hotel or anything," I said. It was something I'd always done, and he knew it. I watched him stand and followed his lead.

"Okay then, whatever you say. What about when you whacked your foot on the bed frame?"

"What about it?" Confused, I stared at him as he took hold of my hand.

"You then kicked the other foot. On purpose." Wide-eyed, he waited for me to respond.

I shrugged, a little sheepishly this time, aware of the door at the front of the plane opening. "I feel, I don't know, uneven if I don't do it." Okay, so maybe that was a bit weird.

Before I could challenge him with my own list of oddities that I had for him, a throat cleared. I realized Nate was already looking forward, his expression calm and maybe a little smug.

A broad-shouldered middle-aged man stood a few feet before us. His gaze was unwavering and a little intimidating. I assumed he was the security Micky had organized from the suit he wore and the muscle he was packing.

"Mr. Broadwater, I'm Matt Tully from Stronghold

Security."

I nodded and offered a tight smile. "Call me Ryan. And this is Nate."

Matt dipped his head in acknowledgment. "I've got Zoe waiting in the car for us. She'll be driving us tonight. I spotted two local paps out front. Chancers. Your bags are all loaded. Border control just needs to do a quick check of your passports, then are you ready to go?"

"Yes, thanks." It was then I realized I still held Nate's hand. Doing so felt phenomenal, eased some of my uncertainty, and reminded me of one of the reasons I was doing this.

After a woman from border control entered and did the necessary checks, Matt rejoined us. "Let's get going then." As we followed him out of the jet, our baseball caps firmly in place, I took a cursory glance at my surroundings.

A scattering of planes of various sizes caught my attention, along with a few people milling around, all focused on whatever their task was. This was ideal. "We should travel this way more often," I said quietly to Nate, who snorted at my side. I wondered if he remembered our conversation as kids.

Once we were in the SUV, Matt turned in his seat from the front. "There's news crews and several paps camped outside your condo."

My stomach dipped.

"Don't worry. We have guys there. We've also made a call to the local PD for crowd control support."

While Matt's face held nothing but clear-cut certainty, and I was sure he was used to this sort of thing, my stomach twisted. Nate's hand on my thigh had me drawing in a breath, reminding me I was not alone in this. Gripping his hand, I forced myself to loosen the tension in my shoulders.

"Ryan." My attention darted to Matt. "Trust me when I say we've got this. We'll get you home and without a single camera shoved in your face. We're on your detail for the next week, but more if needed."

I blanched at that, earning me a reassuring smile from Matt. "Hopefully the buzz will have died down long before that."

I nodded, knowing other pro athletes had been where I was, and while they'd been big news for a while, they weren't regularly in the press anymore. I'd always known that. It was just now I had to deal with being one of them. "Thanks. I'm just so not used to any of this."

Matt studied me for a beat as Zoe said something quietly to him. He signaled he heard her with a nod before we pulled away. "You've stayed out of the media and have done an impressive job of doing so." The wide eyes I shot his way made Matt chuckle, a deep rasping sound. "We had twenty-four hours to prep before you were due back on American soil."

The squeezing of my hand caught my attention again. Nate's warm eyes met mine. "You'll be able to get that back again," he said.

Once Matt turned around to face the road, I pressed a kiss to Nate's temple. He sighed against me and traced his fingers over my chest.

"You doing okay?" I shrugged, not willing to lie to him by saying yes. "Have you still got your phone switched off?"

"Yeah. My phone blowing up was stressing me out."

"You want to let me have it for a while so I can field any calls? I suppose some people who you need to talk to will be trying to get in touch."

Thoughtful to a fault, Nate somehow always knew what I needed and what to say. A genuine smile formed on my mouth. "I love you." I indicated I wanted his lips, and he offered them willingly. The smile I felt pressing against them sent a fresh wave of calm over me.

When I pulled away, I watched as the bright lights from outside danced around on his face. There was honesty, and such love and understanding reflected at me, my heart calmed even further.

"How'd you get to be so brave and awesome?" While my voice was soft, there was no real teasing in my tone.

Rather than spouting off with the sass he would have another time, Nate stroked his thumb across my cheek. "I think you just bring out the best in me. That's what happens when my heart's fit to burst with just how much I love you and with how incredibly proud of you I am."

This man was going to be the making of me. I knew that as viscerally as I knew the sun set in the west.

"When we step out of this car, we can finally start moving forward. You can finally have that whole cake you've been dreaming about."

I chuckled. "I want to share my cake with you. It'll taste better that way."

Nate grinned so wide, I was sure I'd never seen him look so happy. That such a feeling enveloped him now was a hell of a thing. Hope bloomed inside me. It was no wonder I marveled at how this man, this once scrawny eleven-year-old who'd talked me into being his friend, had the power to bring me a peace I'd never been sure I'd find.

Matt's voice cut through the car. "Ryan, you need

to prepare yourself." Steel wrapped around his words, and he sent me an apologetic grimace. "I was informed by Micky not to share this with you." He didn't look too pleased by that instruction either.

Alarmed, I snapped my attention to the road and realized we were on our street. A couple of police cars edged the sides of the road, news vans filled the area, and a large crowd had formed.

The "What the fuck" that fell out of my mouth had nothing to do with any of that, though.

Outside of my building was a small, raised platform. On the ground stood an army of men wearing what looked to be official Vegas Stallions steward vests. It was what was on the platform that had my mouth dropping wide.

At least six of the guys from my new team stood on there.

"Holy shit, is that—? Are they—?" came from my side.

Speechless, I nodded.

The police had done an impressive job of keeping the forming crowds and media at bay. We were able to drive right on through, eventually pulling up outside the underground parking lot entrance.

"What do you want to do, Ryan?" Matt asked. "My offer back at the hangar still stands. We get you in. No one has to see you. No one will bother you."

I glanced at him, about to answer, when Nate gripped my arm.

"Fuck me dead."

"What?" I jerked my head away from Matt and followed Nate's gaze. My heart full-on stopped in my chest, a fresh wave of emotion hurtling into me. Jayden and Sutton stood in the very center of the platform that had been erected outside my building, wearing matching T-shirts, both printed with the words *We love Ryan*.

"I want to get out." How could I not? Matt moved immediately. The door opened, and the volume of the crowd almost had me stumbling. Only Nate's palm securely in mine prevented me.

I focused on the men on the makeshift stage, wondering who'd decided to do this and how they'd pulled it off. From the shit-eating grins on Sutton's and Jayden's faces, I figured I already knew the answer.

With all my attention on them and making my feet move, I zoned out the chaos surrounding us. The shouts and chants became nothing more than a din. I had no clue what anyone was hollering, and even if it was hatred, I didn't give a damn.

I met Phillips, my team captain, first. I didn't even know the guy, not really, yet he shook my hand and pulled me into a back-slapping hug.

"You doing okay?" he said next to my ear.

"Yeah, thanks." I pulled away. "Just, wow... what the fuck is going on?"

He snorted. "Team support, Pride support, all organized by your two buddies." He squeezed my arm, stepped back, and the other players swarmed me. I'd lost Nate's hand at some point, but before I could panic as I sought him out, I spotted him hugging Jayden.

I stepped toward them, also noticing my coach to the side. I did a double take, and he sent me a wink. After acknowledging him with a grateful smile, I looked back at my friends.

"Wait!" Jayden said, thrusting his hand out to stop me.

With the shouts and screams as the soundtrack of the surrealist moment of my life, my soul fucking sang from feeling so much love from these guys. When Jayden indicated his shirt once again, I reread the words *We love Ryan*, and smiled, then Sutton turned, facing away from me.

And Ryan loves Nate. The words detonated the live wire in my heart, made it explode. I stepped toward them, wrapping Sutton in a hug, giving up from holding back my emotion.

"We've got you, man." My friend squeezed a little harder as he spoke.

I nodded and pulled away, rubbing a hand over my face. Uncertain what to do next, I had no doubt the horror took over my expression. If anyone thought I was going to do a speech or some shit, they'd be sorely disappointed.

I had no intention of talking to the media ever about my sexuality.

As if reading my mind, Jayden grinned at me. "You're not expected to do anything. Maybe wave and invite us all in for a beer."

"Really?" That sounded like an ideal plan to me. While I knew there'd be questions and the road wouldn't be easy, I could breathe easier with the solid, strong arm of support, at least for tonight.

"You know I've been on vacation and have no beer or food, right?"

Sutton responded. "All taken care of."

Matt then appeared at my side. "You ready?"

"Yeah, thanks." As we walked away, for the first time I looked at the crowd. In fairness it was mainly the press, but a few pockets of people had gathered, a couple of sweet We Support You signs being waved around, right along with some others I quickly looked away from, not willing to let their hatred ruin this moment.

As we approached the doors, some of the reporters' questions and shouts reached me. I knew better than to make eye contact, let alone answer any of them.

"What do you say to the fans who are saying they'll no longer support a team with men that kiss?"

Despite my tension, I rolled my eyes at the absurdly phrased question.

Some dick in the crowd must have heard the reporter, though, taking up a derisive chant. "Men kissing are sick."

My jaw tightened, and I held Nate's hand even tighter, and then I had no choice but to stop. Frowning, I looked at Jayden, who'd stopped dead in front of us. Fury flooded his features as he peered out at the small piece-of-shit group still chanting vile words.

"The stupid fuckers," Jayden spat, loud enough for me to hear but not enough for it to reach the public. "I'll fucking show them."

My eyes widened at his words, a jolt of adrenaline slamming into me. Jayden did some stupid shit when pushed.

Before I could react, before I could reach out and tell him to leave it alone, he turned to Sutton, grabbed his face, and planted a big kiss on his mouth.

"Holy shit," Nate gasped. Once again, all I could do was look on and nod.

EPILOGUE
NATE

NINE MONTHS LATER

IT TOOK ME LEAVING AFTER MY NINETY DAYS, RETURNING a month later—rather than the initially planned two months—and then perhaps another couple of weeks for the media frenzy to truly stop. But honestly, what completely blindsided the both of us was that it was all concerning rumors of Ryan taking early retirement to move back to Australia rather than him being gay.

And who the fuck knew who started that rumor.

There'd been a few quieter weeks during that time, especially as he didn't confirm anything. Some trade or whatever snagged the media attention for a while. It had been exhausting, especially for Ryan, who seemed to make it his mission to play harder than ever before.

His fierce determination to shut down the hate—because, while his team and the League were impressively supportive, there was no cutting the stupid out of bigots—by playing phenomenally made me as proud as I was concerned. He'd pushed himself hard all season, doing some damage to his ankle that didn't seem to properly heal. And while the fans and media sang his praises after a win, the slightest fumble meant fresh news stories about his sexuality and a new round of hate-filled Tweets would make their rounds.

But we bore it all together. My three trips away to renew my visa had still happened, but the second and third time had been for just a week rather than my planned month. Not only was that because I missed Ryan, but I refused to let him go through any of this alone.

For eight long years we'd done that, and we'd both learned our lesson. Together we were happier, stronger.

Tonight was a struggle to hold back my excitement. As hard as I tried to maintain a sad face and commiserate with the team as they exited from the locker room after their round five loss in the playoffs, the twitch of my lips kept breaking free. Happiness knowing this was all finally over danced around my system. I wanted to grin and cry and jump on a plane and get the hell out of here and be home more than I wanted almost anything in the world. The exception being my man, who'd be stepping out any second.

"You could at least pretend to be miserable." Jayden nudged me. I grunted when he made contact and shot him an evil eye.

"Watch it. Even your elbows have muscles."

He grinned at me, but the usual happiness I was used to seeing from him didn't quite reach his eyes. When he'd flown in alone yesterday, both Ryan and I had done a double take. It took me an hour to finally relax, certain Sutton was going to jump out of Jayden's suitcase or something.

He never did.

Jayden had still played his role, pretended nothing was out of the ordinary, joked and made fun of Ryan, but something was off, and the gaping Sutton-shaped hole usually by his side was the only explanation.

"So you're seriously going to come with us?" I asked him, keeping one eye on the door. Only a couple of players had exited so far.

"Hell yes. I already have a list of everything I want to see and do."

When Jayden had mentioned to me this morning

after Ryan had left that he was considering tagging along with us to Australia, I'd thought he was joking. It didn't take long to realize he was serious.

"I've already called to organize my ticket and make sure they can get me a visa or whatever I need. I'll keep you both entertained on the flight."

I chuckled, sure he would, but none of that eased my concern for the guy.

The doors opening caught my attention. Philips exited with Tucker, both looking exhausted and just a little miserable. A few more players left wearily, wearing similar expressions. And then there was Ryan, his gaze already roaming the small crowd, seeking me out.

Unlike his teammates, he grinned and limped through the crowd. I had no idea how he'd managed to keep playing with the ache of that damn foot. But play he did. Like a goddamn rock star.

I ignored Jayden's snort and his "Yeah, completely devastated," wanting all my attention on the man arrowing straight for me. And then he was here. In my arms. Hugging me. Holding me so damn tightly I was worried a rib might crack.

"You played so well," I whispered against his neck. The whole team had played their hearts out, but the other team had fought just as hard and won with a buzzer beater. "I'm sorry you didn't get through."

Ryan released me, his brows arching high. "That right?"

I rolled my eyes at him. "You know it is. I would have loved for you to get to the finals and win." If he had, I would have cheered the loudest.

"But?"

Jayden snorted again, and I reached out and smacked him on the chest. "But we get to fly home in three days." A thrill of excitement thrummed along with the beating of my heart. It had been an experience being here, living this life with Ryan, but I was so ready for normality.

There'd be things I missed, our friends mainly, but I knew we'd be seeing them again.

Speaking of— "Looks like we'll be having our first guest too." I indicated Jayden, who nudged me out the way and hugged Ryan. I clamped my mouth shut, holding back my chuckle at the wide-eyed expression Ryan shot my way.

"We will?" he finally said, pulling away from Jayden and throwing an arm around me.

"Hell yes." Our friend rubbed his hands together. "I'm so going to ride a kangaroo."

It was impossible to keep my laughter contained. It burst free, my shoulders shaking. Meanwhile, Ryan rubbed a hand over his face, sighing wearily. But he couldn't fool me. He loved Jayden. He'd be pleased that, despite retiring from the League and this having been his final professional game, his friends would still be around.

"Right, beers are needed. You all need some serious cheering up," Jayden shouted loudly, clearly talking to the team as a whole.

As we followed him out, my hand firmly holding Ryan's, I cast him a quick look. "It's the last time I'll ever ask," I promised, "but you sure you want to give all this up?" If he had changed his mind, we'd make it work. Though I wasn't sure how much longer his ankle could hold out if he did stay.

Stopping, Ryan tugged on my hand. I turned and stood before him, inhaling his shower gel and cologne I'd bought him for Christmas.

"The only thing I'll never be prepared to give up is you." He leaned down and brushed his lips tenderly against mine. "Say it," he mumbled against my mouth.

I smiled and pulled back to look into his eyes. "Really?" I couldn't even pretend to be annoyed, not when the way he looked at me made me melt.

"Yes, really." He shook me a little, urging me on.

I rolled my eyes, my mouth twitching as I said, "No take backs." Emotions pushed to the surface, knowing despite the teasing, I meant every single word.

"That's right, baby. No fucking take backs."

Continuing for the exit, we stepped out into the warm evening. And for the first time ever amongst the camera flashes and the call of Ryan's name, my boyfriend hauled me into his arms and kissed me like he absolutely meant it.

BE ON THE LOOK OUT FOR BOOK TWO, **NO MORE SECRETS**. Want to know more about Bar QK? Then visit in **NOT USED TO CUTE**. And please consider leaving a review on AMAZON and/or GOODREADS. Thank you.

Announcement... gah... maybe I should just wing it?!

Before I head back stateside, I just wanted to share with you all that I'm gay. This is something I've ~~needed~~ wanted to say for a long time, and I'm in such a good place that it's a relief to be at this point that I can tell you the truth.

Life is ~~fucking awesome~~ great, especially with my new move to Vegas. I've got an awesome support system--my family, friends, and the League being the best of people. I'm beyond grateful to my Vegas team and the League for their support. Sharing this with you all is easier knowing they have my back. ~~(I hope!!!!!)~~

You know this is super rare for me, showing my face let alone my words like this. But I'm happy to be doing so now. LGBTQ+ visibility continues to be so essential, and I'm proud to be coming out and identifying as part of the community.

So thanks for listening, and I can't wait to be back the court in a few weeks.

I also have a ~~hot as fuck~~ boyfriend who ~~loves me~~ and my ~~gay ass.~~

ACKNOWLEDGMENTS

Thank you so much for taking a chance of my first Australian-American crossover. I had such fun jumping between the two countries.

As always a huge shoutout to my team at Hot Tree Editing. Liv. Keeley, and Donna, I appreciate your support so much.

This book had extra support and from the amazing Annabeth Albert. Annabeth, your alpha feedback was so wonderful. Thank you for pushing me!

Claire at BookSmith Design nailed this book's cover. I love it so hard and am so grateful you know me so well.

A thank-you to Arden and Barb for all of the PA and amid support you offer. You make life so much easier for me so I can focus on my words.

I share a fabulous Facebook group with my gorgeous author wife, Louisa Masters. Our RoMMantics are such hardcore readers and supporters. If you're one of our active members, please know I appreciate you so much.

Louisa, you're my rock, not only in life but in this crazy, wonderful world of authoring. I adore you.

ABOUT THE AUTHOR

I live and breathe all things book related. Usually with at least three books being read and two WiPs being written at the same time, life is merrily hectic. I tend to do nothing by halves, so I happily seek the craziness and busyness life offers.

Living on my small property in Queensland with my human family as well as my animal family of cows, chooks, and dogs, I really do appreciate the beauty of the world around me and am a believer that love truly is love.

To check for updates head to my website:
https://beccaseymour.com
https://landing.mailerlite.com/webforms/
landing/r9f0i4
Plus, join my Facebook group, which I share with the awesome Louisa Masters here:
https://www.facebook.com/
groups/rommancewithbeccalouisa/
On TikTok, follow me here: https://www.tiktok.
com/@beccaseymourwrites

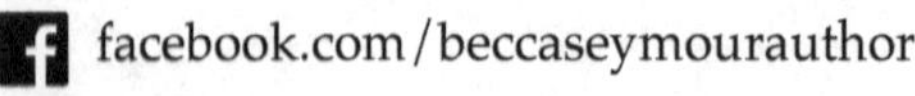

facebook.com / beccaseymourauthor

twitter.com / beccaseymour_

instagram.com / authorbeccaseymour

bookbub.com / authors / becca-seymour